Beatrice 1963
by
Tom Frye

Hang on for the ride!

© Copyright 2020
by Tom Frye

Although this is a work of fiction, many of the places and the events in this story are real. However, names and characters are the product of the author's imagination. Any resemblance to actual persons, living or dead is entirely coincidental.

All rights reserved. No part of this publication may be reproduced or transmitted by any means, electronic, mechanical, photocopying, recording, without prior written permission of the author in care of Storm Haven Press, 6139 Kearney Ave, Lincoln, NE. 68507

In memory of my Grandpa,
Amos Hawkins,
and all those nights
we sat and listened to my
Uncle Richard tell his tales.

To Zack Runyon, that kid
from Tennessee
who made the first 50 copies
of this book available.

The dance of the wind and dust

*All we are is dust in the wind,
is an understatement here in Nebraska.
Because here, it's the dust of
a thousand back country roads,
that keeps the landscape alive.*

*That same dust was kicked up
by the buffalo and horses
of the Plains Indians.
That same dust found its way
into the cabins of
the first pioneers to tread the land.*

*It's the dust of those country roads
that mars and scars the old wood
of the barns, farmhouses, and road signs.
That dust paints a vivid picture
of the distant past, the present day,
and the oncoming future.*

*Particles of dusty DNA
are carried far on strong winds.
Those same winds once
blew winter storms away,
sent tornadoes howling
and screaming across the prairie.*

*Wind and dust created a wild dance,
like barroom betties kicking up their heels.
It's the wind and the dust
that we endure out here in the sticks
of Nebraska.*

*Because if we can survive that,
we can survive anything.*

© Copyright 2019 by Tom Frye

Chapter One
Beatrice, Nebraska Nov. 1963

I had just turned twelve when I first saw a man die directly in front of me. I remember it well, too. Years later, I could definitely answer the question, "Do you know where you were the day President John F. Kennedy was shot and killed?"

Oh, yeah. I could answer that question with certainty. I was standing in my tree fort overlooking the intersection of 8th and Elk Street in small town Beatrice, Nebraska. It was there that I witnessed the shooting that took place. While President Kennedy was mortally wounded by what some would call the magic bullet, a second Kennedy was mortally wounded there before me on the Elk Street intersection by another magic bullet. It was the sixth and final shot fired from a .38 caliber Smith and Wesson that took young Jon Kennedy's life.

My best friend, Declan Connors and I were there in our tree fort having a heated argument about gum. In particular, what gum held its flavor the longest. I know the topic of our conversation doesn't sound serious, but for two twelve-year-old boys who had skipped school for the first time in our young lives, a heated debate over gum seemed to be the most important subject in our small, sheltered world.

Tall and slender as a bean pole, Dec fluffed back his shaggy blond bangs and huffed, "But, look at the fun you get with Bazooka. Why, do you know how many bubbles you can blow with just one chaw of that two-bit, pink squishy stuff? And you get a comic inside of every pack. You can't get that with *Juicy Fruit*, Hawk!"

Hawk is what almost everyone in town had called me since I was little. My real name is Jessie Hawkins, but a long time ago, Dec's dad tagged that nickname on me, and it had stuck. Hawk fit me, having Irish in my family plus a sprinkling of Lakota, an Indian nickname like Hawk was a good thing. Dec always said in the summer time my skin turned almost as dark as my black hair, and made me look like one of the Gypsies who lived down in Blue Springs south of town.

I did some fluffing of my own scraggly black bangs and said, "Comics are a gimmick to get folks to buy bubble gum. You don't need comics if you're a serious gum chewer. Besides, don't you feel a little more grown-up when you buy a pack of *Juicy Fruit*? I mean, penny gum like Bazooka is really kid's stuff, ain't it?"

Dec said, "Who says I want to feel all grown-up? Besides, how many old folks chew *Bazooka*? Ever saw an old fart trying to blow a bubble?"

Dec and I were just continuing our argument about gum when the next thing you know, Henry McGinn pulled to a stop at the Stop sign at the Elk Street intersection, half a block away from our high lookout position there in our tree fort.

Dec said, "Look, Hawk! If it ain't King Henry and his Rolls Royce!"

Of course, Henry McGinn wasn't a king, nor did he drive a Rolls Royce. But he sure acted like one ever since buying that brand spanking new Pontiac. Henry drove that black and white Pontiac like an old lady going to church on Sunday. He smiled and waved at everyone he happened to pass in his prized mobile. It was Chris Catlin who coined the phrase, "Here comes the King riding his coach down the bricks!"

Sitting there at the Stop sign, Henry looked like a Billy Goat with his shaggy goatee and his dark, collar-length hair, craning his long neck as if he were trying to see cars coming from the next county. Only when he was certain that no cars were coming for at least three blocks either way on Elk Street, did he remove his foot from the brake and proceed to place it gently on the accelerator.

And that's when it happened. A young blond man in his mid-twenties came barreling up behind Henry in his junk heap of a Chevy. Dec swore later that the guy didn't brake or try to steer out around Henry in front of him. He simply threw his hands in the air as his Chevy slammed into the back end of Henry's brand new car, not only denting in Henry's trunk, but sending his Pontiac flying out into the middle of Elk Street, where he proceeded through the intersection and came to a stop only after striking the elm tree just west of the Presbyterian church. The blond driver climbed out of his Chevy, looking dazed and confused. Henry sat there in his wrecked Pontiac, staring straight ahead like a boxer who was punch-drunk from taking too many shots to the head. Dec whispered, "Holy Moses!"

I stared down to the street in stunned amazement. Henry was now coming across Elk Street armed with a big, black pistol!

What Henry McGinn was doing driving around town armed with a gun was later speculated about during the investigation that followed. Three days prior to this chance accident at the intersection of Elk, some sinister man had followed Henry's two young daughters home from the movie theater late at night. Henry had reported the incident to Sheriff Mac, and he'd told Mac that he'd actually locked his doors that night, an almost unheard of precaution in our small town. But evidently, Henry had felt his daughters were being stalked and the .38 Smith and Wesson was considered necessary to keep them safe. It just happened to be at hand when Henry literally snapped there on Friday, November 22, 1963.

Henry raised his gun and said, "Jon Kennedy, time to die!"

They both struggled over the pistol. Henry began pulling the trigger. One bullet took out the side mirror of Kennedy's car. Another shattered the back window. Two more made hollow thunking sounds, plowing into the hood of Kennedy's Chevy. Before the fifth shot was fired, Jon Kennedy almost managed to wrestle the pistol out of Henry's grasp. But Jon's struggle was fueled by terror, while Henry's was fueled by rage. And rage beats terror any day. At least, that's what Dec said later. He must have been right, too. Because at the end of the battle between Henry and Jon, it was Henry's rage that won out.

Who knows where that fifth bullet flew? The sixth slug, though, burrowed a hole into Jon's left shoulder, ricocheted off his collar bone, struck his lowest rib, shot back up and plowed a hole clean through his heart, killing him instantly. When we snooped through Dec's dad's files later, we were amazed to read the coroner's report. The path of that sixth bullet had been nothing short of a miracle. That's what Dec said about it anyway. I told him it wasn't right to call it a miracle when it resulted in Jon's death. But magic? That was something we both could agree upon when that lead slug missed so many vital organs. And then, struck like lightning, taking Jon Kennedy out of his life.

As he fell dead to the pavement, King Henry walked back over to his car and sat down on the curb beside it. It was sad. There he was minding his own business. Out driving his prized Pontiac. All jolly and happy. Then in an instant, his life changed.

The first one on the scene was Deputy Tyler Burke. Big, blond and mean, Ty was Sheriff Mac's third in command. Ty Burke had once played football at the University of Nebraska as one of the famous Cornhuskers under the head coach Bob Devaney. Ty had been a great quarterback until a knee injury ended his career as a pro athlete, which resulted in him coming back to his hometown to issue tickets to speeders and to take keys away from drunks at the Blue Lady Lounge on Saturday nights.

Dec whispered, "I hate that guy. Ever since I had a run-in with him down at the rail yards. Ty caught me putting pennies on the tracks to smash flat, but I never did deserve what Ty did to me after that. He took it upon himself to punish me after I called him the name that insulted his mother. Ty made me chew on a bar of soap! Afterwards he threatened me, saying if he ever told Sheriff Mac about the soap-chewing incident, Ty swore he'd tell Mac that he'd caught me stealing undergarments off young Carla Bennet's clothesline!" Which was so untrue. Dec ain't above pulling a good prank once in awhile. But fooling around with a young lady's underwear would have been embarrassing. Ty had him over a barrel. Dec never did tell Mac that Ty had a mean streak in him.

Ty pulled up in the street behind Jon Kennedy's Chevy. He moved like the Tin Man on the Wizard of Oz, when he stepped out of his squad car, his eyes fixed on Jon sprawled dead in the street. He kneeled down beside Jon's body to get a better look at the bloody bullet wound. He then said, "You reaped what you sowed, Jon Kennedy!"

It seemed odd that Ty would even know this stranger to our town. But Ty seemed glad that he was dead. Ty said, "What happened here?"

Henry just broke down and started bawling, carrying on like a kid who had been forgotten at Christmas. Ty went over and removed the gun from his hands, then pulled Henry to his feet and led him back over to his patrol car. He put a weeping Henry in the backseat and closed the door on him. Ty then did something peculiar and mysterious, because it really got our detective instincts kicking in and sent us on the adventure we embarked on later.

Ty walked directly up to Jon Kennedy's Chevy, took the keys out of the ignition, and went deliberately to the trunk of the car. Dec and I stood on tiptoes to see because we had branches blocking our vision. These same clustered branches kept us hidden from the view of Ty as he took a good long look around to see if anyone was watching him.

When he seemed satisfied that no nosey neighbors had come outside yet to see what the commotion was, Ty unlocked the trunk.

The second he lifted that trunk lid, Ty choked out in one long gasp, "Oh, Lord Jesus!"

Chapter Two

Dec and I stood up higher on our toes so that we, too, could see inside of that trunk. Of course, we saw nothing as Ty slammed the trunk lid closed. He was just reaching for the keys still in the slot of the trunk's lock mechanism, when Dec did something stupid.

All this time we'd been watching this spectacle in the street, Dec had completely forgotten about our argument over the long-lasting flavor of *Juicy Fruit* or *Bazooka*. Well, as it was, Dec finally remembered to chew. And after a couple chews, he did what naturally came next. Dec blew a bubble. Dec froze, staring wide-eyed at me. It was like the time Dec farted in church. He simply felt a gas bubble coming on, lifted his leg, and let her rip. Farts make a lot of noise on hard oak pews. Dec's ripper was no exception. It turned every head in Saint Joe's congregation. Even Father Murphy, our parish priest, was left speechless at the thunderous explosion. And before he could carry on with his sermon, Dec shifted the blame to me! "Hawk!" he gasped in feigned amazement.

I turned red with shame as everyone in the congregation at St. Joe's wrongly assumed that I had let the fart in church. Declan, son of Cormac Connors, sheriff of our small town, was always the diplomat. Why take for instance the name of our town. Some kids at school got into a debate one day about how it's pronounced. Most were of the popular opinion that it should come out as Bee-at-trice, while some said it was named after some judge's daughter, and therefore should be pronounced as Bee-a-trice. When Dec spoke, everyone listened. If they didn't, rumor was his dad would come in the middle of the night and put you in jail, forcing you to share the same cell with Oscar the monkey that Harv Brindle kept in a cage as a pet.

Dec's words were the last on any subject, because no one wanted to end up locked in a cell with Oscar, except maybe Hiney Scrabble, the only one who had bragging rights when it came to wrestling with Oscar. He was the only one in our town strong enough to give that chimp a run for his money. One night, Sheriff Mac and his two deputies had to extract the big chimp out of Harv's Tavern when he escaped from his cage. Mac and his two deputies took Oscar to the ground, wrestled him around some, and then along came Hiney, who ended up taking Oscar by the hand and leading him back to the cage on the side of Harv's oak tree beside my vacant lot. No kid in our school ever wanted to test the theory that Sheriff Mac would do his only son's bidding and arrest his fellow classmates so they could spend a night in county with big ol' Oscar. Funny how rumors like that get started. The last thing Mac would ever do is terrorize some poor kid on a whim from his son. No, Mac was the most fair-minded upholder of the law I had ever seen. And to think that he would even consider doing something that mean would be absurd.

    I knew firsthand Sheriff Mac's idea of justice. The first time we ever got caught cobbing candy from Lawrie's Shop, old man Lawrie phoned Sheriff Mac and told him he had two hooligans in custody. Mac showed up, apologizing to old man Lawrie. When Mac got us down to the jail, he escorted us inside the jail house. Silently, he led us into the back room where the cells for prisoners were, and there he seated us in two chairs facing one of those cells. Inside of it lay Rome Kowski. The big ogre was sound asleep, his mouth a big O within his bushy gray beard. Mac then turned and without saying a word, left us seated there.

    Dec and I sat there, fidgeting and fretting for nearly three hours. Not once did Rome wake up from his booze-induced coma. We both just sat there, not even whispering to each other for fear our hissing voices would arouse the sleeping giant. At the end of those three hours, Mac came striding down the hall leading to the cells, looking every bit like Clint Walker, the cowboy hero of the TV western, *Cheyenne*. Big and handsome, his sheriff's outfit fitting him like a second skin, muscles rippling on his large frame, every black hair on his head neatly combed into place and slick with *Brylcreem*. And then Mac quietly said, "How do you think Mom would feel about this, Declan?"

    Dec's mom had died two years ago of cancer, and the last thing that Dec would ever do is disappoint her, so I'm figuring Mac had made his point as he finished with, "Mom would be disappointed to know you ended up being a jailbird. Is that what you want?"

Dec said, "No, sir. No way, no how."

That was it. Mac let us go, and just before shooing us out of his office, he reached out with both of his massive hands and ruffled our hair.

I wished right then and there I had him for a dad.

Without really thinking, Dec had blown that gigantic bubble and froze. It was like that big pink bubble had a life of it's own. And *Pop!* suddenly echoed between the branches and carried all the way over to Ty Burke reaching for those keys. Ty looked directly up at our hiding place. Big Ty started across the street. He was almost there, and could almost see us trying hard to blend with the branches, when my dad stepped out of the work shed to one side of our house some distance behind our fort. "What in hell happened over there, Ty?" Dad asked.

To our instant relief, Ty Burke turned away from our hiding place and joined my dad as he walked over to stare down at Jon Kennedy laying dead there in the street. A few minutes later, Sheriff Mac pulled up in his squad car. A minute after that, my Uncle Bill, the fire chief, pulled up in his fire truck with four of his men. While Ty filled Sheriff Mac in on the details of finding Jon Kennedy gunned down by Henry, Uncle Bill discovered the billfold that had fallen from the man's pocket. He scooped it up and took the liberty to open it and read the guy's driver's license. Uncle Bill let out a shrill whistle. "Well, now, this guy's name was Jon Kennedy! What's the chance of two Kennedy's being shot on the same day? One down in Dallas, the other one right here!"

"I'll be damned!" Deputy Noah Berry said as he joined Sheriff Mac thirty feet from the tree where we were hidden. "Absolutely ironic, don't you think, Mac?"

Sheriff Mac said, "More like tragic and sad."

It wasn't long before twenty nosey neighbors filed out of the surrounding houses, some lining up on Elk Street while others gathered in a curious huddle on 8th. Dec and I didn't know then what took those folks so long to come out of their houses to investigate the shooting that must have sounded like cannon fire in our small town. Later, we learned that those folks had been glued to their TV sets, sadly watching events unfold in Dallas, where some man gunned down President Kennedy.

Sheriff Mac said, "Noah, you and Ty drive Henry down to the station. I'll wait here for the tow trucks and Clive from the mortuary to show up. Soon as I get this mess cleaned up, I'll be down to question Henry."

"Sure," Noah said, turning to greet my dad as he walked across the street. Dad and Uncle Bill had hair as black as crow feathers, but where Bill was beer-barrel round like a weathered old keg, Amos was lean and trim. The difference between the two brothers, my dad once said, was on account of their two different professions. Dad, being the town's tree trimmer, had to use his body every day, climbing trees like a jungle monkey, balancing on spindly branches that even squirrels wouldn't dare set paws on. "Yes," Amos said one night at our dinner table, "the reason I stay in such good shape is that I'm active every day, while you sit on your fat ass waiting for a fire to start somewhere!"

Everyone at our dinner table laughed, Bill the hardest, because he never did take offence at my dad's kidding.

"Did anyone see what happened here?" Sheriff Mac called out to all the neighbors gathered on Elk Street. Dec and I shared a knowing look. We knew. We could tell Sheriff Mac about the shooting. But we weren't supposed to be there. We were thought to be in school. How could we explain what we were doing in our tree fort in the middle of a school day?

An argument suddenly erupted down there in the street. Deputy Noah boomed. "I'm not taking any guff off you, boy!"

Big Ty towered over Noah by a good six inches, but squat, broad-shouldered Noah was standing right up to him and not backing down an inch. Ty growled, "I won't be having you order me around, Noah!"

The thing is, no one there thought it was anything out of the ordinary when Ty refused to simply follow Noah's orders. The two lawmen were always having a spat about one thing or another. It just seemed natural that Big Ty would go blowing off at Deputy Noah, refusing to obey any order he might have given. Sheriff Mac, kneeling down beside Jon Kennedy, looked up to offer Big Ty a stern look.

Ty gave a defiant snort, then stomped over to his squad car, climbed inside, and after starting it up, he promptly drove Henry down to jail.

Which is how Jon Kennedy's car keys got left in the trunk lid.

Which called out to Dec and I up there in our tree fort.

Which led to nothing but trouble later.

Chapter Three

Hiney Scrabble and Chris Catlin pulled up in the street next to Sheriff Mac in their tow trucks from Catlin's junkyard, south of town. Being real quiet so Mac down there in the street didn't hear us, I whispered, "Both cars are both gonna end up at Catlin's. Think anyone's gonna notice those keys are still sticking out of that trunk?"

Dec said, "Ain't like Sheriff Mac not to notice something like that. I'll bet he searches both cars before Hiney and Chris cart them away."

We watched Hiney approach Mac, looking to him for instructions. Huge and brawny, dressed in his blue denim overalls, Hiney looked like a mountain man. His long, red hair hung loose about his shoulders and a bright bushy beard covered up most of his face. Dec once saw Hiney lift a horse off the ground by standing under it and hefting it up on his shoulders. He was big and strong like a pro-wrestler, which came in handy in his line of work as a tow truck driver out at Catlin's junkyard.

Hiney didn't talk much, which doesn't mean he was stupid or not too bright. It was just in his nature to speak only when he was spoken to. Chris Catlin whistled, then loudly declared, "Mac, it looks like Jon Kennedy was driving around town armed with a gun, too!"

Then, wiry, dark-haired Chris reached inside the Kennedy car and removed a pistol from the front seat. As Chris handed it to Sheriff Mac, I thought, *The man was a complete stranger to our town, so how did Chris know his name?*

"What in hell?" Sheriff Mac said in disbelief. He opened the cylinder on the .22 pistol, checking on the status of its six bullets. "Two of these have been fired," Mac said to no one in particular.

He called my dad over to talk with him, asking if he had heard any shots being fired. I think he was trying to determine if maybe Henry hadn't killed Jon in self-defense. Which would have changed things considerably. Dec and I knew, though, that Jon Kennedy hadn't so much as even drawn his pistol, let alone fired it. Which we badly wanted to tell Sheriff Mac, but we couldn't. Instead Dec and I walked down to the Blue River west of town. It was only the only route to take if we didn't want to be spotted. Besides, if we took the trails that ran south along the Blue, we could make it to Catlin's junkyard a mile outside of town in a jiffy. By then, we were both determined to see what Ty had seen in the trunk of the Kennedy car. Because when Hiney and Chris hauled those cars away, Mac never noticed those keys dangling from the slot in the trunk of Kennedy's car. It was because of the extra gun that Sheriff Mac found himself distracted.

As Dec and I walked down to the dock at the Blue River, our eyes fixed on Mose Hadley's motorboat tied off there, he said, "Do you want to walk all the way out to Catlin's?"

I asked, "What if we get caught?"

Dec replied, "Man, you worry too much, Hawk! Or should I call you Chickenhawk?"

Stung to anger about him calling me a name, I snapped, "What if Mose Hadley planned to go fishing? What if while we're cruising upriver to Catlin's, Mose finds his boat has gone missing?"

By then, Dec and his beagle dog, Cooper, had clambered aboard the twenty-foot boat, complete with a small Captain's Cabin built over the steering wheel. "Brawk! Brawk! Chickenhawk!" Dec teased, smirking at me as he opened the cabin door.

My own dog, a Pit bull named Badger, followed Cooper aboard, leaving me standing alone on the dock. I said, "I know it will save us gobs of time, but if we get caught Judge Neely will send us to the looney bin! I get sent to the State Home, my brother will kick my butt."

Dec knew how explosive my 18-year-old brother was. He'd witnessed his rage one day while he was home for a visit. Mom later said he wasn't on his meds. Dad broke three knuckles whooping his butt for what he did to Dec. Richard had made these Balsa wood airplanes that he hung from the ceiling in his bedroom by wires attached to the ceiling. In a breeze blowing in from the open back door off the porch, those planes would spin back and forth, narrowly missing each other as they swung from the ceiling. Dec got carried away that day he started tossing aluminum foil balls up at Richard's air force that dominated every patch of his ceiling. Several planes collided in midair, and several wings sheared off and fluttered down to the floor.

The second Richard appeared at his bedroom door, he came charging into the room and he lit into Dec, slugging him in the face and chest. I wasn't trying to be a hero. In fact, my first thought was to run out of the tornado of flying fists being leveled on poor Dec. But I didn't. I jumped on Richard's back, circled my legs around his waist, and wrapped my arms around his neck. I then hung on like a rodeo rider, riding a mad bull. Richard stopped hitting on Dec, leaving him with a bloody nose. As I clung to his back, I was terrified of the beating I was going to get if I let go. I choked Richard so hard, he spun around to the right, wheeled back around to the left, tottered off balance, knocking over his dresser. He then dropped down to both knees, wavered there for a full minute, and passed clean out.

Dec did a masterful job of steering us through cross currents sweeping in at the mouth of the Big Indian when we reached the intersections of the two rivers. He guided that motorboat right up alongside a sandbar, and Cooper and Badger excitedly sprang out of the boat and darted up the river bank to romp in the fields beyond.

I followed the dogs over the side of the boat, a line in hand to tie us off with. Dec cut the engine and it spluttered to an abrupt halt, leaving us in silence for long moments. And then sounds came back to our ears. The smooth hiss of the river passing by. Birdsong from a copse of trees on the west bank. The wind blowing through the leaves high above our heads. Cooper and Badger fiercely barking as they ran through the field out of sight above us.

"Best see," Dec said, "what those two mangy mutts scared up."

He landed in deep sand beside me. After inspecting my tying job, he said, "Good job, Hawk. You tied a really fine knot there."

I said, "Well, I should have been the one to drive the boat, too. After all, that's how the Hawkins' clan ended up in Beatrice. My great-grandpa was a river boat captain. It's how he met my great-grandma. There was a flood over in Ohio, along the route he drove his big steamer. When a flood swept through Ohio, he rescued Rebecca Bower. They married, traveled up the Mighty Mo to Brownsville, then the Platte to Salt Creek, then the Blue and on into Beatrice. That's how the Hawkins clan ended up here in the sticks."

Dec and I stood for long moments, watching our two hounds chasing a rabbit. Badger, with his longer legs, outdistanced Cooper, the short-legged beagle. Before long though, Cooper changed tactics. Instead of bounding through the thickets lining a copse of elm trees, he stationed himself along the trail that doubled back out of the stand of trees.

In this way, Badger did all the work. Staying right on that rabbit, running himself ragged as he tried to keep up. Soon, one rabbit springing ahead of my dog, turned into two, and then three. Those rabbits were having a hay day, springing ahead of Badger. I think they were confusing the hell out of my dog, leaping one way and then another, able to change directions within a split-second.

Badger worked one rabbit away from the rest of the gang, forcing him to double back toward Cooper. Poor Cooper would have sprung out and nabbed him, too, but suddenly out of the blue, a big dark shape came hurtling out of the hedgerow, bowling both of our dogs over.

It was Dum-Dum, the Catlin junkyard's guard dog. Though 'guard' would be a laughable joke to any who trespassed in the yards after dark. Dum-Dum was a strapping black Lab and he didn't have a mean bone in his body. In fact, most customers who ventured to Catlin's place, had a good laugh at his expense. Especially the days he thought he was a pig, and went rolling in every mud puddle he could find. Most folks greeted by him had to shoo the dog a safe distance away, for he was usually covered head to tail in a slimy coating of black mud.

"Dum-Dum!" called a voice from the small woods between us and Catlin's junkyard. The big lab began wagging his tail as a slender, raven-haired girl stepped out beside a tree as if materializing like a magical forest dryad. Katherine Catlin, the only daughter of Daniel Catlin, owner of the junkyard, came from a long line of Irish gypsies. With her dark, smooth skin, her doe-like brown eyes, and her wild tangles of black shoulder-length hair, Kat greatly resembled a fairy princess.

She had once stood up to Big Ty when he'd caught some middle school kids drinking down near the tracks. Ty had lined those seven kids up in a row, marched them out to the old railroad bridge, and ordered them to jump off and plunge down into the dark waters thirty feet below. Kat and her brother, Chris, happened to be fishing beneath the old Northern Pacific bridge. They had watched Ty badger those kids, and heard all of them begging Big Ty to let them go, swearing they'd never drink again.

Ty had just been pulling out his pistol when Kat and Chris strode to the middle of the old bridge. Those drunken kids hightailed it and ran from the bridge. So there were no real witnesses as to what happened next. The way rumors spread, Chris leveled Ty with one punch, knocking him out cold.

Kat actually told me the true story later. Contrary to popular belief, Chris never landed a fist on Ty. He'd simply scared him so bad by speaking up on behalf of those bawling kids nearly wetting themselves, the dumb galoot had dropped his gun. No one ever did explain why he'd pulled it on seven unarmed kids in the first place, but Ty had dropped his pistol and it fell down, slipping through the railroad ties, landing on the pylon ten feet below.

It had been Kat who climbed down off of that bridge and retrieved Big Ty's pistol and returned it to him.

But it was Chris who walked away a hero that night.

Chapter Four

Kat had once given Dec a bloody nose over *Red Hots*. Dec assumed that he had been a genius the day he discovered how to create his own brand of candy. He had combined a handful of those little *Red Hot* candies with cinnamon oil and tamale juice. The stuff was so hot, Dec had to use rubber gloves to mix the three ingredients together. He'd even cried during the process, with real tears running down his cheeks as he fiddled with the pot, the spoons, and the strainer he used to produce his creation.

As it turned out, Dec's first guinea pig was his last.

He'd made a fifty-cent bet with little Bobby Brazer that he could not keep a mouthful of his new candy in his mouth for more than two minutes. Bobby and Dec shook on it, and out came the candy stored in one of those metal cigar holders. Dec had Bobby pour those little babies into his mouth, so that neither of them got the scalding juices on their hands. Be as it may, Kat happened to be riding over to Bobby's house to babysit him. She took one look at Bobby retching, bawling, and going into cat-fight crazy mode, as those little pellets of extreme fire exploded in his mouth. Kat turned on the garden hose. She practically shoved that sucker down little Bobby's throat as she crammed it into his mouth. A second later, a strange gurgling sound came burbling up from the depths of his stomach. Dec sniggered at little Bobby thrashing around like a mad loon, and Kat launched herself directly at him.

Dec took up a boxer's stance, all set to take Kat out with a one-two punch. But his one-two was trumped by her first, second, and third fast and furious punch to Dec's left eye, his chin, and to his nose. A bright red explosion of blood burst from his nose as he sailed backward and landed hard on his butt. Kat had delivered those punches with all the swiftness of a tiger attack. After that tromping he took from the Gypsy girl, Dec asked her older brother to teach him how to box so that no girl ever tromped him again. After a four-month training session, Chris made him square off with Kat in their ring in their old barn. Kat took it easy on him. Chris would not allow his sister to show-off and Kat was too kindhearted to beat Dec a second time.

"Keys?" Kat said, quite suddenly. "Keys in the trunk of that Chevy!"

Dec and I followed her over to the Kennedy car, now determined to find out what Ty had discovered in there when he took a peek back in town. Kat let out an angry hiss when she saw the dark-haired girl crumpled in the trunk, her head propped up by the spare tire. The three of us were shocked that Mary Kay's life had ended so tragically. Someone had killed her and dumped her in that trunk. I felt the loss more than those two, for Mary Kay was Lakota like me, and had always seemed more like family than friend, Mary Long Soldier, the sweet girl who worked the concession stand at the Lyric Theater. One time, during a movie, I got up to get me some candy corn. I did not have an extra nickel to cover the cost, and Mary simply slid that box of candy corn across the counter, and kindly winked at me. That's the kind of person she was, good-hearted and beautiful, with her long, black hair and her amazingly green eyes. She was always smiling, too, and when she did that I just had to smile back at her, like maybe it had inspired me.

"My brother," Kat said, "was going to marry her . . ."

Her eyes filled with tears, a crease appeared on her brow. At that moment, Kat looked like the fierce battle-maiden, the Morrigan, for with her raven hair flowing over her shoulders and the angry glare in her eyes, it looked like some Celtic spirit had spiraled down through her Gypsy bloodline and taken over her.

"Mary Kay," she harshly said, "did not deserve this!"

That's when Mary Kay opened her eyes.

And whispered, "Where am I?"

It took all three of us to help her climb out of the trunk, for she was really woozy. "Someone drugged her!" Kat snapped, angrily.

Kat closed the trunk lid, then helped us lead Mary Kay to the row of junked cars at the edge of the junkyard. As we settled Mary Kay down on the far side of a red Ford station wagon, the sound of gravel crunching beneath car tires came to us. We looked out to the road some distance from the junkyard. "A patrol car!" Dec said. "We best hide!"

    We watched Big Ty drive through the gates of Catlin's. He parked behind the Kennedy car, killed his engine and climbed out. Ty looked in our direction, but we hunkered down behind the junked Ford, our eyes in line with its windows which allowed us to see all the way across the junkyard without being seen. He walked over to Jon Kennedy's car and turned the key that had been left there in all the commotion back in town. "Sorry, sweetheart," he said. "Shouldn't have been so damned greedy, Mary Kay. Now look at you, deader than a door nail. Jon is dead, too. Killed by King Henry over on Elk Street. And that leaves me the only keeper. Finders keepers, losers weepers."

    Ty opened the lid of the trunk and let out a startled, "What the hell!"

    Behind the Ford, the three of us looked worriedly at Mary Kay slumped against the side of the car, as if maybe in her groggy condition she might answer him. But she had fainted and was out for the count.

    Big Ty hauled a large suitcase out of Kennedy's Chevy. It was heavy, because Ty had trouble carting it over to the trunk of his car. Once he deposited it into the trunk, he slammed the lid closed. Our dogs, content to chase rabbits down by the Blue, came to check on us. We raised our heads and peeked through the windows of the Ford. As the three dogs ran up to give Ty a friendly greeting, he scanned the rust buckets around him suspiciously. My heart did flips flops as Big Ty lowered his hand to his pistol holstered at his waist.

    Dec and I were both rising to our feet, when the loud roar of a Harley filled the air and a biker came thundering into the junkyard. He was a big Indian with long black hair, reminding me of Will Sampson from the Charles Bronson *Hickock* movie. He rode toward Ty, whirlwinds of dust kicking up behind his motorcycle. He parked behind the Kennedy car, killed his bike, and lowered his mirror shades, revealing the greenest eyes I'd ever seen. The Indian put his kick stand down and dismounted. He bent down and scooped up Cooper, cradling him in his arms. The three of us remained hidden behind the car, listening to the two men talking thirty feet in front of us. "Afternoon, Deputy," the Indian said, holding Cooper and stroking him behind the ears.

Ty snapped, "You're late, Ghost! We were supposed to cut that deal two days ago! I've got buyers!"

Ghost kneeled down, allowing Dum-Dum and Badger to sniff him. "It's not your buyers you should worry about. It's the men from New Orleans. How many conspiracies can you juggle? This ledger? This gold? Twelve angry bikers known as Vandals?"

Ghost settled Cooper down beside Dum-Dum and Badger. All three dogs appeared to like the Indian and wouldn't leave him alone. He said. "You've been playing me. Been working out the deal for two months, and I've never once seen evidence that you are a serious player. These men from New Orleans? Give them what they came for, Deputy. That gold is going to take a lot of people down. Give them the gold and walk away a rich man by landing me a buyer for that ledger."

Ty laughed. "You saying it is worth more than—"

"Worth more than gold," Ghost said, "that doesn't belong to you."

Ty said, "What are my odds? Two thugs. Twelve Vandals. A sleazy lawyer. A greedy bail bondsman. I've got an Ace in the hole."

Ghost said, "Aces and Eights is the hand Wild Bill held the night he got his head shot off up there in Deadwood. You've got a lot of Jokers running wild in your town. I'd throw in my hand if I was faced with those odds. Find a buyer for that ledger and be done with this deal."

Minutes later, both the Indian biker and Big Ty drove out of Catlin's junkyard, leaving in their wake swirling clouds of dust. After they drove off, Chris stepped outside. The tall, dark-haired Gypsy kid just stood there, staring at us still standing behind the Ford. Kat said, "Chris, we've got Mary Kay here! She's been shot up with some kind of dope!"

"Sweet Jesus!" Chris said, running over to find her still slumped against the car. He hauled her to feet and walked her on into the house. Kat said, "You two should return to town. This is something we must deal with on our own. We'll take care of Mary Kay."

As she joined Chris inside the house, the dogs and I followed Dec back to Mose Hadley's boat. As we trudged across the field to the river, Dec and I were in a daze, not sure what we had stumbled upon. I said, "What if Ty saw us? What if he told Sheriff Mac we skipped school? What if when we get back to the docks there's a Sheriff's posse waiting for us? What about Mary Kay being stuffed in that trunk? What does Ty and Jon Kennedy have to do with each other? What if there are more shady people involved in this?"

Climbing into the boat, we both heard Chris Catlin let out the most sorrowful wail we'd ever heard from up near the house.

His pitiful cry tore through our hearts and would haunt us both for a long while to come.

Chapter Five

Fifteen minutes later, Dec steered us around the bend in the Blue, where we saw two men having a fight up on the river bank ahead of us. "That's Hiney!" I said, staring at the huge man going fisticuffs with Roman Kowski. Those two big brutes were wailing away at each other. Roman was wildly throwing haymakers, his fists barely landing on Hiney's brawny body. Hiney wasn't feeling those little bee stings either. For every fist that whizzed past his nose, he landed a meaty thwack that rocked Roman all the way to his toes.

It was Badger and Cooper who spoiled the moment. The two dogs started barking anxiously at the two brawlers up on the river bank. Badger ran back and forth on the deck of the boat, whining and carrying on like he was going to a fire. Cooper howled like he'd treed a big raccoon, his, "Arrooo! Arooo!" carried all the way down river.

Upon hearing the dogs, Hiney took a fist to the eye. Another of Rome's fists plowed into Hiney's nose, and blood spurted through the air. I grabbed onto Badger, clamping a hand over his mouth. Dec tried to catch Cooper, but the wily little dog dipped, dodged, and darted away like a scalded squirrel, leaving Dec's outstretched hands empty.

And that's when we suddenly had troubles of our own to deal with.

The boat engine spluttered and died. That old engine growled like a cornered badger and gave up the ghost. Dec looked at me. I looked back at him. There was bewilderment in his eyes. There was fear in my own. If we didn't have a running engine when we reached the cut in the channel ahead of us, we would be swept right over the dam some two-hundred yards in front of us. It was a five-foot fall to the river below.

My little sister, Donna, had once been catching frogs near the dam, when she fell into the river. She had been swept away by the rushing water and swept over the dam. In that black water she had been churned like weekday work clothes thrown into the Sunday wash. That terribly swift water had her bouncing like a cork, slammed to the river bottom, sucked back to the surface, twirled round and round, then sucked back underwater again. Yes, she lived, but my Uncle Bill nearly drowned pulling her out of the mad-dog suck of that river.

I could tell Dec knew how desperate our situation was. I could tell, too, that he was tempted to jump overboard and swim for the nearest shore. But I wasn't about to go into those swift, deep waters. And I wasn't risking the life of Badger to have him follow me. Dec said, "Either we abandon ship, or we take the rodeo river ride, down and over the dam!"

From the nearby bank, we heard Roman squawk, "You sum bitch!"

He then did almost a perfect cartwheel down the set of wooden stairs stretching from the upper bank and down to the shoreline of the river. That poor fool must have made twenty clunking sounds as his head, his elbows, his butt, his knees, and his clodhopper boots came in contact with the rotten boards of those steps. We didn't see the mighty punch that sent Roman clumsily falling down the staircase, but we did see Hiney scoop up a large burlap bag the two men had been fighting over.

The red-haired giant carefully slung that sack over one meaty shoulder. He laughed out loud, spraying blood from his smashed nose all down the front of his overalls as Roman somersaulted into the river.

"You shouldn't have tried to kill the babies," Hiney said. "Rome Kowski, you are a bad man! A cruel, bad man!"

Dec and I, however, had no more time to see what Hiney did next. Cussing and muttering, Dec cranked hard on the wheel. All his straining and pulling had little effect on the direction that boat was going. It was headed right toward the middle of the dam. Cooper and Badger started barking. Badger ran over to me, head-butting me gently. Cooper ran back and forth from bow to stern, whining, yipping, and growling.

Still cranking hard on the wheel, Dec looked ahead of us and his eyes got round as Aunt Betty's silver-dollar pancakes! He cried, "Hawk, we're going over in the next two minutes!"

My eyes closed as I said the first earnest prayer I had said in the last five years. I suddenly heard Dec say, "Oh, holy Jesus!"

We were then thrown forward on the deck as the boat came to a complete stop right there in the middle of river. In total amazement, Dec and I looked over the stern of the boat to see Hiney Scrabble standing chest-deep in water in the middle of the river, and holding onto the tow rope of the boat with one hand. The big goliath still had the burlap bag slung over one shoulder and he was having one heck of a time juggling both the rope and the bag around to keep from losing his grip on either.

"Gotcha, boys!" Hiney said, acting as chipper as the collection priest on Easter Sunday. "Hiney won't let you drown!"

It was a miracle! The boat was not moving! It was being pulled down stream by the suck and flow of the river, but Hiney, with a big grin on his furry face, was keeping it in place by holding onto the tow rope with one hand, keeping us from going over the dam.

Having recovered from Hiney's last powerful punch, Roman had dragged himself out of the river. He stared at us for long, silent moments. As if suddenly realizing the trouble we were in, the big scruffy man came to life and ran up the stairs, shouting, "I'll go get Sheriff Mac!"

Hiney must have stood there in the middle of the Blue River pulling on that rope for close to half an hour. By the time, Sheriff Mac and Uncle Bill got down to the same stairway Rome had rolled down, Hiney was huffing and puffing like a forge billow. It was his brawn against the powerful pull of the river. And he was determined to win.

Mac and Bill borrowed a canoe from Les McAdams who owned the bait shop a block upriver. On such short notice, it was the best they could get to rescue us. A boat with a motor would have served the purpose better, but with the situation getting beyond desperate, the canoe would have to do. "Hold on!" Mac called, as he paddled to get out to the middle of the river. "We'll get you out of the drink in a mad minute!"

Hiney gave a loud laugh, his guffaws echoing across the water. "Speaking of drink," he chuckled, "a shot and a pint be a good reward for saving these hooligans!"

The first thing to go into the canoe as Mac and Uncle Bill pulled alongside Hiney was the burlap bag he'd been holding onto all this time.

He'd slung it around his thick neck as he fought the suck of the river, and he looked mighty relieved as he flung it aboard the canoe and it landed at Mac's feet.

Dec took that old saying that a captain goes down with his ship literally, because as Mac latched onto the side of the boat, he tossed Cooper over into Uncle Bill's arms. Once his beagle was settled at Bill's feet, he sent Badger over the side and flying into the middle of the canoe. Turning to me, Dec said, "You're next, Hawk. Don't fall in the river!"

Thirty seconds after I launched myself over the side of Mose Hadley's boat and landed in the canoe, Dec was safe beside me. Mac, in the stern of the canoe, paddled with firm and even strokes, turning us around and heading us back to the bank. "Hiney?" Mac called over one shoulder. "Hold on just a little longer! We'll be back to get you!"

Looking all lonely like in the middle of those dark waters, Hiney called back, "Sheriff Mac, you better hurry! I'm getting awful tired!"

When we pulled up alongside the dock at the end of that stairway, Uncle Bill tossed me to Roman standing on the dock. Bill then flung Dec into Rome's outstretched hands. Badger leaped onto the dock and Bill gently handed Cooper over to us waiting to catch the smaller beagle.

It was just as Mac and Uncle Bill got that canoe turned around that we heard a mighty roar from the middle of the river. Unfortunately, the boat finally won out. Hiney lost his footing, and being attached to the boat by the rope wrapped so tightly around his one arm, he was drug behind the craft as it careened toward the dam thirty feet downstream. That current was too strong. The last we saw of Hiney before he went floundering and flailing over the dam, was him coming untangled from the rope and that rushing water carried him on over and dumping him in the madly churning waters six-feet below.

A second later, Mose Hadley's boat shattered on the rocks below. Tears sprang to Dec's eyes as he whispered, "We killed Hiney!"

Mac and Uncle Bill desperately searched for any sign of Hiney in that churning white water at the bottom of the dam. They had to paddle backwards to keep from being swept over the dam, too. I was just standing on my tiptoes so I could see over the dam from the dock nearly sixty feet away, when Dec bumped into me as he tried to get away from the burlap sack that was moving at his feet. Badger and Cooper growled at the sack. "Here," Rome said, reaching down to grab the burlap sack. "I'll take care of that. They're going in the river where they belong."

Badger took a protective stance, his hackles raised and a serious growl contorting the features of his face. My dog did not want Roman to touch that sack for some reason, and I had to step up to the plate and back him. Even if it meant slapping Roman's big hands away as he reached out to snatch it up from the dock. Roman's look of surprise turned into an ugly sneer. Snorting in disgust, his eyes strayed past us to the burlap sack. "Maybe you peckerwoods," Roman snarled, "should have been drowned when you were little, too!"

Badger stopped the irate man dead in his tracks as he lunged at him. One part of me wished that my dog would bite Roman. The other part of me, however, knew that once a dog in our town bit someone they were considered vicious and needed to be put down. Fortunately, Badger grazed the fly of Rome's overalls with his teeth. Cooper tore into Rome's booted feet, nipping and snarling and carrying on like he was a wild Bengal tiger. The big man literally danced a jig there on the dock. Rome cursed at us in some strange jabbering, then darted up the stairway and disappeared when he got to the top of the bank. Dropping to one knee to calm Cooper, Dec said, "He sure wanted that sack to go into the river."

Kneeling down beside the burlap sack, I slowly opened it and looked down at three tiny furry faces peering back up at me. "Puppies?" I said. "Rome was trying to drown them! And Hiney was trying to save them!"

Dec said, "And we killed poor Hiney stealing that boat, Hawk."

On the far bank, Mac shouted, "Bill, he's coming to the surface!"

"Haruff!" exploded into the air at the bottom of the dam. "Arrrrr!" came next, and finally, "Holy Jesus, this water is cold!"

And there, risen from the dead, was Hiney Scrabble, the hero of the day, truly still amongst the living.

Chapter Six

Sheriff Mac was not pleased with us as he led Dec and I away from the Blue River. We wished he had hollered. Cussed us out. Shouted our names in anger. But Mac carried the burlap sack to his patrol car, and ushered us and our dogs into the backseat, refusing to give us so much as a peek as he drove us away.

He stopped first at my house, passing along those three rescued pups to my mom. She was always saving unwanted kittens, puppies, and once even nursed Harv Brindel's pet monkey, Oscar, back to life after the chimp caught himself a bad fever. My mom, Martha, said it was a shame that Harv kept Oscar locked up in a cage high up on the side of a tree. She said it wasn't natural for any creature to be cooped up in a cage like that. Dad shared with us a few stories about other chimps in other small towns. Dad said there were seven caged chimps living out their days confined to steel cages situated high up off the ground.

I often stopped by his cage to chat with him. The big chimp seemed to like my company as he always gave me his undivided attention while I would jaw away at him. Three times now, I had tossed him up a banana. He got all excited each time I did so, catching those bananas and eating them with quite hoots coming from somewhere inside him. After that, Oscar always looked forward to my visits.

My mom took those puppies off of Sheriff Mac's hands. She said she'd force Badger to be nice to them, and make sure he knew they were now going to share our fenced-in backyard. We followed Mac into our backyard when he handed her the burlap sack full of puppies. Dec told her how Rome Kowski had been drowning them in the river, then said they were special due to Godly intervention when he sent Hiney down to the river to save them. A stern look on his face, Mac said, "Martha? Would you see to Cooper for a short time? His master is headed to jail. He'll be around later to collect him, if that suits you."

My mom whistled at the beagle who had sat all this time in the backseat of Mac's patrol car. Cooper took one look at my mom and sprang out of the car and darted inside the yard. At least, Mac did not tell my mom why he was carting us down to jail. Mom would have cuffed me upside the head before Mac had us back in the patrol car.

Mac's silence haunted us all the way down to city jail.

When we got there, Deputy Noah greeted us in the main office, grinning as usual. Mac escorted us past him and into the first cell. Noah's cheerful attitude quickly faded when Mac told him about our theft of Mose Hadley's boat. A sad-eyed look was all he could muster as he locked us into that first cell. Dec and I sat down on the bottom bunk, sadly accepting the fact that we were criminals. As if to confirm it, Henry McGinn, in the next cell, said, "Good little boys never steal boats."

King Henry's eyes were all bloodshot and he raked his fingers through his scraggy beard as he said, "It was my row boat that your brother stole from my back alley one night last year. Your dad had been drinking, when he and your mom got into a knock down drag-out in your kitchen. Your dad, Hawk, has one fierce temper. Mac arrested him for hitting your mom. He put him right here in this cell, the one with the window overlooking the alley."

Henry laughed. "Yep, Richard rode your old horse down here with a length of chain, intending to bust your dad out of this jail. He threw a chain through this window above me, when Amos threw it right back out at him. He told Richard to go on home as he would be out in the morning. Disgruntled, Richard took his chain and horse, and turned around and started for home. When lo and behold, he spotted my boat all slathered in moonlight next to my garage. He tied my boat off with that chain, attached it to the harness of your horse, and drug my boat all the way down the alley to home! Sheriff Mac followed those drag marks the next morning down my alley, and found my bottomless boat parked up against your dad's work shed. Ha, he arrested Richard and hauled his butt back down here! So, while your dad was getting released from jail, Richard was going to jail! Funniest thing I ever saw!"

I had never heard this story before. My brother was always in trouble. It is why he was always being locked up in the State Home. Henry cackled like a mad hen. I looked toward the office and saw Sheriff Mac heading toward the door. Deputy Berry asked, "Sure you don't want my help, Mac? I could go tell Henry's wife about the shooting."

"No, Noah," Mac said. "I'll deal with Henry's wife."

With that, Sheriff Mac went out the door to tell Henry's wife that he had snapped and shot Jon Kennedy dead. Dec looked over at Henry in the far cell. "What were you carrying a gun for, Mr. McGinn?"

Henry suddenly slunk down on his bed, his eyes shifting in fear to the window above him. "They are watching! They've been stalking us every night for a week! They follow my daughters around town after dark! They watch my wife at the grocery store! They peek in our windows at night! They are relentless! They are fox-crafty, like marauding coyotes! And they want what has been stolen from them!"

"Who, Mr. McGinn?" I asked.

Henry whispered, "Ghosts of the Templars! And they are many, and one never knows when the ghosts walk among us!"

Henry hunkered down on his bed, putting a pillow over his head like a little kid afraid of the dark. It was in Henry's silence that we settled in for the long haul, figuring we were destined to stay the night there.

Dec nudged me with his knee to rouse me. I stirred and perked up my ears to hear Kat's voice coming from the office: "Deputy Noah, my pa said you were Cingane of the Three Rivers province in Romania. Is this true?"

Noah leaned forward in his chair, peering at Kat with a keen look in his eyes. "The Gypsies of Blue Springs swear I am the grandson of a Cingane Chieftain. Let's just keep that our secret, okay?"

Noah stared down at her for several seconds before he glanced toward the jail cell. Dec and I quickly closed our eyes, pretending we were still sleeping. We had to lay for quite some time before Noah was convinced we were not eavesdropping on their talk. When he at last looked away, Dec and I opened our eyes to slits to peer out there in the office.

"I was scrapping," Kat said, "two cars hauled out to our place. I found Mary Kay in the trunk of Jon Kennedy's car!"

Noah sat up straighter in his chair. "Mary Long Soldier? But why?"

Kat said, "My brother was seeing Mary, and now she's hiding out to our place. But Christian is mad as hell. You have to find him. If he follows through with his vow, he will spend the rest of his life in the state pen. Chris has a gun! He is out to kill Cliff Loyd, the bail bondsman. Please stop him!"

Noah left the jail in quite a hurry. Kat went along with him, probably figuring if the deputy found him, she could be there to talk sense into Chris, who was obviously distraught over what had happened to his girl friend. King Henry said, "Loyd is deep in with the Knights! He's one of their ambassadors!"

Dec looked over at Henry, his nose all scrunched up. "What are these Knights all about, Mr. McGinn. Don't you think if they are that dangerous you should have been letting my dad in on their secret? You say they been stalking you? Why? How come you're so interesting to them?"

I thought Dec sounded a little like Sherlock Holmes, carrying on one of his investigations. It was a masterful performance for a junior detective, especially since he cut to the chase with his questions. Henry blinked like an owl in bright sunlight as he looked across the cells to Declan. "Told you never know who the ghosts are, didn't I? Why, your dad might be inside the circle, Declan Connors. That Kennedy boy was sent here to get back their gold."

He looked past us outside the cell and the front door of the jail house swung open. Henry hunkered down on his bed, slid his pillow over his face, and muttered, "Broken vow, broken knight!"

Big Ty entered the jail, eyes fixed on the office ahead of him. It was only when he reached his desk that he noticed us seated like two little monkeys inside the cell. Ty said, "What did you do, boys?"

Dec said. "We cut school out of respect for President Kennedy. We could not finish school we were so upset over it. Our teachers were crying. Our classmates were crying. Johnny Bolis barfed chocolate milk all over the lunchroom room floor. It was getting sadder and grosser by the moment, so we cut out. We were minding our own business up in our tree fort when . . ."

Damn it! I immediately thought. *Shut your big mouth, Declan! Do you even realize what you're saying! You're gonna give us away and as stupid as Big Ty is, he might put two and two together!*

Ty's entire demeanor changed. He now glowered at us. He'd acted peculiar when he saw Jon with that bullet hole in his chest, like he was glad Jon was dead. I wanted so badly to let him know we'd seen him at the scene of the shooting, and also out at Catlin's when he'd opened the trunk and didn't find Mary Kay in there. I especially wanted to tell him we'd seen him take that suitcase from the trunk of Jon Kennedy's car. But I kept my mouth shut. To my relief, Mac stormed in and informed Ty that Chris was armed with a gun and hunting for Loyd.

Things kicked into high gear as Mac sent Ty out searching for him. Mac let us go without even a lecture. He told us we would be expected to work off paying for Mose Hadley's boat starting tomorrow, but he didn't seem as mad at us as we expected. He sent us on our way from the jail with a gentle pat on Dec's back and a ruffling of my thick, black hair. "Home to bed," Mac said, sending us on our way.

Chapter Seven

It was dark by the time Dec and I reached the cut off to our houses. Mine was down the street at Elk Street, and his was two blocks away on Ella. We could see lights in Grandma's house located between the two. Rebecca Bower had been rescued by my great-grandpa Amos, who was friends with Samuel Clemens down in Hannibal, Missouri, where the two became steamboat captains. Amos had whisked Rebecca away from the Ohio floods, bringing her to Beatrice in the 1800s. While Amos continued to ply the Missouri, Rebecca remained here. It was a house fire that 10-year-old Billy Hawkins got burned in one night. Doctors wanted to amputate his legs, but Rebecca doctored him with her Lakota medicine. Later, Uncle Bill became the Fire Marshall of Beatrice. All because Gran B used her Native medicine on him.

I liked to visit her because she would open up her windows, throw wide her doors, and then scatter bird seed on the kitchen floor and invite birds and rabbits right into her house. Most of my friends said she was, "That weird old lady on Elk Street who lets rabbits poop in her pantry!"

Dec and I were always welcome at her house. It was dark inside of Grandma Becky's den. Shadows seemed to leap out at us as she ushered into the room, backlit by a low burning fire in her wood stove. She offered us seats on her couch. She took a seat in her favorite rocker near the stove. Her recliner was occupied. Chris Catlin looked like he was going to leap out the nearest window. I looked over at the pistol that lay beside him on the nearby end table. "My dad," Dec said, "heard that you were gunning for Cliff Loyd. I am sorry about Mary Kay."

"She's pregnant," Chris said.

A sudden and long silence followed.

I asked, "Is it yours?"

"Hawk!" Dec nearly shouted.

"Jessie Hawkins!" Gran B scolded.

Chris turned his sad-eyed gaze on me. "You know nothing of the Cingane. Before there were Catholics, before there were even Christians, my Gypsy folk helped hide the baby Jesus when King Herod demanded all babies be killed so that they could not be rivals to his kingship. It was the Cingane who whisked Mary and baby Jesus off to Egypt to escape this baby purge. The Cingane saved the world with this deed. Gypsy folk live by a code of honor. Until Mary Kay and I are married, I would not sleep with her. Although it crushes my heart, Mary Kay has an unborn baby with an unknown father."

It became quiet there in Gran B's den, only the crackle of popping embers inside the wood stove filled the air. Letting out a long sigh, Chris said, "Jesse James, a 33rd degree Freemason, left caches of gold belonging to the Knight's of the Golden Circle across dozens of states. After the Civil War, the Knights tried to start a second uprising against the Federal Government. The James-Younger Gang funded plans for a second Civil War. At the Minnesota bank robbery of 1876, Jesse broke his ankle, and fled down the Missouri to the west of Lincoln, forty miles from here. There he discovered a hideout known as Robber's Cave. King Henry's grandfather inherited a map and Tyler used this map to get two gold bars out of that cave. They hid it with Loyd at the courthouse. Then Mary Kay became entangled in their scheme."

Dec and I stared at Chris, hardly believing that the girl he loved had been mixed up in something so bizarre. We devoured the Hardy Boys and Nancy Drew series whenever they hit the shelves of the Beatrice Library. But this was way beyond dime novel mysteries.

Chris said, "There are men coming. Mary Kay went to the Gypsies of Blue Springs, who have an underground network. The Cingane have connections with shady people. The information she passed onto them went to the Memphis Mafia. That suitcase Ty took from the Kennedy car? That was only half the gold. Right now, Mary Kay is being guarded by a handful of Gypsy folk out at the junkyard. But if these men come, they will want to deal with her. In fact, that is what this Jon Kennedy was doing when he shot her up with dope. The only reason he did not kill her is, he was trying to make her tell him where the other half of that gold is."

Dec and I left Gran B's house at a little before nine o'clock. Chris had accepted her invite to stay the night there at her place to keep him out of mischief. He was still miffed at Loyd for the conspiracy that Mary Kay had been entangled in, but he was smart enough to know not to interfere with these men coming to town to deal with Loyd. Something had been nagging at Declan as we left Gran's house. He said, "Henry knew about these Knights. He said, *'You never know who the ghosts are. Your dad may be inside the circle.'* What if that's true, Hawk? What if there's secret society stuff going on right here in town? What if my dad already knows about this gold?"

"King Henry," I said, "is four pickles short of a peanut butter and pickle sandwich. How could you put any stock in what he said? Besides, these Knights are connected with the Klan. The Klan hate black folk. Your dad is good friends with the Hadleys, the only black family living here. He even went fishing for carp with Mose on the Big Indian. Your dad is not a racist and treats Mose kindly."

Dec still didn't look too sure, as if Henry's words had put some kind of poison pill in his brain, and that poison was slowly spreading, making him doubt his own dad. Mac was kind and gentle. He spent time with his son, and made his friends all feel welcome whenever they came to visit at their house. Dec loved him fiercely, so I know it was a blow for him to have listened to Henry's yakking. We both stopped as Kat approached us from down the street. In one long breath she said, "Men just pulled up to the courthouse. They ordered Sheriff Mac to get your dad, Hawk."

"Let's do some spying," Dec said. "On the day of the Corliss murder trial last July, Hawk and I climbed up the fire escape on the side of the courthouse. We slipped through a window on the third floor. We wormed on our way on our stomachs out onto the catwalk above Judge Neely's courtroom, and watched the court hearing. Just like Shadow Ninjas."

As we headed to the courthouse, I told Kat, "Chris is over at Gran B's. She talked sense into him. That was stupid of him to go after Loyd, but I can understand he's just concerned about Mary Kay."

Kat nodded and said, "Mary Kay first told me about the baby, asking if I knew of a Gypsy witch—"

"Witch?" Dec asked. "Gypsy witches flying brooms? Gazing into crystal balls? Casting spells? They kill babies and then remove them from the woman's privates. Are you saying a gypsy witch was gonna help Mary Kay lose her baby, Kat?"

"No!" she said. "There is a Cingane healer in Blue Springs. She advised Mary Kay to turn to Saint Sarah, patron saint of the Romani. During the persecution of early Christians, Lazarus and the mother of John and James, sailed to France. Sarah, a native of Egypt, was chief of her tribe on the banks of the Rhône. She had visions that the Saints who had been present at the death of Jesus would come by boat. The sea was rough, Sarah floated toward the Saints on a cloak thrown on the water and helped them reach land by praying."

Dec said, "My dad claims the Romani are nomads who travel in house wagons. Some have psychic powers. They can see the future. They can levitate, travel by astral projection, invoke curses, and channel spirits. Romani that practice that aren't serving God, they are serving the Devil."

Kat said, "The Romani were traveling Egyptians, exiled from Egypt for hiding the baby Jesus from King Herod. Cingane is a Christian sect, deemed heretics, because we are neither Hebrews or Gentiles. We believe in the Melchizedek priesthood that Jesus is the King-Priest who will redeem the world. Roma groups are all over the world, Spain, France, Germany, Denmark, Norway, Sweden, Poland, Hungary, Turkey, and Lithuania. Mary Kay prayed to Saint Sarah, who instructed her to talk with the Cingane Chieftain, who in turn contacted the Freemasons of Charlottesville, who contacted the secret cabal of Knights."

Kat followed us up the fire escape to the open window leading to the third floor of the courthouse. It was a three-story stone building with tons of oak woodwork inside. Benches in the courtroom were all carved of oak wood from trees that grew wild down along the Big Indian River. Before stepping through that window, I said, "Dad said Indians had a village beside Big Indian creek. He said those oak trees used to create the inside of the courthouse were infused with wood smoke from a thousand campfires of those same Indians. He once had me sniff the benches inside the courtroom to see if I couldn't detect the smell of wood smoke. All I could smell was the furniture polish those benches were slathered in.

"Dad knows a lot about the Pawnee, natural-born enemy of the Lakota. Tribes clashed to claim hunting grounds. The Lakota, Pawnee, Blackfoot, and Crow all fought bloody battles right here on the courthouse lawn. The only reminder of them hangs in the main entryway. It is a picture of a band of Lakota riding horses on a buffalo hunt. There's a lone brave at the front of the hunting party. His face is blurry and you can't see his features very well, but atop a layer of white powder, he has a jagged yellow lightning bolt down the left side of his face, and blue hailstones on his right cheek. Crazy Horse, greatest war chief of the Oglala Lakota. The reason his face is all blurry is because he refused to have his picture taken. Sitting Bull, Red Cloud, American Horse, Little Big Man sat still long enough for their images to be captured on film, but never Crazy Horse. Dad said he feared once his image was captured, he would be trapped in only one realm. For a war leader like Crazy Horse who had the magical ability to ride through a hail of bullets, his image captured like that, would never allow him to ride in this realm and the Otherworld.

"In 1860, Crazy Horse fought in many battles against the Crow, Shoshone, Pawnee, Blackfeet, all enemies of the Lakota. He fought in the Sand Creek Massacre, the Battle of Platte Bridge, the Battle of Red Buttes, and Fetterman's massacre. In 1867, Crazy Horse fought in the Wagon Box Fight. The Lakota suffered heavy casualties, but Crazy Horse came out of the battle untouched by even one bullet. Dad said his secret, and why he was never even grazed by a white soldier's bullet, is he rode in both worlds."

As we climbed in that window at the courthouse, I wished we could blend with the Otherworld, because then like ghosts, we could sneak up on those holding a meeting below and they would never even know we had been there.

Chapter Eight

We snuck up onto the catwalk above the hallway of the courthouse. There, we belly-crawled our way up to the spindles of the catwalk railings, peeking through with our cheeks pressed against them to watch the show below us. Mac stood before the door of the sheriff's department. He had his arms folded in front of his chest. Beside him, Noah struck the same defensive pose, looking cantankerous.

The three men were dressed in suits, their black shoes so shiny they reflected light in the courthouse hallway like reflectors on road signs. One was big and bald, looking like *Sgt. Rock*, the Comic book Marine. The second man was slim and cocky, reminding me of the Asp from the *Little Orphan Annie* cartoons in the Sunday Funny papers. The third man reminded me of a bear dressed in a fancy suit, for he had long brown hair and a full beard. If anyone was the godfather of these mafia men it had to be this third guy, for as crusty as they appeared, Rock and the Asp showed him great respect, offering him a chair to sit in. The large man sat down, thoughtfully stroking his long beard.

If I had to compare my dad to anyone, it would be Beatrice-born movie star, Robert Taylor AKA Spangler Arlington Brugh. Only thing is, Dad wore wire-rimmed glasses that made him look like a college professor more so than the tree trimmer he actually was. And unlike Robert Taylor, my dad was not a hero of any sort. Amos Hawkins was just one of those regular kind of guys, and not a soul in our town spoke ill of him. His usual greeting to most everyone he met was a cordial, "How'd do?" Which in proper English meant "How do you do?"

Come to think of it, Dad had a might funny way of talking. When I listened to him jawing at the dinner table, I would hear things like:

"That sum bitch."

"Quicker than Jack the Bear."

"Those clouds is thick as pea-green soup."

"Queerer than a three-dollar bill."

"Worthless as tits on a boar."

"People in hell want ice water, too!"
"Slower than a three-legged dog."
"Took off like a scalded dog."
"Smarter than a box of rocks."
"Slower than molasses at Christmas time."
And last but not least, "Well, I'll be go to hell!"

As a kid, sometimes it boggled my mind. But it also may be where my love of language and words all started, too.

The moment Dad walked in down there in the entry way of the courthouse, the bear in the suit said, "My name is Silas Vance. And you are Amos Hawkins, correct? In case you did not hear the news down here in Beatrice, President John F. Kennedy was assassinated at 12:30 this afternoon in Dallas, Texas."

Silas withdrew a folded sheet of paper out of the inner pocket of his suit jacket. He handed the paper to my dad seated there in the chair looking like a school boy in trouble for cheating on his test.

Dad unfolded the paper and opened it up.

"What is the title, Mr. Hawkins?" asked Silas.

"Flechette," Dad quietly said.

Silas said, "What is a flechette, Mr. Hawkins?"

"An umbrella gun," Dad said, with a little quaver in his voice.

Silas said, "But that's not what you called it when you tried to patent this contraption back in 1960, is it?"

Dad said, "I named it the Rainy Day Gun, on account of most users would be carrying it when it rained."

Silas asked, "What purpose could a weapon like that serve?"

"My daughter," Dad said, "was followed home one night. We never did find out who the stalker was, but later, I tinkered around in my workshop and came up with a way to keep my daughter safe on late night walks here in town. A year ago, Darlene and my oldest daughter, Lily, were in a car accident. Lily, at 20 years-old, had been killed. Darlene suffered a broken jaw and a broken arm. She had her jaw wired shut because of that car wreck, which would have made it impossible for her to scream had that stalker ever caught up to her. As it was, she was walking home from movie theater in downtown Beatrice. The moment she left the well-lit downtown street, some burly guy followed her. She said she could hear his footsteps and the crunching of gravel as the guy walked about a block behind her. He started to close the distance between them, when Darlene spotted her younger sister, Donna, walking ahead of her. She took off at a sprint, grabbed Donna by the hand, and rushed her along down the sidewalk. The guy behind them clomped down the sidewalk at a run.

"Darlene and Donna ran up onto our porch. They rushed inside, slamming the door closed and turning to find my wife coming out of the kitchen. Donna told Martha of their stalker. Martha turned off all the lights in the house. And since I was away on tree-trimming work in the next county, she went and snatched up the iron poker from the wood stove. Darlene and Donna crept around inside our dark house, peeking out of windows to see if they could see the creeper outside. Darlene pulled back a curtain and peeked out, only to have the creeper peeking right back at her! She screamed and those wires on her jaw went flying in all directions! A minute later, Martha heard the knob on our front door turning. She swung that poker and clobbered me as I came through the front door. With a bleeding head, I grabbed up my shotgun and went out to patrol our yard. I never did spot the creeper, but later I created my Rainy Day gun for Darlene. After trying that gun out on watermelons, my brother, Bill, urged me to patent the umbrella, so I sent paperwork to the Library of Congress, but my patent was turned down due to the fact someone else had fashioned umbrellas into weapons."

Silas said, "Flechette. The name is French, meaning little dart. They've been used since World War I. Methods of launching vary, from a single shot to thousands in a single round. Lazy Dog bombs they were called during the Vietnam War. They might seem like a simple weapon, but they are complicated to create. Did you sell your work to anyone? The flechette you created could not have fallen into the hands of any unsavory characters, right? What do you know about the shooting?"

Dad said, "That the shooter was arrested by the Dallas Police seventy minutes after the shooting. He also gunned down a Dallas policeman."

Silas said, "Three shots were fired. President Kennedy and Senator Connally sustained injuries from those shots. The President, fatally, and Connally is still in serious condition. We've concluded that an audio recording of the shooting indicates there was an additional gunshot. There is a high probability there were two gunmen. One shot at long range with a sniper rifle. The other at close range using the gun hidden inside an umbrella. A perfect disguise for a gun. Who would suspect a man carrying an umbrella, except for the fact that it wasn't raining prior to the shooting. Still, we have to consider the probability that this second shooter got close enough to the car to fire his flechette. Which brings us to how your second weapon ended up in Prairie View Texas, less than fifty miles from Dallas, the place of the shooting."

Dad said, "My sister's husband is Dr. Bird Whitcomb, a skilled surgeon who lives in Prairie View, Texas. They live there on a farm. My sister wanted one of my special-made flechettes to shoot gophers making a nuisance of themselves in her garden. I made her one and shipped it to their home. But, you certainly don't suspect Dr. Whitcomb had anything to do with this shooting. Bird was there in the Dallas ER trying to save John Kennedy's life! Why would you even suspect a prominent surgeon of being involved in any of this?"

"I'm not insinuating a thing," Silas said. "I'm asking how your weapon ended up in southern Texas. We confiscated Dr. Whitcomb's flechette, and now we're going to have to ask you to turn yours over to us. This is after all related to the assassination of a United States President and to the shooting which took place here this afternoon."

It was Mac who asked, "How are the two related?"

Silas said, "Besides the fact that two Kennedys were shot on the same day, don't you find it a coincidence that the workshop where this umbrella gun was first created, is less than a block away from the sight of the shooting? Before you cite Henry McGinn for murder, don't you think you should consider that the victim was also armed with a gun?

And with the feud between the Kennedy and Hawkins clan never being resolved? Could be Amos Hawkins took a shot with his umbrella gun to get the whole shoot-out going down there on Elk Street."

Mac shook his head. "So, that's what you're doing here, Silas. You're here to defend Henry—"

"I'm here, Cormac," Silas said, "to make sure you don't embarrass yourself by taking this shooting to trial. When jurors hear that Kennedy had a gun, that the creator of this umbrella gun was in his workshop very near the shooting, the element of doubt will play pretty heavy on the minds of not only the jurors, but also the judge, don't you think?"

Chapter Nine

The three of us slipped back outside the window of the courthouse. We clambered down the stairway of the fire escape and were way beyond the courthouse sidewalk before any of us spoke.

"Who in the hell," Dec asked, "is Doc Whitcomb, Hawk?"

I said, "Dad's sister married Bird. They moved to Prairie View, Texas. Bird comes back here once a year to hunt with Dad and Uncle Bill. He's coming here this week for Thanksgiving. Dad and Bird both loved John F. Kennedy, and neither would want to harm him. However, my Aunt Lily is a strange old duck. She refuses to sit in the regular seat of any car. Instead, she sits down on the floor in the backseat. One time, while I was riding along with them, Aunt Lily planted herself on the floorboards behind Bird, and yakking a mile a minute, 'Bird? Be careful now, Bird! Stop at the red lights, Bird! Watch out for other cars, Bird! Slow down, Bird! Keep your eyes on the road, Bird!' When we finally pulled up in front of our house, Lily exited the car and said, 'Good job, Bird!'"

Dec said, "Odd duck, for certain, Hawk."

Kat said, "I've been watching the News most of the day, and the shooting of President Kennedy actually made me cry. It was a sad, tragic event that shook everyone up."

I said, "We have our own affair to deal with. We know you talked to Noah. We were locked up in a jail cell, listening when you came to the sheriff's office. We also heard from Chris about this stolen gold. Instead of telling Mac about Big Ty taking that suitcase out of Kennedy's trunk, why don't we find out where he hid that gold? Tyler Burke is cold-hearted. No way he will tell us where he hid that gold, but what about Mary Kay?"

"She don't know," Kat said. "She claims Henry hid the share they stole. Ty has half. Henry the other half. And these Knights want both halves returned to them. And Mary Kay is in the middle of this deal."

Dec fell strangely silent after that, simply waving at us as he faded off into the darkness. I walked Kat to Gran B's. She decided she would call home, check in with her dad, then stay the night there at Gran's to keep an eye on her brother. As I saw her to the door, Gran B stepped outside and handed me a ten-dollar bill.

"Hawk," she said, "be a dear, why don't you? Stop by Gracie's on the way home and pick up the book I had her bind for me. You can bring it by tomorrow, just don't lose this money, honey."

I slid the ten-dollar bill into my pocket and kissed her good-bye.

Mary Kay and her mom lived alone over on Ella Street. Gracie was as kind-hearted as her only daughter, quick with a hug or a kiss. The moment she saw me approaching her front porch, she ushered me inside. Gracie Long Soldier like most Lakota women I'd met, was pretty, her long, black hair braided and hanging over one shoulder. As our town librarian, she had learned the art of book binding.

Gracie held up a finely-crafted leather-bound ledger. "Please take this to your Grandma," she said. "Mary Kay phoned me from out at Catlins, telling me of the trouble she was in on account of Loyd. I'm relieved Mary Kay will be staying at the Catlin's until this thing blows over. Ty came inquiring about Mary Kay, but I told him nothing. Loyd also paid me a visit, asking where she is. Do you think King Henry knew about her baby? Do you think that is why he shot that young man?"

Too surprised to answer her, I mumbled, "I don't know."

Gracie planted a kiss on my forehead and then ushered me and that ledger outside and into the night.

I got the creeps as I rounded the next block and could see my house some distance ahead of me. I had the awful feeling someone was watching me. Tucking the ledger up under my chest, I turned around to look down the dark sidewalk behind me. I could see only shadows beneath the trees, beside houses, beside bushes, and beneath the light pole at the end of the block. I suddenly realized the bulb at the top of that light pole was not working. Either that, or someone had shot it out. For kicks, my brother, Richard, often shot that bulb out with his BB gun. It would shatter and then came an explosion of purple lights. Those bright purple colors would slowly fade down to only a crackle of reddish light before the filament inside the shattered light would go black.

But Richard was locked up currently in the State Home for his delinquent behavior. Either the bulb had burned out or else someone else had put it out, so the sidewalk below would be dark and shadowy.

I had a full block to run to my door, but just as I hunkered down into a starter's position, I heard gravel crunching behind me. I spun around, searching the entire block. There were cars parked up and down the street. There were four or five houses with lights on inside with most residents probably watching the ten o'clock News, Weather, and Sports. A low trickle of sound drifted from beneath the cottonwoods at the far end of the block. There was a black smudge there, sidling up against those ancient giants. A smudge that transformed into the large, slender form of a man stepping out from the bushes beside the cottonwoods fifty feet away.

I wheeled around and ran directly into the old oak situated to one side of the cracked sidewalk beneath me. I slammed into the tree and sprawled on the lawn, the ledger landing beside me. I dizzily clawed my way up the bole of the oak tree, my eyes shifting upward to see an ugly face ten feet above me. Oscar the monkey was seated there in his tree-side cage, peering down at me with his large yellow eyes. The big chimp gave a soft hoot and pressed his face through the bars of his cage.

Whoever was walking down the sidewalk must have seen him for he stopped, hesitant to step forward. As I turned around to look, the footsteps thudded directly toward me. A cold, clammy hand locked on my chin and slammed me back against the oak tree. I felt the terrible strength in the guy's hands as he locked his other hand around my throat. Even as my eyes traveled up to look into the Asp's dark eyes, I heard a loud *Click!*

I heard a deep voice say, "Leave off, Mister! Leave the boy alone!"

The hand came away from my throat. There was a flurry of movement and the Asp suddenly turned and ran, disappearing into the night. I looked up into the cold, blue eyes of Lawrence Shank. The tall, dark-haired, bearded man slid his flashy six-shooter back into the holster he wore strapped around his lean waist. Lawrence Shank stood there looking like a skinny scarecrow dressed in a Sunday morning black suit, complete with a black tie and a white dress shirt. He also wore a black cowboy hat, cocked to one side of his head.

Lawrence had a fire in his blue eyes. He then noticed me looking up at him, and he smiled. I nearly fainted from the shock of that alone. The town killer was now grinning at me. Back in the 40's, Lawrence had snapped one night. God only knows what drove him to murder his wife and his daughter. "Maybe a mental illness," Mom said, since she worked with the mad and insane out at the State Home. "Or maybe he didn't want them to suffer any more that this life had to dish out."

Judge Gilbert gave Lawrence a choice. Either he could spend the next twenty years locked up at the State Pen or he could serve his country by going off to fight in the war against the Germans. Lawrence chose the war, and surprising to everyone who knew of his cold-hearted murder, he fought so valiantly, that he was awarded several medals. He came back to live out the rest of his days, here in Beatrice, pretty much scaring the hell out of most people when he started walking around town carrying those six-shooters in his twin holsters.

Sheriff Mac once confronted him about going around armed like a gun slinger, but for some reason he allowed him to keep his guns. After all, Lawrence used them up and down the tracks leading in and out of town to shoot rats. He set himself up as the town exterminator, and anyone who had vermin problems hired him to shoot them dead. For some reason, my dad and Uncle Bill liked Lawrence and didn't give him no truck nor stick their noses into his business. And each Christmas and Thanksgiving, they made sure Lawrence didn't go hungry down there in the boxcar he lived in beside the rail yards.

One time my brother was shooting bottles down beneath the old railroad bridge outside of town. Lawrence appeared on the bridge above him and beckoned to him to come up to talk with him. Richard reluctantly climbed up the embankment to reach the old bridge. When he got there, Lawrence handed him one dollar and asked him to run down to Blackstone's and buy him a pouch of Red Man. When he returned, he said Lawrence looked a might surprised. He never expected my brother to hand him the tobacco and the change he had coming to him. He was so tickled, he said, "The son of Amos is such an honest young man. You've never murdered anyone, but you're damned proud of your John Dillinger reputation you've built as the town's most notorious delinquent due to your criminal activities. You need to change that, son."

He then tipped him a dime for his troubles.

Above Lawrence and I, Oscar gave a soft hoot. We both looked up to the big chimp staring down at us, a rather sad look in his big eyes. "He don't belong there," Lawrence said. "One of these days, his master, Harv Brindle and I are gonna have words. After that, that monkey is going to go free. Best watch yourself, young Jessie Hawkins. Trouble is coming, no doubt."

I figured Lawrence had been there somewhere in the darkness, listening in on our last conversation for the night. "Thanks," I said, forcing myself to smile. "I'd been in more trouble if you hadn't come along."

"Can I give you some advice?" he asked. "Don't go the way of your brother. That's no kind of life for you. He's spent more time locked up then he has freed. Dead ends lead to dead ends, boy."

I nodded, picked up the journal, and ran for home. Once inside my bedroom, I slid the ledger beneath my bed, figuring I would look at it first thing in the morning. I then turned off my bedroom light and peered out my window to see Lawrence tossing peanuts up to Oscar seated there in his cage near the sidewalk.

I thought, *The town killer, who feeds peanuts to the town chimp.*

Chapter Ten

The following morning, things took a creepy twist. At sunrise, I heard a scream piercing the air outside. I then heard Oscar hooting as he ran past my bedroom window. But that didn't make sense since Oscar was locked up in his cage. The horrible scream came again, and it caused shivers to run up and down my spine. Badger barked. The three puppies he had been sharing his blanket with on my bedroom floor, began yipping in high-pitched puppy voices.

I clamped a hand around Badger's nose, shutting him up. The puppies peered up at me, fear in their dark eyes at the sound of Dad running down the hall outside my room. The spring on the front screen door whined and Dad said, "Good God almighty! Martha! Call the police!"

Mom moved down the hallway to our dining room phone. I walked out into the hallway, Badger and the pups behind me. Sirens wailed from Uncle Bill's fire station on Court Street. And then, more sirens wailed like wolves howling at a midnight moon as they neared our house. The whole damned town awoke to the bizarre cacophony of sirens and barking dogs. Badger was determined to do his part in letting us all know there was good cause to be alarmed. The three pups joined in.

"Shush, Badger!" Dad said. "Hawk? Quiet them dogs down!"

I kneeled down there on the porch, trying to get the dogs to be quiet. "Shush," I said. "Got enough racket going on to wake up sleeping Jesus!"

I heard Dad say, "Gawd, who would have done such a wicked thing?"

I stood to my feet, Badger and the pups milling around me. I stared at Oscar's cage ten feet off the ground and bolted to that oak tree. Oscar was no longer inside of it. No, now there was the bloody form of a man scrunched up inside the cage. Sirens wailed from the nearby street. Two fire trucks came screaming down Court Street. Sheriff Mac came barreling up 8th Street in his patrol car. And soon, we had a crowd of nosey neighbors joining my dad beneath the blood-covered man huddled up there in Oscar's cage. It was Clifford Loyd, the bail bondsman involved with Big Ty in the theft of that gold.

Uncle Bill used several ladders to get Loyd out of Oscar's cage. He had a difficult time removing the hunting knife driven through Loyd's wrists pinning him to the tree. All the blood running down from cuts on Loyd's face made me sick to my stomach, and I would have fell back onto our porch if Dec wouldn't have latched onto me and said, "Sit down! You look as pale as Caspar the Ghost!"

As he settled me beside the dogs and the puppies, in a hushed voice I told him about the creeper who had been run off by Lawrence Shank last night, but before Dec could respond, Big Ty parked behind the two fire trucks. The sirens shut down. The only sound now was the chatter of the crowd that had gathered some distance from Oscar's tree. Noah herded the gawkers away from Harv Brindle's front lawn. Ty headed for Oscar's tree. For the next several minutes, Ty hovered over the firemen as they loaded Loyd into an ambulance. Taking one last look at the departing ambulance, Sheriff Mac said, "Deputy Burke, head over to the hospital. Take a statement from Cliff."

Ty stood frozen there in the street as a dozen Harleys came roaring down Elk Street, a motley crew of long-haired, bearded men seated on them. Each of the leather-clad bikers offered Ty an ugly scowl as they cruised past him. And then coming from the opposite direction was the big Indian who had met with Ty at the junkyard. Ghost stared at Oscar's empty cage, revved his bike, and raced away down the street.

The moment Big Ty drove away in his patrol car, Dec leaped off our porch. "Come on!" he hissed. "Let's be Investigators!"

After shooing the three puppies back inside my house, I got dressed, then followed Dec to our alley. Once there, I hopped on my old black Schwinn while Dec climbed aboard my brother's three-speed Sting Ray. Badger and Cooper trotted behind us as we peddled down the street.

Hiney Scrabble's truck came out the alley right in front of us. Hiney slammed on his brakes, while we practically did a face plant on the side of his old rust-bucket of a truck. Dec dug his underwear out of his butt and sat there on the bike adjusting himself. He muttered, "Geeshus, Hiney! You about made us hood ornaments on your truck!"

Hiney said, "You boys going for another boat ride soon? That be some ride, huh? Sheriff Mac be plenty mad, right?"

Dec said, "Yes, now we got to help pay for Mose's new boat. That was mighty nice of you to save them pups, Hiney. What's wrong with Rome Kowski? How could he be so mean as to drown those poor pups?"

As Hiney sat there, trying to come up with an answer, Dec came up with an idea. "Want to help us with a secret mission? Like a James Bond mission. Give us a lift to the hospital on Jackson."

Climbing out of his tow truck, Hiney scooped up Cooper and placed him in the bed of his truck. He then picked up Badger and did the same with him. After tossing our bikes into the bed with the dogs, he opened his passenger door and ushered us into the cab. When we got there five minutes later, Hiney dropped us behind the hospital's rear loading dock. We saluted Hiney as he drove away, leaving us and the two dogs near a copse of cedar trees. Snapping his fingers, Dec said, "Stay put right here, and guard our bikes."

Badger and Cooper stationed themselves by the trees next to our bikes. They watched us as we trotted over to the loading dock where Pete Dooley was busy at work unloading cases of pop from his delivery truck. "Need some help, Pete?" Dec asked him as we walked up beside the open end of the back of his truck. Pete gestured at two cases of soda still in the back of his truck. "Sure, just don't drop those cases or they'll be exploding pop cans firing off all over the place. Nice of you to offer."

As I carried the first case over to the loading dock by the back door of the hospital, Dec made up a good story. "We've been sentenced by my dad to community service. We got to help out all around town when we see someone needs help. So if we help you load all this soda inside, could you let my dad know we did the work?"

Pete gestured at Dec to take the last case of pop off of his truck. "Sure, Mr. Declan. I can always use the help from two strong young strapping lads like you two. But why'd you take Mose Hadley's boat?"

Sliding the case of pop across the dock to me so I could lift it up onto the cart with the first one, Dec said, "Ever read Mark Twain? Two wild sprites settled into our bodies. We just had to take that river trip. Besides, we saved some puppies."

"Puppies?" Pete said, a bit puzzled.

"Yep," Dec said as we followed Pete inside the hospital. We walked beside Pete with him straining to keep that two-wheeler on a straight course to the first pop machine on his route. Ty's loud voice echoed from out of the emergency ward: "I'm on official police business here, Doctor Wilson! I need to question Loyd about who assaulted him!"

Doctor Wilson blared, "This man has suffered severe trauma, Deputy! Wounds to his wrists! Cuts to his face! Let me do my job here, cleaning his wounds and medicating him! And then you can question him! He'll be staying in room 233! Go! Get you a coffee from the lunchroom!"

Ty stormed out of the emergency ward and stomped all the way into the cafeteria. He walked right past us, not even noticing we were there. We followed Pete down the hall to the next pop machine. It took us thirty minutes to help him unload those cases of pop. When Pete finished his job there at the hospital, he said, "I'll tell Sheriff Mac I appreciated the help with your community service."

We thanked him and scurried off down the hallway to the elevator. When we got off the elevator on the second floor, Dec casually walked over and scooped up a vase full of brightly colored flowers situated on a cart. Evidently, some nurse had been delivering them to individual rooms, and stepped away from her duties for a moment. So, quick-thinking Declan carried that vase with us as we made our way down the hall to room 233.

We passed four nurses on our harrowing trip down the hallway. But for some reason, those flowers got us warm smiles from the nurses who all seemed to be patrolling those halls in sort of a daze. It then occurred to us as we passed by the TV midway down the hallway. A report of the assassination of President Kennedy came from the TV, leaving most of those nurses sad. It was why Dec and I were a minor distraction to them as we walked down the hall and directly into room 233. Placing the flowers on a night stand beside the single bed in the room, Dec followed me into the room's bathroom. Once inside, we hunkered down on the edge of the bathtub and closed the door. Ten minutes later, a nurse wheeled Loyd into the room in a wheelchair and got him settled into bed. Big Ty was hot on their heels. He came tromping in to get his statement. "Who did this to you, Clifford?" he asked.

Loyd said, "Big, bald bulky guy. Other guy was a weasel. He talked funny. These guys want their gold. What did you do with it?"

"I hid one bar away," Ty said. "But Mary Kay stole the other one from your office and Jon Kennedy tried to get her to give it back to him. She wanted financial support for that baby. It was your baby, right?"

Loyd said, "It was someone else. Someone else she told about our plot, too. And that's why we're in trouble."

Big Ty snapped, "Where would she hide it?"

Loyd said, "Find out who got her pregnant, and you'll find that second bar of gold. They belong to the New Orleans mafia. They've got a large network. Find their gold and give it back to them."

And that's when Doc Wilson walked into the room. "Deputy, my patient needs his rest now. Time for you to leave."

As Ty exited the room, Loyd said, "Doctor? I've got to use the can."

Dec and I froze, wishing we were Ninjas who could whisk ourselves away. "Mr. Loyd," Doc said, "the meds I administered in the ER are going to be kicking in soon, and we wouldn't want you to risk a fall."

"But I gotta go!" Loyd growled at her.

"I'll summon a nurse for you," the good doctor said. "She'll help you with a bedpan, Mr. Loyd. It will just be a minute."

Dec and I sat there for maybe the longest minutes of our life, listening to the nurse working on doing her duty with Loyd, keeping him right there in his bed.

Our own sighs of relief coincided with Loyd's sigh of relief at one and the same time.

Chapter Eleven

The dogs were gone when we exited the hospital and our bike tires had been punctured with a sharp object. "Big Ty!" Dec growled. "I'll fix him if he did anything to Cooper or Badger! I'll tell my dad everything we know about this damned gold!"

Badger and Cooper would not have left on their own, not when we had ordered them to stay put and watch our bikes. And we fretted over what Ty could have done with them. Dec even brought up a nasty rumor he'd heard about Ty removing strays from the city pound so he could use them for target practice out at the city dump. Sheriff Mac had been summoned to the dump by Alvin Plimpton, who had discovered seven dogs, shot to death by some cruel unknown shooter. Mac had confronted Ty about it, but he lied about it. After that, no more dogs were found dead at the dump, but I think Mac had his suspicions about his deputy being involved. I don't think Mac liked Tyler much after that incident.

We were halfway home when Dec started waving his arms like a man stranded on an island who spots a plane flying above him. Deputy Berry pulled up in the street in front of us. He shut off his engine and climbed out of the patrol car. "You boys seen that damned Oscar? That chimp is on a tear! He was spotted over on Lincoln Street by Mrs. Rivers. He was then spotted by Kyle Waters. Three blocks later, Norm Bridges chased Oscar away from his dog pens. Lyla Creek claimed Oscar started banging on her door! Paul Van Squirt used a garden hose to douse the chimp with cold water. With Loyd's attack and Oscar running wild through town, it's been one helluva morning!"

As Noah carried on with his tirade, I was astounded by all the names he'd used of the people in our town. It was a known fact that a number of marriages had left a lot of folks connected by names that had to do with water. Bridges, Waters, Rivers, Creeks, and Van Squirts were all related in our little town.

Dec said, Nope, we ain't seen hide nor hair of Oscar, but we sure do need a ride back home, Deputy Berry. Could you give us a lift?"

Noah helped us load our two bikes into his trunk. All the way back home, he looked like one of those blue herons hunting fish down in the Blue, turning his head this way and that, searching for any sign of the rampant chimp. Dec and I thanked Noah for giving us the ride, and as he pulled away from the curb to continue his monkey hunt, Big Ty drove up in front of my house. And he did not have our dogs with him.

"Where's our dogs?" Dec demanded to know.

"Shut up, you little peckerwood!" Big Ty growled as he came around the side of his car. "I gave your dogs a lift over to Rome's place. Badger is papered according to Rome. He wants to enter him in the next dog fight down there in Blue Springs. But your beagle, Declan, is probably gonna be used for target practice. Ha, you should have seen his face when Rome came outside, carrying his new leever action Winchester!"

Dec and I were truly petrified. Ty had doomed our two dogs. If a man like Rome could drown puppies in the river tucked inside a burlap sack, he was capable of shooting Cooper as well as throwing Badger into a dog fight. Ty said, "You snot-nosed little cons are going to give me some answers. How come when I was out to Catlin's, your dogs were out there? How come you boys were at the hospital? I came out of the hospital to find your flea-bitten mutts! I did some backtracking after King Henry's shooting yesterday. My snooping took me right off of Elk Street into the vacant lot beside the Hawkins' house. I stood beneath the branches of that oak tree, where your tree fort is."

Dec and I stood there, fighting to remain silent. If we so much as uttered a peep about any of Big Ty's questions, we knew he would then know everything we knew. He would then have a good reason to silence us over that stolen gold. We felt like we were standing in a deep hole, with Ty looking down at us with a shovel full of dirt in his hands.

And that's when Hiney Scrabble pulled up across the street in his tow truck. When Ty saw who was riding with him, he said, "You're interfering in a criminal investigation!"

Hiney climbed out of his truck, with Badger and Cooper hopping out of the cab behind him. "These dogs don't be no criminals, Deputy,"

Hiney said, shooing the two dogs across the street toward Dec and I. We dropped to our knees, hugging our dogs, greatly relieved to see them. Hiney said, "Rome be spitting mad like a wet civet cat! Rome gonna use his new rifle on Cooper. Rome and Hiney had words, then Rome's Winchester sink like a stone in the Big Blue River!"

"You tossed Rome's gun in the river?" Ty asked, blinking in disbelief.

"Yep," Hiney said. "The gun be easier to toss than that big bulhunk!"

Ty snapped, "I'm placing you under arrest!"

Ty whipped his handcuffs out of the leather holder on his belt. Hiney said, "You don't got to arrest me, Deputy Burke. When Rome cool down, Hiney will buy him a new rifle to make amends."

"Too late!" Big Ty snarled. "You're heading to jail!"

At that point, my dad stepped out of his work shop at the back end of our vacant lot. "Tyler? What are you doing?"

"Arresting this big, stupid fool!" Big Ty snapped.

"Ty," I said, "carted Badger and Cooper over to Rome's junkyard. He wanted to throw Badger into a fight and was gonna shoot Cooper!"

Big Ty turned his red-hot glare directly at me. "Look, you little shit!" One of the notorious Hawkins' clan! I know all about your troublesome family! Your older boy locked up out there at the State Home! And I know about the running rum with the Kennedy clan!"

"Careful there, Deputy," Dad said. "You're speaking of things you've only heard. Did you really take my son's dog over to Rome's?"

"Yes!" Big Ty answered.

"He," Hiney said, "wanted Rome Kowski to use his new gun on Cooper. But I bring the two dogs back to the little boys here."

Ty slipped his handcuffs back in their pouch on his gun belt. His face turned red and he stormed off toward his car. Dad followed him out into the street. "Tyler, next time you do anything this cruel to my son, I'm going to ask you to take off that badge. You are a bully with a badge, and there's only one way to deal with a bully."

Ty started to lower himself into his car seat, but Dad reached out and latched onto his arm. "Do you understand what I am telling you?"

Big Ty fell backwards into his patrol car seat. Two minutes later, he started up his car and without so much as looking at my dad, he drove away. Dec and I stood there, staring in amazement at my dad still standing there in the street, a steely-eyed glare in his dark eyes.

Dad walked over to us boys, trying to downplay what we'd just witnessed. "Take your dogs out back. Your mom is cooking dinner, and someone needs to relieve her of puppy duty."

"Sure, Dad," I said, having just a little more respect for him after him dressing down Big Ty like he'd done. Dad said, "Hiney, thanks. Stay for dinner. I'll have Martha set an extra plate."

Hiney smiled gleefully, looking like a kid on Christmas morning. The laughter that bubbled up from Hiney's ample belly cut through the tension, but I knew this was the calm before the storm, because Ty would not forget the dressing down Dad had given him.

Chapter Twelve

Dec and I entered our backyard. We were immediately set upon by the three rambunctious puppies. It was obvious, at even two months old, they were Staffies. Uncle Bill once told us that in Chicago, terriers like these were called Pit bulls on account of them being forced to fight in pits against bulls and bears. He called them Staffordshires, and told us that the Little Rascals had one named Petey. He said that if you raised a dog right there was no meanness in them. My own dog, Badger, was nothing more than a big baby.

As I kneeled down to be head-butted by the three little clowns, Dec said in a low voice, "What was Big Ty saying about the Kennedy clan?"

"We're not supposed to talk about that," I said.

Patting his leg to get the attention of the three pups, Dec kneeled down beside me next to Cooper and Badger. He said, "Dad said the Kennedy's were rum-runners, that they made moonshine and ran it all over southern Nebraska. He said, these same Kennedys once spelled their name Cennedi, that they came from a clan out of northern Ireland. They were related to the same Kennedy's in Washington."

Dec bent down, his face in the grass, his butt up in the air, allowing two of the pups to gnarl on his cheeks. I picked up the runt of the litter, a Brindle female, and nuzzled the top of her tiny round head with my mouth. I said, "The Kennedy clan ran shine and rum all over five counties back in the day. The Hawkins clan wasn't involved with them."

Dec placed his face in between the two males of the trio, and huffed and puffed to rile them both up.

"My dad," I said, "had five brothers, Perry, Bill, Eddie, Jessie, and Tom. When he was young, Eddie got hit by a train. Perry and Gus took after my gramps and drove steam boats down the Mighty Mo. Perry once steered the Hannibal down the Mississippi before that old boat gave up the ghost and sank to the muddy bottom. Hannibal, the greatest military generals in history, is who the river boat was named after. So, too, was Hannibal, Missouri that Mark Twain wrote about in his books."

I snuggled my face down in the grass, closing my eyes so I didn't get my eyeballs scratched out as two of the pups clawed and nibbled at my cheeks and nose. When I sat back up, spilling them backward so that they rolled in the soft grass, I picked up the little Brindle and placed my chin on her head. She planted her head against my chest.

I said, "In 1857, the Hannibal, sailing up the Missouri River from St. Louis to Nebraska City, ran aground near Kansas City. While it was stranded, 35 passengers aboard, went exploring. When they reached Nebraska City, they divided into two parties, one of them came upon the site where the DeRoin Trail crossed the Big Blue. They settled there, and named it after Julia Beatrice Kinney, the young daughter of Judge Kinney, a member of the explorers party."

Dec got this far away look in his eye, as if he were looking back in time and seeing the first citizens of our town leaving that stranded steam boat and walking cross country until they came to the Big Blue. "We should find that gold," he said. "Our town was founded by explorers. So we ought to follow in their footsteps."

Picturing Mary Kay slumped in the trunk of that car, I shook my head like a wet dog. "No, we don't need that kind of trouble."

After dinner that night, Mom had Dec and I run a piece of her apple pie over to Gran B's house. Still feeling creeped out by the men who had beaten up Loyd, we took Badger and Cooper with us. Gran opened her door and ushered us inside. She then asked what that business between Dad and Big Ty had been about that afternoon. I told her the story and said, "Dad really surprised me by standing up to Big Ty."

Gran B tried to lighten my load by saying, "Gutsy your dad is, but also a great sense of humor. Tell Declan some of his stories that had us all slapping our knees after Sunday evening dinners."

We sat there on her couch, our dogs at our feet, and I proceeded to tell some knee-slapping stories: "Since Amos Hawkins was of Lakota heritage, some snooty white lady walked up to him in downtown Beatrice one day, held up her hand, and gave the traditional Indian greeting, saying, 'How!'

"Dad grinned at her, offered her a sly smile and said, 'Me already know how! Me want to know when?'

"Another time, he got pulled over by a cop while driving the wrong way down a One Way street over on Grant. The cop asked, 'Didn't you see those arrows?'

"Dad grinned at him and said, 'Why, no, Officer, I didn't even see the Indians!'

"Dad used to sneak a drink during the middle of the day, hiding his whisky bottle in the outhouse. My little sister, Donna, found it one day and filled it with Apple Vinegar. Amos snuck out there, swigged the contents of the bottle, and ended up throwing up his cookies. He paid her back for the prank by placing her on the back of their one horse they had. While Donna was getting situated on the horse's back, Dad hit it with an open hand on its hind end! That horse took off flying down the road, into the ditch, across a field, with Donna clinging terrified to its reins! A farmer who saw her flying past him, told Dad the next day, 'Man, that girl of yours sure can ride!'

"Once when Dad and Mom got into a heated argument, Dad drove his buggy downtown and bought a big block of ice. He drove it on home and pulled up beside Mom who sat fuming in her rocker on the front porch. Dad dumped that big block of ice at her feet and said, 'Here, old lady, sit on that and cool your ass off!'

"As far as humor goes, Mom and Dad were evenly matched. Mom once saw a mouse on our kitchen table. She screamed so suddenly that the mouse had an instant heart attack and keeled over and died! The next day, Mom took that mouse and placed him between two slices of bread and took it to work at the State Home. There, during lunch, she put the mouse sandwich down in front of her good friend, Mrs. Allen. She had the mouse sandwich up to her mouth before she saw the tail sticking out. She screamed and flung it across the room! The other workers talked about that mouse sandwich for some time after that!

"Then there was the time, Mom asked Dad to go down and buy her three bras at Penny's in downtown Beatrice. Not having a clue about her size, the clerk asked Dad what size he wanted, and Dad got frustrated trying to explain her breast size without embarrassing himself. When the clerk asked him, 'What? Are they the size of an egg?'

"Dad promptly said, 'Yes! Fried eggs!'

"On my 7th Birthday, Dad made me a hot fudge sundae using an ice cream dipper on mashed potatoes. He heaped fudge, whipped cream, nuts and a cherry on those mashed potatoes. I gagged when I took my first bite. He handed me a glass with Cherry soda in it, and when I tipped it to wash that dry taste of potatoes out of my mouth, there were tiny holes in the top of that glass and I got sprinkled by soda pouring out of them. The best prank I unfairly took the blame for was when Dad handed me a joke box and instructed me to hook the contraption to our toilet. It had an air pressure hose attached to it and set off a little recorder that blared out a farting sound and then a man's deep voice said, 'Hey, I am working down here!'

"As luck would have it, my Aunt Alice sat on the rigged toilet. Dad, seated in the kitchen, listened to the loud farting sound and then the voice, 'Hey, I am working down here!' Aunt Alice fell off the pot, and peed all over herself she was so startled by the voice. Dad shuffled the blame off on me, saying, 'Hawk, how could you?'

"So, thinking I would pay him back, I got the biggest shock of my life. I was carrying a load of packages to Dad's car. He opened his trunk. I dropped the packages inside. When he slammed the lid shut, I placed my knuckles along the crease of the trunk, pretending he had slammed my fingers in his trunk. Dad went into spastic cat-mode trying to get his keys back out of his pocket. Once he swung the trunk open, I wiggled my fingers in front of him and started laughing. Dad let loose with a barrage of red-hot words that parted my hair right down the middle!"

Chapter Thirteen

When we were ready to leave, Gran B asked, "Did you pick up that ledger from Gracie?"

"Derp!" I said, slapping my forehead. "Forgot about it, Gran. It's safe beneath my bed. Can I bring it by tomorrow?"

She said, "That will be fine, Jessie."

We ran back over to our house, the dogs trailing behind us. Quietly, we snuck into my bedroom so I could show the ledger to Dec. Gold letters on the front cover spelled out, *Black Hawk Holy Man*. A sheet of folded paper tucked inside the ledger slipped out and fell to the floor. I picked it up. Taking the sheet of paper back outside with us, we darted over to the oak tree, ordering the dogs to stand guard. We then climbed up to our fort. After cranking up our Coleman lantern, I unfolded a map. I zeroed in on that drawing like Superman using his X-ray vision. At the top of the page was a bear standing on his hind legs. Trailing down from him were paw prints that connected with a capital E and the drawing of a locust. At the tip of his tail was an owl in a tree, and near the Blue River was a stockade and an X in the center of the island fort.

Dec said, "In *Treasure Island*, pirates marked where they buried their loot. That's Standing Bear Trail! According to the map there's a river fort on that island near South 136th and East Locust! Folks found safety in forts. Fort Laramie was a hot bed for wild west heroes like Wild Bill Hiccup, Wyatt Burp, and General Lemon Custard! Wild Bill was a soldier, scout, lawman, gunfighter, and gambler. He spied for the Union during the Civil War. While he was recovering from an attack by a grizzly bear he killed with a pistol and a knife at Rock Creek Station near Fairbury, three men came to collect a debt from the station master. Wild Bill shot all three men. On the way to trial in Beatrice, he stopped at the home of the lady he'd made a widow by killing her husband. He gave her $35. The trial lasted fifteen minutes, and Bill was cleared of murder. Who do you think was more famous, Hawk? The cowboys of the Old West or the Indians?"

I said, "According to Gran B, I'm a descendant of Red Cloud, who was not there when Custer died. Red Cloud's Wars made him so famous, they named Red Cloud, Nebraska after him. Standing Bear was more famous. In school, I did a report on him. Chief Standing Bear became the first Indian granted rights under our law. Because of the Treaty of Fort Laramie, the government gave the Ponca reservation to the Santee to end Red Cloud's War. By spring, many Poncas died of starvation, including Standing Bear's son. He promised to bury him in the Niobrara valley, but General Crook had him arrested. Standing Bear sued for being imprisoned in court in Omaha. During the trial, he raised his right hand and said, 'This hand is not the color of yours, but if I cut it, my blood will be the same color as yours. God made me, and I am a man.' After that, the judge recognized the Indian as a person and Standing Bear was elected to the Nebraska Hall of Fame."

Turning off the light on the Coleman, Dec hid the map in our comic book stash stored in a wooden box. We climbed down the side of the tree, giving our dogs a pat for being such good guards. Badger growled, looking off to the west, where a cluster of cedars bordered the street beyond. The tiny ember from the man's cigarette betrayed him. He flicked it through the air, and like a firefly, it spiraled down into the grass. He was a large man with long, dark hair.

Dec whispered, "Injun Joe!"

"No," the man laughed. "Ghost Running Thunder. Why don't we have a talk, boys? You're not afraid of me, are you?"

We turned then and ran for home, our dogs trailing behind us.

That next morning, Mac summoned Dec and I down to the courthouse in order to make restitution for Mose Hadley's boat official. Mac walked us into Judge Neely's office, presenting his plan to keep us off of probation. Judge Neely, an old man with a walrus-like mustache, agreed with Mac's idea. After sternly lecturing us, the judge walked us back to Mac's office where Noah stood holding a broom and a dustpan.

Judge Neely said, "Deputy Berry? The miscreants are all yours. When they finish with your office, have them march back to my office!"

As Judge Neely turned around to return to his chambers Andy Tate, our town lawyer, entered the court house. Andy looked like Atticus Finch in that *Mocking Bird* movie. He was tall and wore round spectacles like my dad's. He was dressed in a three-piece suit. Andy said, "I'm making a motion that you set bail for my client, your Honor."

Sheriff Mac came out of his office and said, "Andy, he shot a man in cold blood. I strongly urge you to reconsider freeing him."

Andy said, "Sheriff, did anyone witness this shooting?"

I stood there, holding the dustpan and looking directly at Declan. He stood a foot away from me, holding the broom, looking right back at me. We both badly wanted to tell Mac exactly what we witnessed there in our tree fort. It was on the tip of our tongues to speak up then, and had we spoken up, instead of protecting our own hides, Henry would have stayed in jail until his trial, locked away safe from harm.

Andy said, "Henry fired his weapon in self-defense. The victim of this shooting was also armed. Correct, Sheriff?"

Judge Neely said, "This is the first I heard there were two guns at the scene. Just where did you get this information?"

Andy said, "Deputy Tyler Burke. Rumor has it that Deputy Burke was involved in a secret order that began in Kentucky in 1854 with five Freemasons who wanted to create a golden circle of slave holding territory in the Southern States. Chapters were called castles and they had 50,000 members across every state. In 1860, the start of the Civil War got in the way of that plan. Agents of this secret order infiltrated Federal arsenals. Took control of small towns. Collected guns. Burned and plundered. At the end of the war in 1865, the Order went underground. The Knights of the Golden Circle ceased to exist, yet there are rumors of Sentinels all over the country, guarding caches of hidden gold buried by Jesse James, who committed at least 70 robberies in his time."

Andy was interrupted then by heated wrangling between Mac and Judge Neely. Several seconds later, Neely released Henry on bail, and

Andy drove away from the courthouse with King Henry seated in the front seat of his car, pleased as punch.

Later that afternoon, Dec and I, busy with the broom and dustpan in the cells, overheard the conversation taking place in the office. Noah said, "Mary Kay is safe and sound out to Catlins. She'll be moving back into town once these thugs from New Orleans are gone. Cormac, when my Carey passed four years ago, I swore I'd never find another woman. Gracie, however, makes me happy."

"Noah," Mac said, "I've been watching you turn into a sad, forlorn fat man these last four years since Carey passed, and I've known about you secretly meeting with Grace Long Soldier. So what?"

Noah said, "Gracie knew of the James gang connection to Robber's Cave, and how they made a stopover at the cave in Lincoln, where they stashed gold. She asked me to consult with an old Cingane healer down in Blue Springs. This old gypsy sooth-sayer knew right off that I was of the blood—"

"Of the blood?" Mac asked him.

"Yes," Noah said. "I am related to the Cingane folk in Blue Springs. At Gracie's request, I met with the old gypsy woman, who used a crystal ball to scry for information. I said two words, *Jessie James*, and she peered into that damned crystal ball and went cryptic on me. Her hoodoo voodoo rambling gave me the heebie jeebies!"

Noah cleared his throat, then said, "*The bear looks to the monkeys, the monkeys look to the tree of the horned owl.*"

"What the hell?" Mac said.

"Yep," Noah chuckled. "Not a clue, Mac, not a clue."

Chapter Fourteen

The shrill ring of the telephone echoed across the office. Noah answered the call. We heard him say, "Oscar started a stampede down at the rail yards, Mac! We best get down there!"

We waited a few seconds more to make sure the two lawmen were gone before creeping out of that middle cell. Dec's eyes narrowed quite suddenly. He looked past me and into the cell where Henry McGinn had been in during his jail stay. Dec darted inside that cell and ripped a sheet of paper off the wall taped to it with Scotch tape. He held it up for me to see. "This bear is an exact likeness of the bear on the map we discovered! Mary Kay didn't draw that map. Henry did!"

I had barely folded that piece of paper up and stuffed it into the back pocket of my jeans, when Noah came running back to the office. He shouted. "Oscar caused a stampede in the yards!"

He rushed over to his desk and scooped up four bananas. Noah allowed us to ride along down to the yards, sirens blaring, red lights flashing. He laughed out loud as we hit the slant in the street going into the train yards and the cruiser's four tires actually left the ground. Ahead of us, Angus cows ran all over the yards, clogging up the six sets of train tracks that brought trains from the Burlington and Union Pacific to the yards. Bananas clutched in his hand, Noah ran to join Mac chasing cows in the middle of the tracks. A dozen railroaders from the shops joined them and for the next thirty minutes, our train yards looked like a scene from *Rawhide*, only instead of Will Favor and Rowdy Piper chasing those scattering cows, it was Mac, Noah, and a whole crew of railroad folks.

Dec and I spotted a black shape careening away from the stampeding herd of cows. Oscar moved like greased lightning as he then darted in between two warehouses at the front of the yards. "Want to try to catch him?" Dec asked, climbing out of the cruiser.

We ran to the front end of the rail yards, and entered the old corrals inside an enormous barn where the cows were kept to be shipped out on cattle cars. They were now empty with corrals stretching all the way to the open double doors seventy-feet in front of us. Although we could hear the commotion at the back of the barn, we were alone there in that dark building, and it was kind of creepy. Dec skidded to a stop in front of me, and I ran directly into him. That sheet of paper slipped out of my back pocket and fluttered down to the ground.

I bent down to scoop it back up, when I heard a sudden *whoosh!* And a flying knife sliced into the paper, ripping it right out of my hand and carrying it ten feet beyond us and into the closest corral. The blade made a solid *Thud!* as it was buried three inches deep in the wood at the back of that corral, pinning the paper to the wall. Two men stepped out of the shadows behind us. They were the men who had come to town with Silas Vance. Rock and the Asp.

Asp spoke in a slight Cajun accent, "Hand me da knife, boy."

Dec walked into the corral and pulled the knife from the wall. He came back out of the corral, holding the knife in one hand and the paper in the other. Snatching the knife out Dec's grasp, Asp next snatched the paper away and unfolded it in front of Dec's face, inches from his nose. "See dis bear? Who draw him?"

Dec said, "It don't mean nothing. It's just doodles."

Asp reached beneath his suit jacket and drew out the map. He had snuck into our tree fort and stolen the map. There was a flurry of movement, and Asp had his lock-blade beneath Dec's chin. *Click!* came from the shadows beyond the corrals. Lawrence Shank moved forward, one of his pistols in his grasp. He was dressed in a long black duster and wore a wide-brimmed cowboy hat. He had shaved off his scraggly beard, leaving a thick black mustache, resembling Doc Holiday, the famous gun fighter. Lawrence said, "Put that knife away, Mister."

Wisely, Asp closed his blade, slipping it back inside his pocket. He glared at Lawrence and raised the map, flashing it past Dec's face. "That," Lawrence said, "belongs to the boy. Give it to him."

Peering down the barrel of Lawrence's pistol, Asp cursed and handed the map to Dec, saying, "Dis be the second time you interfered in my bidness, gunslinger! Next time, gone be your last!"

As we emerged from the barn, Lawrence was already halfway across the train yards on his way to his home in the rail car situated on the west end of the yards. He tipped his hat, then headed on his way. Kat came running from the rail yards. She said, "I came over the Blue River bridge just as Noah coaxed Oscar down off the roof of the park shelter. He was dangling a banana in front of him and almost had him inside his patrol car, when Mac and a gang of railroaders steered a herd of cows off the bridge! And then, Oscar swiped the banana out of Noah's hand! Noah fell back into the open door of his patrol car on his butt, and those stampeding cows ran up and over the bridge!"

Dec held the map up.

"And what is this?" she asked, studying the map.

Dec said, "It came from Gracie, but the artwork is King Henry's."

Kat said, "So, Henry drew this for his niece to find?"

"His niece?" Dec asked. "Why would Henry draw a map for Mary Kay? When was she supposed to find it? Do you think he hid the stolen bar of gold? My head is filled with a mad pack of wild, buzzing hornets!"

"Come," she said, turning around and walking back inside the barn. Kat led us to a ladder leading up to a trapdoor in the ceiling of the barn. The three of us sat down on the front edge of the barn, sixty-feet above the train yards. From our high vantage point, we had a bird's eye view of Mac and the railroad gang herding cows back and over the Blue River bridge. Mac had them under control, too, as he and his posse forced those cows to head back toward the rail yards.

Directly below us about a hundred yards away, we saw Oscar spring up behind a box car at the west side of the tracks. "Oh, oh," Dec said, watching the big chimp appear in front of the oncoming herd of cows.

Mac and Noah, moving steadily along behind the cows did not see Oscar about two-hundred yards in front of them. But in the next few seconds, those cows spotted the chimp and they turned tail and run back at Mac and his railroad crew. And that's when we saw a large, muscular black man riding into the rail yards on Rosie the elephant. Mose Hadley owned a dairy farm on the west side of the rail yards. He was a giant of a man, and as he swept the wide-brimmed hat off his head, his shiny bald dome reflected sunlight.

Seated on Rosie's back, Mose flung his arms out wide, shouting at those cattle to get back into the yards. The Hadley family had once traveled in a circus and had settled down here in Beatrice. They lived down by the rail yards with many of their exotic animals. My favorite was Rosie. Every Saturday, Dec and I helped Mose take Rosie down for her weekly bath in the Blue River. That river was ten feet deep and it was a might spooky to sit on Rosie's back as she swam in the dark muddy waters, but still it was a thrill to ride on an elephant.

"That was smart," Dec said, "Mose using Rosie to herd the cattle back into the corrals at the edge of the yards. I bet those dumb cows think Rosie is just some giant bull that they had better cow to."

Rosie played her part well. Soon she and Mose had the loose cows back in their pens. As Mac came running up to thank Mose for his help, the big black man slid down from Rosie's back. After shaking Mac's extended hand, Mose ran to greet Oscar off to one side of the tracks. Mose and Oscar came together then, and tears sprang to my eyes, their show of affection for each other moved me, and I had to quickly wipe them from my cheeks. Minutes later, Mose and Oscar were gone from the yards, more than likely headed back to his cage in Mose's Ford truck.

We sat there on the roof of the barn for ten more minutes. As Mac walked Rosie back down to the Hadley place, Kat told us about the map Gracie had passed to us through that ledger. Dec and I felt like junior detectives as Kat unraveled the plot involving the stolen gold. The story she told us was way better than any Hardy Boys mystery, far more complex than a Nancy Drew book.

Kat said, "Rivermoon is the name of the research facility nine miles south of town. It's an island near East Locust Road. Since it was created by rocks hauled in from the rock quarry near Holmesville, a deep trough of water encircles it. It's owned by King Henry, it's been in his family for years. He rents it out to some weird government agency who conducts research on monkeys. Henry allowed us to visit the island and Mary

Kay and I got to help feed the monkeys. Important research goes on there. We were only allowed there because Mary is Henry's god-daughter, not really his niece, but Mary Kay calls him Uncle Henry.

"Your brother, Hawk, went to the island before he got locked up out at the State Home. There's an old, burned-out fort out there. Richard and Chris talked King Henry into letting them camp out in the ruins. Henry joined us around the fire. He told us about the gold inside Robber's Cave. He said he had a map left to him by his grandfather. Henry started blabbering about Templar knights in Jerusalem. The Ark of the Covenant. Oak Island. Scottish Freemasons. The Civil War. The Knights of the Golden Circle. The Sons of Liberty. Two days later, Ty snuck inside Robber's Cave and stole two bars of gold. By the time Henry learned that Mary Kay was mixed up in the theft, Kennedy kidnaped Mary and Henry shot him dead over on Elk Street. Now we got men in town searching for the gold, one which Tyler has and the other Henry hid in a Hoot owl tree that Sentinels call markers. Henry revealed to Mary Kay that he was a Sentinel, watching over a cache on Rivermoon."

Kat lowered her voice as she added, "Something escaped from its cage out on that island. Henry stopped taking us girls out there, and now armed security guards patrol Rivermoon. Rumor is, it's a Chupacabra. The Mexican word, chupa, means to suck, and cabra, means goat. The beast attacked goats in Puerto Rico, then in America, Russia, and the Philippines. People in Puerto Rico call it El Vampiro de Moca, the Vampire of Moca, where 150 pets were bled dry through holes in their neck. Some say it is a reptile, with wings."

Sitting there in broad daylight, listening to talk about this creature made me think of all those Friday night episodes of *Creature Feature*. Just thinking of going out to that island made me shiver.

Chapter Fifteen

It was dark by the time we got back to my house. We were nearly plowed over by Mose Hadley, who did a two-step shuffle to keep from colliding with us. He shouted, "Oscar! Get back over here!" But Oscar veered off at the end of the block and vanished into the night. And that's when we heard Hiney roar. We ran through our vacant lot and into the alley. There, Hiney kneeled beside Henry sprawled on the ground, a knife buried in his right shoulder. Hiney said, "The Asp Man stuck Henry with his knife, then weaseled away down the alley!"

Hiney scooped King Henry up into his arms, carried him over to his tow truck, then headed to the hospital. As we watched him go, Ghost stepped from behind Dad's work shed. The biker was just reaching inside his jacket, when Mose delivered a swift upper cut to his chin that catapulted the big Indian off his feet. A silvery object sailed through the air, landing beside him as he settled into a crumpled heap before us. "A badge?" Mose said, staring down at the small shiny badge in disbelief.

Having heard all the commotion, my dad came out of his shed. Turning to Mose, he asked, "Who the hell did you knock out, Champ?"

Dec said, "Injun Joe is an undercover cop! And Mose just knocked him into next Wednesday!"

Dad and Mose lifted Ghost to his feet and assisted him on into our house. Dec and I followed them, looking on as they got the man situated on the couch. Gran B came out of our kitchen, placing a wet cloth on the forehead of the dazed Lakota. As Ghost began to come around, Gran dabbed at his head with the wet cloth. By the time Sheriff Mac showed up ten minutes later, Ghost was fully recovered. Mac read his badge and said, "What the hell's a private investigator doing in my town, Agent Gabriel Running Thunder?"

Ghost said, "Investigating a secret society that dates back to the Civil War. Cloak and dagger stuff. Ever heard of Mark Twain? It was a term meaning the water in the river was deep enough for a boat to get through. Twain belonged to a secret society, Wolf's Head, who had information about the Golden Circle. Twain was born after the appearance of Halley's Comet. He died the day after the comet returned. Natives considered him a Thunder Dreamer. Black Hawk was a Thunder Dreamer who died at Wounded Knee. At the Cheyenne River rez in 1889, he created a series of drawings of Lakota rituals. His drawing of him riding a Buffalo Eagle depicts his connection to a Thunder Being. Gran B served at the Cheyenne rez as a healer. She left there with his ledger. I thought if I proposed a book by Sam Clemens and Black Hawk's ledger it might draw out my prey during a book auction. I'm investigating a murder that took place here in 1956. Dr. London was involved in creating fake books. He lived on a farm near Beatrice. Someone killed his entire family and took the fraudulent books and vanished. So far, Loyd and Tate have become involved in a bidding war over the Black Hawk ledger. Loyd, Tate, and Mr. Craig, president of the Vandals."

"Vandals?" Mac said. "I don't associate bike gangs with rare books."

Ghost laughed. "You hurt my feelings, Sheriff. Don't think a biker would read books? You underestimate us. Clubs are moving away from beer drinking, drunken brawls, and raising hell on their iron horses. Clubs are becoming involved in fund-raising for a lot of good causes, especially ones involving troubled kids. Some of us are the good guys."

Mac said, "Says the biker who stealthily entered my town to solve a murder that took place in 1956? How do I know you're not a bounty hunter? And why involve this fine lady in such a covert operation?"

Gran B said, "I'm more than happy to help Agent Running Thunder. A ruse is a deception that is pulled to trick someone. A rube is an Idiotic person easily fooled. As to the original text? No serious rare book buyer would have considered the ledger that Gracie bound to be the genuine text. Early on when bidders contacted me, I informed them I was having the ledger perfect bound. Not one bidder protested. Loyd, Tate, and the Vandals are still bidding on it."

Ghost said, "After the Civil War, Boys' books took off like a rocket with over 100 books geared for young readers. These authors opened up new worlds for millions. All of those authors are long dead, the scratching of their writing pens long silent, the click-clacking of their typewriters never more to fill a room. Legends in the literary field. To make a fortune off their last works, Dr. London taught his family how to produce authentic-looking works of famous writers:

"Edgar Rice Burroughs, who wrote the *Tarzan* series.
"Abraham Stoker, who wrote the *Dracula* story.
"Horatio Algiers, who wrote many stories about wayward boys.
"Johann Wyss author of *The Swiss Family Robinson*.
"Lewis Carroll author of *Alice in Wonderland*.
"Mark Twain author of *Tom Sawyer*.
"George MacDonald author of *The Princess and the Goblin*.
"Robert Louis Stevenson author of *Treasure Island*.
"Rudyard Kipling author of *The Jungle Book*.
"J. M. Barrie who wrote *Peter Pan*.
"Beatrix Potter author of *The Tale of Peter Rabbit*.
"Kenneth Grahame author of *The Wind in the Willows*.
"A. A. Milne author of *Winnie the Pooh*.
"J. R. R. Tolkien author of *The Hobbit*.
"T.H. White author of *The Sword in the Stone*.
"C. S. Lewis author of *The Chronicles of Narnia*.
"Alan Garner author of *Elidor* and *The Owl Service*.
"Roald Dahl author of *Charlie and the Chocolate Factory*.
"Gracie finished the *River Kings* story allegedly written by Samuel Clemens. Henry turned in that story last night. The binding is drying. It will be up for bidding by morning. The hook that catches the fish. Tate and Loyd are Freemasons. Both are connected with the Golden Circle. And that story was written expressly for one of them to bite on."

That next morning, everyone in town was in mourning over President Kennedy's assassination, and yet there were a lot of folks alarmed over the knifing of Henry. The phone had been ringing off the hook during our cleaning duties, and since Mac had assigned Ty phone duty, he was trying to put terrified callers at ease. While I swept the cells, Dec snuck into the evidence room to borrow the London murder file. That evening after dinner, Dec and I climbed up into our tree fort to take a look at the file he'd confiscated. "Gross!" I gasped at the bloody crime scene there in the London family's kitchen. "It took a lot of rage to make such a mess of them. Who could stab two little girls like that?"

While Mrs. London and her two young, blond-haired daughters, had been stabbed once in the chest, it was Dr. London who took the brunt of a most savage attack. Although, there was no color to the photos, the deep black lines in and around the doctor's neck made it look as if his head was about to fall off his shoulders.

"Sweet Jesus!" Dec said. "These are disgusting!"

"True," I agreed. "Wonder what this means, the nanny dog was first suspected of the brutal murders by the lead investigator?"

"Nanny dog?" Dec asked. "Staffordshires were known as nanny dogs. Owners had them to watch over their kids as protectors and guard dogs. Badger would have been known as a nanny dog. This London was an evil creep. It says he was a dog breeder who engaged in dog fighting. He had an award-winning Pit bull named Bear. Poor dog was involved in a lot of fights. So, he was suspected of killing the entire family."

"Yes," I said, "but later it was determined that Bear was stolen along with the collection of rare books created by London. An autopsy proved the family were killed by knife wounds, and not a dog attack."

"Those poor little girls," Dec said. "If the killer wanted to kill their dad, why did he have to pick on them, too?"

I said, "A witness, even a little girl, could tell on them later. Which means those little girls might have known the killer. Which means, he might still be wandering around our town."

That night, I had a really bad nightmare. Badger woke me up with a soft growl. "Shhhh, Badger!" I whispered. "It's okay."

He growled again. I opened my eyes and sat straight up in bed. There at the foot of my bed stood a blond-haired little girl. She wore a white night gown. Dec and I had once snuck into the town cemetery late one summer night, taking his Polaroid camera with us to prove there were ghosts out there. But all we'd come away with that night were shadows. Not one picture that any paranormal expert could swear were ghosts.

But this little girl sent chills down my spine.

"Who are you?" I asked.

"Callie," she said. "I died because my father made someone really mad at him. Men the night of the murder. But boys when my father made them so mad they killed us. Can you tell someone my secret?"

I shook my head. "What secret?"

Tears trickled down her cheeks. "You are just a silly boy, aren't you? You don't even know what goes on out there, do you? If I told you, would you tell someone who can help?"

I asked, "Sheriff Mac? Even if you told me your secret, he would be really mad at Dec and I for snooping."

She then began to fade. "Silly boys should never be trusted to do the right thing." She paused, looking quizzically at Badger.

"Is that Bear?" she asked. "Or one of Bear's puppies?"

I placed a hand on my dog's head. "No, this is my dog, Badger."

"Badger?" she said. "Funny name for one of Bear's pups."

She was then gone, vanishing before my eyes.

I was so shaken up by the spooky dream, I didn't even tell Dec about it the next morning, thinking he would think I was disturbed like my brother. That I might need help. That I might be mental. Instead, I told him he needed to return the unsolved murder file to the evidence room.

Chapter Sixteen

We were getting ready to leave the sheriff's office that next afternoon, when three men came through the front doors of the courthouse. Mose Hadley carried a shotgun. Hiney Scrabble had a hickory stick slung over one shoulder. And Lawrence Shank had his two six-shooters in his holsters. "Deputy Burke," he said, tipping his cowboy hat back on his head, "deputize us to help Sheriff Mac hunt for the man who put a knife in Henry."

Ty said, "You'd only cause more trouble. Leave your guns here with me and all of you mosey on home."

"Leave our guns with you?" Hiney asked, perplexed by his request.

Mose asked, "Why? When we might need them for the bad guys?"

Big Ty drew his gun. He snapped, "Weapons on the desk! Then hands in the air and into those cells!"

Mose placed the shotgun down on the desk. Hiney's hickory stick landed on the desk next. Lawrence reached across the desk and latched onto Ty's gun hand, slipping his index finger in between the hammer and the firing cylinder. Ty pulled the trigger. That hammer coming down on Lawrence's finger must have hurt something fierce, but he simply whipped the gun out of Ty's grasp. Slipped his finger out from beneath the hammer. Tossed the pistol high in the air. Caught it as it fell back down toward the desk. Spun the pistol to the left. Then back to the right. All the while keeping it spinning until it became a silver blur. He leveled the pistol at Ty. Using his thumb, he opened the cylinder. He flicked the six bullets out of it. They plunked down on the desk. A second later, the pistol clunked down next to the six bullets. Lawrence Shank did an astonishing thing then. He drew both pistols from his holsters. He spun those babies around, creating twin flying stars of flashing silver. He finished his dramatic performance by tossing the guns in the air, exchanging them with both hands. He then slipped them back into his holsters. Hiney and Mose quickly followed Lawrence out of the sheriff's office, leaving Ty standing there seething with rage.

By Thanksgiving evening on the 28th, the Asp was still loose in town. Uncle Bird, who been in the emergency ward in Dallas when they brought President Kennedy in, was still deeply troubled by his time spent with our President during his last few minutes of life. Bird and Lily did not join us for dinner. As darkness fell that evening, Mom set two extra plates on our kitchen table. One, for Dec since he would be left alone at home due to Mac's duties. And the second plate for my brother, who was to be released for the Thanksgiving break.

Being first at the table that night, only I saw Dad pick up Richard's plate and put it back in the cupboard, telling Mom he'd gotten bad news about Richard's release. He'd been caught selling cigarettes at the State Home and staff had discovered over two-hundred dollars hidden beneath my brother's mattress. Richard claimed he'd been saving it so that he and his girlfriend could run away to Mexico. Dad and Mom did not even wonder about this alleged girlfriend, but I wondered for the rest of the night who she might be.

Mom outdid herself with her pumpkin pie, covered with gobs of whipped cream. Dec and I had seconds, and after feeding scraps to the dogs and the three puppies out back, we waddled back to the table, burping quietly so as not to get scolded. Dad, however, pulled his old "pull my finger" stunt and let out the loudest fart we had ever heard. We laughed, impressed with Dad. After dinner coffee was served, Dad and Uncle Bill poured their hot coffee in saucers to let it cool. Dad slurped his coffee straight from the saucer. Once the table was cleared, Mom and my two sisters busied themselves in the kitchen doing the dishes. They sounded like a gaggle of hens clucking in the hen house as they carried on. Uncle Bill said, "John Kennedy, the 35th President, was shot riding in a motorcade in Dallas. Bird was on duty at Parkland Memorial when they rushed Kennedy into the ER. He was dead ten minutes later . . ."

Bill's words trailed off as our back door swung open and Silas Vance stepped inside. We all sat there in surprised silence as he said, "He came to Dallas to mend political differences among Democratic party members. His motorcade route through Dallas was widely reported in newspapers several days before he came. 200,000 people showed up. As his limousine entered Dealey Plaza . . . "

Silas stopped and looked at my dad. "Amos? Am I welcome here?"

Dad sat there, saying nothing. Silas pulled up a chair and sat down at our table. He said, "At 12:30 p.m. shots were fired. Governor Connally was hit in his upper back by a bullet. Mrs. Connally testified that President Kennedy raised his arms in front of his throat. She heard another gunshot and she was covered with fragments of skull, blood, and brain. A shot entered Kennedy's back, penetrated his neck and exited his throat beneath his larynx. The same bullet penetrated Connally below his right armpit and exited his chest below his right nipple, then entered his arm above his right wrist. The bullet exited just below the wrist at the inner side of his right palm and finally lodged in his left inner thigh. That was the magic bullet. A second shot struck the President and entered the rear of his head and passed through his skull, creating a large hole on the right side of his head. Governor Connally, seated directly in front of the President was seriously injured, but his wife pulled him onto her lap, and closed his chest wound, which was causing air to be sucked directly into his chest around his collapsed right lung. He survived.

"One witness testified, he saw a puff of smoke from behind the fence along the grassy knoll beyond the street. A railroad switchman, in a two-story tower, had a view of the stockade fence as well, and saw four men milling around. Another witness, sitting across from the Book Depository, looked up to see a man with a rifle take another shot from a window on the sixth floor. Two witnesses watching from windows of the building's fifth floor, said they heard three gunshots directly over their heads and cartridges dropping on the floor above them.

"There were at least 104 eye witnesses as to the direction from which the shots came. Most thought the Book Depository. A few thought the grassy knoll. One witness swore that shots were fired from three different angles, with none of them coming from the Book Depository, where Lee Harvey Oswald fired his rifle from. And then there is the theory that a second shooter positioned on the nearby grassy knoll, in direct line with the President's car, raised and fired a flechette, an umbrella gun, much like your creation, Amos."

It was spooky talk for us boys to be listening to. Some man had killed our president, using a rifle that most hunters would use on a deer at long range. If even the President of the United States wasn't safe driving in a parade and waving at the American people, how could we even feel safe in our hometown? And the knifing of King Henry hit Dec and I like a double whammy. How would we ever feel safe again?

Silas said, "Abraham Lincoln was elected to Congress in 1846. John Kennedy was elected to Congress in 1946. Lincoln was elected President in 1860. Kennedy was elected President in 1960. Both lost a child while living in the White House. Both were shot in the head. Lincoln's secretary, Kennedy, warned him not to go to the theater. Kennedy's secretary, Lincoln, warned him not to go to Dallas. Both were assassinated by Southerners. Both were succeeded by Southerners. Both successors were named Johnson. Andrew Johnson, who succeeded Lincoln, was born in 1808. Lyndon Johnson, who succeeded Kennedy, was born in 1908. John Wilkes Booth was born in 1839. Lee Harvey Oswald was born in 1939. Booth ran from the theater and was caught in a warehouse. Oswald ran from a warehouse and was caught in a theater. Booth and Oswald were assassinated before their trials. Oswald was shot and killed while being transported from the Dallas police department to city jail. That Oswald acted alone was the conclusion of the FBI. However, in the coming days, a number conspiracy theories will arise. On November 24, when Oswald was shot, the autopsy revealed the bullet entered the left side of his abdomen, damaging his spleen, stomach, aorta, vena cava, kidney, liver, diaphragm, and eleventh rib before coming to rest on his right side. Another magic bullet, you might say."

And then, just like that, Silas Vance stood up from our table and walked out of the back door, leaving us all in hushed silence.

Chapter Seventeen

We were back in school after Thanksgiving break when a call came over the loud speaker, "Dec Connors? Jessie Hawkins? Report to the principal's office at once!"

Big Ty met us in Principal Darby's office. He acted all official, too, dressed in his uniform, his blond hair neat and in place. He didn't even look at us as we sat down in chairs before Darby's desk. Instead he asked, "Did Sheriff Mac tell you I'd be picking the kids up for a drive, Mr. Darby? The Beatrice police are hard at work trying to solve this vicious assault on Henry McGinn. I'll have the kids back here before lunch."

He escorted us out to his cruiser and ushered us into the back seat. All during the drive south of town, Dec and I peered out the window. We passed several farms and at the end of a winding gravel road, we came to a metal grate in the ground, a typical cattle guard. After driving onto Bud Spence's ranch, Ty drove us to a hill overlooking a pasture. Below us we could see a valley stretching to the east and west, and at the east end of that valley we saw a sight that made us sit up in our seats. Ty gestured at Badger and Cooper one-hundred yards ahead of us, attached to chains staked to the ground at the head of that valley. "Ever hear of Dog Soldiers?" Ty asked. "Figured you'd know of Cheyenne Dog Soldiers, Hawk. They would tie a leather cord to their ankles and secure themselves in place by driving a stake into the ground. They would then fight their enemies to the death."

I was close to tears as I looked to our two dogs staked off just like those Dog Soldiers he was talking about. "The knife man, Sal Vera," Ty said, "stabbed Henry. Our little town will never be safe again, if we don't get him to leave. In order to get him to do that, I want that map you two have squirreled away somewhere."

Ty picked up a walkie-talkie on the seat beside him and said, "Sal?"

Seconds later, the ratta-tat-tat of a screaming dirt bike echoed across the pasture to the west. I looked to the rider ripping his way across the field. It was Asp, that Sal Vera guy who stabbed Henry. Sal brought his dirt bike skidding to a stop forty feet away from the dogs. He then whipped his bike around and tore off across the field, heading back to the west, until he vanished in a cloud of dust.

We felt it before we saw it.

The entire patrol car began to shake.

A loud rumble filled our ears.

We felt a disturbance coming through the seat.

It felt like an earthquake.

Then came the thunder.

I looked off to the west. There, nearly half-a-mile away was a wall of huge, furry bodies coming across the pasture at a run. Buffalo! A herd of the bison that belonged to Bud Spence. They were stampeding, stirred up by that maniac's sputtering dirt bike coming up behind them.

Dec launched himself up and over the seat, landing in the front seat. Before Ty could stop him, he opened the passenger's door and dove out. The second he hit the ground, he sprang up, latched onto the back door handle, and flung the door open, freeing me from the backseat. I followed Dec as he ran to save our dogs. Ahead of us, those buffalo were coming fast. Glancing up at their big, shaggy bodies, Dec began pulling on the stakes that doomed his dog to a most painful death by trampling buffalo hooves. Cooper hunkered down, shaking in terror. Dec yanked on the stake attached to the chain anchoring Cooper to the ground. He fell backwards as he tore up the stake. Dec scooped Cooper up into his arms, and prepared to get trampled.

As I ran up to the second stake, Badger pranced around me. Unable to free the stake from the ground, I flung my arms under his chest, lifting him off the shaking ground. Hugging Badger against my chest, I took one alarmed look at the buffalo coming on fast. Badger wriggled free of my arms and dropped to my feet. I stepped in front of him and into the path of the oncoming herd. One second before impact with the lead bull, an explosion of dust pummeled me. Pellets of gravel nicked my cheeks. Strong winds forced me back. Badger whined. I cried. Then a shaft of shimmering light tore through the fabric between the realms and six Lakota warriors stepped between me and the stampeding herd. From photos Gran B had shown me, I knew who they were:

   Sitting Bull, his twin braids trailing over his broad shoulders.

   Red Cloud, an eagle-proud look in his eyes.

   American Horse, his bear-claw necklace glinting in the sunlight.

   Black Elk, his long hair flowing free as was his custom.

   Spotted Tail, a raccoon tail trailing from his war bonnet.

The sixth Lakota wore a single eagle feather and a yellow lightning bolt down the left side of his face. The rest of his face was covered by white powder and blue hailstones. He was dressed in a long, white leather shirt with over 200 ornaments on it, marking him as a Shirt Wearer. And perched on his right shoulder was a white owl, his animal protector.

   "Crazy Horse!" I gasped.

   He placed the palm of his hand on the head of the lead buffalo, stopping the great beast in his tracks. He spoke to the bull and told him not to harm me because I was in truth, his little brother. To the Lakota, the buffalo were considered their brothers, sent there to the plains to supply them with food, tools, shelter, and warm robes for the winter. Crazy Horse whispered to the owl perched on his right shoulder. At once, the white raptor flew above the heads of the other Lakota war chiefs and aided them as they guided the rest of the herd out around Crazy Horse, keeping them from trampling over me and Badger. The shambling beasts ran out and around us, plowing into the barbed wire and electric fencing at the east end of the valley.

   A moment later, the bull lowered his head and began to graze on the grass between us. Behind him, I could see Sal flying away on his bike. I blinked several times and wiped at my eyes, trying yet failing to see some sign of Crazy Horse and the other Lakotas who had saved me, but they were gone, as if they had magically slipped back into the Otherworld without leaving a trace.

   Mindful of the bull calmly grazing before me, I kneeled down to unfasten the collar linking Badger with the chain. As I freed him, he head-butted me gently. Dec looked to the green Jeep coming through the herd of buffalo. Ghost braked patiently for bison to move out around his Jeep, then drove forward. In the next second, he sprang out of the Jeep. Ty came from his cruiser, a shotgun aimed at Ghost. With his free hand, Ghost latched onto the shotgun, removing it from his grasp, dumping Ty on his big butt. Ty stared at the badge Ghost showed him. "You fooled me with all that talk about that ledger, Agent. You've got one helluva disguise, that biker get-up and you being an Indian—"

"First American," Ghost said. "My ancestors, the Lakota, were a branch of the Seven Council Fires, with warriors like Sitting Bull, Touch the Clouds, Black Elk, Red Cloud, Spotted Tail, and Crazy Horse."

All of these years, being Lakota, my long hair set me up for mockery in school, but as Ghost named those figures, I felt proud to be a part of the Seven Council Fires, and wanted to embrace my heritage.

Ghost snatched his badge out of Ty's grasp. "Deputy," he said, slipping his badge back inside the inner pocket of his jean jacket, "I'll let Sheriff Connors know you're out rounding up roaming buffalo, but in regards to the gold? Give it back to these men. Let them begone from this town."

Ty said, "That little Indian boy there has a map leading to it, and there's a lot more than just two gold bars to deal with!"

I sat in silence as Ghost drove us back to town. Dec talked excitedly in the back of the Jeep about the stampeding buffalo. As Ghost drove, he said, "I've heard of horse whisperers before, but I've never met a buffalo whisperer! That was amazing how you handled that enraged bull! I saw a buffalo once in Wyoming throw a grown man thirty feet into the air! Imagine if he had rammed you at a full run like he was in!"

I looked straight ahead, not sure how to respond. Concerned about me, Dec leaned forward in the backseat, patting me on the shoulder. I said, "I didn't do anything."

Dec started to disagree with me, declaring that I had not only stopped that bull in his tracks, but that I had parted the herd, diverting them away from me. "It wasn't me," I said, causing him to stare at me in confusion as I told them about the intervention of the famous war leaders of my People. "Gran B always talked about the Otherworld, just beyond this realm. A real place where our ancestors gathered. She spoke of it as if it was just another country beyond ours. She told me she was looking forward to heading there when her time on earth was through."

Ghost looked over at me, a slight smile on his face. "You had a visit, Hawk. Some call it big medicine. The creator of the universe is Wakan Tanka the Great Spirit. Lakota holy men have a connection to this force. All animals are spiritual beings, buffalo, horses, elks, wolves, bears. The sacred pipe is the Lakota medicine man's direct connection to Wakan Tanka. If a vision seeker is visited by a Thunder Being it is his duty to share the vision, or he disrespects the Thunder Beings. You need to share your experience with your grandmother. She could better explain to you what actually happened out there, and better yet, why.

"In that ledger of Black Hawk's is his vision of Thunder Beings, drawings of Lakota religious ceremonies, including buffalo transformation ceremonies. The buffalo transformation ceremony was carried out by members of a society of holy men known as Buffalo Dreamers. There were also Elk Dreamers, Deer Dreamers, and Wolf Dreamers. Black Hawk included drawings of these societies in his collection of drawings."

Chapter Eighteen

Ghost suddenly changed the subject. "I'll take you to Sheriff Mac so you can report the danger Ty placed you in."

After we dropped off the two dogs off at our place with the puppies, we headed to the courthouse. When we arrived, Ghost let us out on the front walk, then headed back out to Bud's place to help round up the buffalo. Dec and I soon discovered that Sheriff Mac was gone on business with the State Patrol in Lincoln, 40 miles to the north. Deputy Berry was there in the sheriff's office, however, flirting with Gracie Long Soldier. Dec told Noah about the dogs being staked out and about the buffalo stampede. All the time he talked, I kept thinking of my dad's threat he made to Ty. I wanted to see the big galoot knocked down into the dirt after taking a good pounding by my dad, but I was worried that my dad might get himself in trouble if he went too far.

Gracie sat there on an office bench next to Noah's desk. She patted the bench beside her and urged us to join her. As we did, I looked over to the newspapers on top of Noah's desk and spied the leather ledger partially concealed by the papers. Gracie said, "Gran B asked your dad to retrieve it from your room, Hawk. We are soon to have a meeting with those rare book collectors that Agent Running Thunder is attempting to flush out. Isn't this exciting? We might help solve a murder."

Noah said, "That book sale will have to wait now, Gracie."

As Noah took the ledger from her, Mose Hadley came rushing in from the hallway of the courthouse. "Buffalo!" he cried. "Bud Spence just called! There's a whole herd of those critters on the loose!"

Before Noah could respond, Cliff Loyd came through the door into the sheriff's office. Behind him came Andy Tate and four grungy-looking bikers, all wearing the patch on the back of their leather jackets that read, *Vandals*. Ty's words came back to me, *"A sleazy lawyer. A greedy bail bondsman. Twelve angry Vandals."* This mis-matched group of men were all involved in the conspiracy that Ty and Ghost had been talking about out at Catlin's junkyard.

Loyd said, "The buyer I represent bids ten-thousand for the ledger. Ten-thousand in cash. I have it down the hall in my office, Deputy Berry."

Andy Tate said, "The rare book collector that I represent is offering twenty-five thousand, Deputy."

The big biker president barged his way up to the counter. With his gleaming bald head and the single gold hoop he had in his left ear lobe, he looked like Mr. Clean from the detergent commercial. He banged a tattooed fist on the counter, snarling, "I already told that Deputy Burke the buyer who sent me to this little po-dunk town made his bid of thirty-five grand on that rare piece of work. Our payment would seal the deal."

Mr. Clean leaned across the counter, and snatched the ledger out of Noah's grasp. The biker stood there, looking down at the leather-bound book, unaware of Mose Hadley glowering at him from only a foot away. "Mose?" Gracie said. "Be a dear, and retrieve that, please."

I've never seen anyone move so fast in my life! Mose let loose with a wicked right hook that connected with Mr. Clean's chin, knocking him clean off his feet. The other three Vandals launched themselves at Mose, raining down a flurry of savage punches. Taking up a boxer's stance, the big black man simply shrugged them off, jabbing with his left fist and wielding a right upper, hammering them with devastating force. He struck one biker so hard, he lifted him up and off his feet and sent him crashing down on the counter behind him. A second biker was stunned as Mose's fist plowed directly into his chest, sending the guy smashing through the window and hurtling into the hallway beyond. The third Vandal took a punch to the chin and Mose finished him off with a left hook to the side of the head, leaving him in an unconscious heap on the floor.

Dec and I exchanged looks of wonder at Mose's boxing talent, and Gracie crossed the space between us, patting Mose gently on his left cheek. "Thank-you," she said. "I can always count on you."

"You're welcome, Grace," Mose said, grinning fiercely.

Before Noah left to deal with Bud Spence's buffalo, he asked us to stay at the jail to keep Gracie company. He then locked up the four dazed Vandals, leaving the keys to the cell with Gracie in case we had an unexpected fire at the jail.

Dec said, "That was amazing how Mose cleaned the floor with those four bikers!"

Gracie said, "Two-time Olympic Champion! Mose left Beatrice a Golden Gloves Champion, then rose through the ranks until he took two gold medals at the Olympics! He don't talk about his boxing days nor is he a braggart. Mose is just a right humble man who works his dairy farm. The only thing I've ever heard him brag about is the day he caught that big old carp on the Big Indian!"

Dec whistled in astonishment. "All this time we thought Mose was just a simple dairy man. And yet he won boxing matches that earned him gold medals? I'm going to ask Mose to teach me how to box! I mean Chris Catlin makes a good coach, but if I could fight like Mose one day, no one would ever mess with me again!"

When Sheriff Mac arrived back in town that evening, Dec and I hightailed it down to the sheriff's office to find out what Mac was going to do with Ty. Turning to us, Mac said, "Boys, Noah shared with me some disturbing news concerning Tyler. Sit yourselves down and let me hear it from both of you. Sounds like I need a new deputy."

A moment later, Gracie and Gran B showed up there in the sheriff's office. The two women stood side by side beyond the counter as Noah escorted the four Vandals out of their cells. The bikers joined the two women beyond the counter as Loyd, Andy Tate, and Ghost walked in.

"Thanks for coming," Mac told Loyd and Tate. "It appears all of you gentlemen were involved in a bidding war over a rare ledger. Andy, your buyer is a legitimate collector of items rare and valuable in the antiquities market. And Loyd, your buyer's bid is burning a red hot hole in your office safe."

Mr. Clean said, "Hell, we had the highest bidder in this game, and the old lady still wouldn't budge."

Mac said, "Rebecca? Just exactly what did you lose on this deal?"

Gran B said, "Clifford Loyd bid ten-thousand dollars. Andrew Tate bid twenty-five thousand dollars. Mr. Craig, president of the Vandals, bid thirty-five thousand dollars on said ledger. By all of my accounts, Sheriff Connors, I am out ten-dollars on this particular deal."

Loyd's brow furrowed with a deep crease.

Andy Tate looked like he was constipated.

The four Vandals glared at Gran B.

Ghost said, "No serious book collector would make such outrageously high bids on text considered illegitimate once they were perfect bound as this was. In order to weed out frauds, she informed the buyers you represent she was having the ledger bound before selling it to you. Only one, a rare book dealer in California loudly protested. The *Black Hawk* ledger is fake. So, too, is the *River Kings* by Sam Clemens. In fact, I had both fraudulent books produced to help solve a murder. Do any of have anything to say to that?"

Sheriff Mac gave them all a short amount of time to speak, but when not one of them did, he pointed to the door, indicating they could all leave. Andy, Loyd, and the four Vandals did so in quite a hurry.

The next morning, during our cleaning duties, the door to the sheriff's office opened and Ghost entered, followed by a bearded, long-haired man dressed in biker leathers. The guy was short compared to Ghost, but he had thick, muscular arms and he moved with the grace of a tiger, slipping in the door behind the big Lakota.

Mac asked, "Agent Running Thunder? Who is this?"

"Rod Kramer," Ghost said, "President of the Nine Poor Knights. He and his club are responsible for breaking up dog-fighting crews all over Nebraska. Rod and his eight-man club have rescued hundreds of Staffies destined for the dog-fighting ring in the past ten years. They've come here to retrieve a papered mama dog and her litter of pups. Some legitimate breeder has instructed him to purchase this dog and her three pups. I vouch for them, Sheriff. They are good-hearted men, speaking for dogs who cannot speak for themselves."

Mac actually crossed the office to reach out and shake the biker's hand. "Good to know that someone is removing these dogs from the hands of cruel men. Nine Poor Knights? As in the Templar order? Any significance to the name?"

Rod's smile creased his thick beard. He adjusted the black bandana he wore on his head, making him look like a pirate. "The name is an euphemism in regards to how we consider ourselves outlaws of society, humbly fighting what some might say is a lost cause. The only thing we have in common with the Templars is, we try to stay far away from open fires, and we never ride our bikes on Friday the 13th."

For some reason, Ghost and Mac laughed at this. Dec and I stared at them, puzzled as to what was so funny. Mac said, "Nine Poor Knights who defend helpless dogs, I welcome you and your gang here to town."

"Club," Rod said. "We ride in a club, Sheriff, not a gang. We are just nine scruffy bikers out for a good cause. Some in law enforcement consider our method a little unorthodox, but when the time for words is over, our fists certainly get the job done. We've come to retrieve a mama dog owned by a hard-headed mule of a man. You may want to intervene to keep the mule from turning into an ass. We've heard he tried to drown the pups. We're taking them, too. We'd appreciate any help you could offer us."

When Mac turned to us, Dec and I snatched up our coats and stocking caps and ran toward my house. Rod and his eight Knights fell in behind us they cruised the bricks away from the courthouse, and though I did not vow to become a future club member when I got older, I did vow that I would own a Harley one day. When I explained who Rod was and what he intended for the three pups, Mom was on board right away, and she kissed the heads of each pup as she passed them off to the bikers. Two of the largest members of Rod's club tucked two of the pups inside their leather jackets. Rod gently tucked the female pup inside his jacket and said, "Would you boys like to visit them one day at their new home?

Why, right now, these puppers are a little under weight, but in a few short months, they will be pushing eighty! And rest assured, boys, the owner of this dog rescue ranch loves dogs more than he does most people. They will be well taken care of."

When Rome Kowski pulled up to our house, Rome handed the pups' mama over to Rod for a mere ten-dollars, and he was fidgety as a gerbil on speed as Rod and his Knights stared intently at him all the time Mac was talking to him. After watching that, I was glad I wasn't associated with the dogmen who were out there in the path of the Nine Poor Knights on their crusade. Any dogmen on the radar of these bikers were going to be in a lot of trouble, especially if they got caught mistreating dogs.

I caught the conversation between Ghost and Rod as the club prepared to leave town: "Where did this Kowski," Rod asked, "ever get a papered female pit?"

Ghost replied, "Probably stole her from some breeder. The thing is she is safe now, no fights in her future."

"No," Rod said. "Just makes me curious where a lug like that came to own such a beautiful dog. She is truly a nanny dog."

And for some reason, it reminded me of the London's award-winning dog stolen by whoever murdered their family.

Chapter Nineteen

As Dec and I sat round our campfire beneath our tree fort there in the side yard, Badger and Cooper woofed a warm greeting as Chris helped a pregnant Mary get settled on a half log close to the fire. I offered Kat my own seat, and she sat and stretched out her hands to the warmth of our fire. Mary Kay said, "So, you two ended up with Uncle Henry's map. Funny how a secret society started in 1854, still has an impact to this day. The Knights of the Golden Circle hid their troves in dozens of states. Jesse James passed through Nebraska as a member of the secret society, and yet John Wilkes Booth, who killed President Lincoln, was one, as well. Rumor is the Ku Klux Klan was an offshoot of the Golden Circle. The word, kuklo, is Greek for circle."

Dec asked, "Why all these references to knights?"

Chris said, "Knights Gallant is what Jesse and Frank James were called as guerilla fighters. Their commanders were Knights of the Iron Hand, William Quantrill and Bloody Bill Anderson. Jesse was a Scottish Rite Mason, who buried the gold he stole under a grid that employed coded maps. These hidden caches had to be protected by lifelong guards, sworn to secrecy. King Henry achieved the ancient Scottish Rite of Freemasonry, and yet as a Sentinel, he betrayed his vows. Scottish Rite is one of the bodies of Freemasonry only a Master Mason may join."

Dec asked, "What's a Templar?"

Chris said, "In 1099, Christian armies captured Jerusalem from the Muslims. During the Crusades, pilgrims in the Holy Land, were killed as they crossed through Muslim lands. In 1118, a French knight started a military order along with eight knights, calling it the Poor Soldiers of Christ, their headquarters being in the ruins of Solomon's Temple. The Order became known for its code of conduct and their white habits marked by a red cross. They became defenders of the Crusades and were highly skilled warriors, forbidden from retreating unless totally outnumbered. The Templars built dozens of castles and won hundreds battles against Muslim armies. In the late 12th century, Muslims retook

Jerusalem and the Knights Templar moved their base of operations to Paris. There, King Philip plotted to bring them down, because the Templars refused him loans he demanded. On Friday, October 13, 1307, he had members in France arrested, including the order's grand master Jacques de Molay. Pope Clement disbanded the order in 1312 as commanded by King Philip. While the Knights Templar disbanded 700 years ago, the order went underground and remains in existence to this day. Currently, there are several international groups styled after the Templars, who aim to uphold the values of the original order.

"Historians claim that the Templars guarded the Shroud of Turin, a linen cloth believed to be placed on Jesus's body before burial for hundreds of years after the Crusades ended. Some say the Shroud was created by cloth that came from the 13th Century, that the bloody impressions of a long-haired, bearded man on the cloth was none other than the Templar leader, Jacques De Molay, who was wrapped in the Shroud after being tortured and killed."

The sudden clap-clapping of applause startled the five of us. Badger and Cooper growled as Sal Vera stepped out of the shadows beneath our oak tree. Sal said, "A history lesson from one of da Gypsy rebels who were as much a part of world history as these Templars. And now, you be dabbling with dat gold that belongs to another band of knights."

A knife appeared in his hands. "You Cingane," he chuckled, "always sticking your nose in where it don't belong."

I latched onto Badger's collar and Dec did the same to Cooper. Sal told Chris, "I want dat map dis boy got. What you say, Injun boy? Get me dat map? Or shall I cut off one dem ears of yours?"

Brushing past Badger, Sal latched onto the front of my jacket and hauled me up and over the fire, planting me beside him as he swung his knife up to my right ear. The sharp blade slipped through the strands of my long hair, grazing the top of my ear. I heard a voice say, "Let go of my brother!"

Sal released me and wheeled around to face my brother. I blinked in astonishment as I saw that Richard, too, was armed with a long knife.

I'd once seen a Gypsy knife fight down in Blue Springs. It had been between two would-be chieftains as they fought to earn that title. Those men had moved like lightning, their blades mere flashes of silver in the moonlight. In fact, they moved so fast, stabbing, slashing, poking with wildcat swift attacks, I did not even see the knife slide into the loser's shoulder that night. It was over with as soon as it had started.

There was my brother pitted against the Cajun knifeman as he came to my defense, their silver blades snicking against each other as they attempted to savagely stab each other there beneath our tree fort. The thing about a knife fight, either one of the fighters draws first blood or someone gets stabbed. In the movies, the knife-fighting scenes begin with grabbing wrists, and then a long, fierce struggle begins as the fighter tries wrestling the blade out of his enemy's hand. There is a lot of huffing, puffing, and straining as the sharp blades come close to ending the fight. In the movies, usually the knife is knocked out of one of the fighter's hand as other delivers the last stab, ending the fight.

But this knife fight was a lot different than the movies. Sal started out by grabbing onto Richard's wrist, but as wiry as my brother was, they did not stay connected for long. My brother looks a lot like Charles Bronson, with high cheek bones and a long, narrow face, with definite signs of Lakota in his features. He wears his coal-black hair in a Marine-style buzz cut, courtesy of the barber from the State Home. Unlike Sal who was slightly muscular, Richard was lean as a scarecrow. And yet what he lacked in muscles, he more than made up for with his speed. The five of us sat before the fire watching as dozens of slashes and savage lunges were deflected by Sal and Richard. They carried on their wild dance for three long minutes, with neither of them drawing blood. How they had managed to keep stabbing at each other, with neither taking a wound, was a miracle.

I sat there amazed, and wondering where my brother had learned such skills. It became obvious that Richard had done this more than once before. I could only imagine what it took for him to summon up the courage to face off with someone as fierce and deadly as Sal Vera.

And then Richard slipped through Sal's guard with an overhand lunge, his knife leaving a line of crimson on his cheek. Mary Kay gasped as Richard performed a rapid backspin, turning completely around in midair to plunge his knife deep into Sal's right shoulder. Sal stepped back, fighting to maintain his balance. Grimacing, Sal reached down and slowly pulled the knife from his shoulder. He stood there, now armed with two knives. "You Apache? You fight Geronimo."

Richard offered him a smirk. "Lakota," he said.

"Ah," Sal said. "You fight den like dat Crazy Horse."

Sal swayed, dropping Richard's bloody knife. His knees suddenly buckled and he fell backward. Springing to his feet, Chris caught him before he fell into the fire, and maneuvered his unconscious form to one side of the crackling blaze. Richard said, "Should have let him burn."

Appearing there beyond our firelight, Gran B scolded Richard, saying, "Good Lord, what mischief are you up to? Shame on you!"

Richard stood there, his shoulders slumped, his head hanging low. I felt sorry for him and despite all the times he'd been mean to me in the past, I said, "He was saving me from this thug, Gran."

"Oh, hush, child!" Gran B said. "If I call for an ambulance, he'll end up at the emergency ward, then Sheriff Mac will get wind of this. And Richard Hawkins will be headed back to the State Home."

I nearly gave my brother a hug to thank him for saving me, but I knew he would not like it, especially in front of his friends. And so, I stuck out my hand and said, "Thanks for saving me."

Richard said, "Don't mention it. You're ugly enough. Just think what you would look like with one ear. We can't have that, can we?"

Tears welled up in my eyes. I thought, *Why in the hell do you have to be so hard? I'm your only brother and you just risked your own life to save me, so why can't you just accept my sincere thanks?*

A moment later, Rock pulled up in the street beyond our vacant lot. After settling Sal into his car, he drove him away.

Chapter Twenty

As Gran led us into her house, Richard said, "Hawk, go get me the map. I'm getting the treasure. If we claim all that gold, who cares what Ty did with the gold from Robber's Cave?"

Dec said, "Stolen gold is cursed. Ever heard of Black Beard's ghost? In Irish folklore, a geis is a curse. In all the pirate stories I've read, a violator ends up dead or they break out in boils or leprosy."

Richard stood there between the wood stove and Gran's rocker, a puzzled look on his face. "So, you're saying this cache of gold is cursed?"

Dec said, "Don't know, but I am telling you why Hawk and I would never be foolish enough to claim it. No boils for us. No leprosy either."

Dec had everyone in Gran's den considering this qeis he spoke of. Kat looked over at Chris. Mary Kay looked up at Richard. I wondered where Dec had come up with this talk of curses. It applied to grave robbing, but I never heard it applied to treasure hunting.

Dec said, "Kat spoke of this Chupacabra. Maybe, this flying monkey is someone who actually got changed by a geis placed on that trove."

Gran asked, "Do you know how that cache got there in the first place?"

Chris and Richard gave her blank stares. Mary Kay and Kat peered at her curiously. Dec nodded, indicating he was listening. I offered Gran a puzzled frown. She instructed Dec to remove a brick from before her wood stove, creating a hole in her hearth. He reached into it and drew out a satchel. He gave it to Gran. She opened it, removing a book and three bronze arrowheads. Gran showed us the long-haired men engraved on each medallion: Custer, Wild Bill, and Buffalo Bill Cody.

She raised the book. "*River Kings by Samuel Clemens*," she said. "Henry McGinn wrote this as part of Ghost's ploy to trap a rare book collector. It's hard to tell which is fact and which is fiction."

We all sat there enthralled by the story read to us by Gran B:

"William F. Cody, born in 1846 in Iowa, moved with his family to Kansas. Before the Civil War, Bill's father was speaking at a trading post where pro-slavery men met. His anti-slavery speech so enraged one man that he stabbed him with a knife. After his death, 12-year-old Billy, struck by gold fever, was on his way to the gold fields, when he met Wild Bill Hickok in Junction City, Kansas.

"In 1860, while driving a freight team, Wild Bill was attacked by a bear. He killed the bear, yet was severely injured and sent to Rock Creek Station twenty miles from Beatrice to recover. While there, he and Billy Cody rode out to Fort Blue River to sign on as scouts for the US Calvary. It was then that a company of Confederates rode up to the gates in front of a Lakota war band in hot pursuit. These Confederates had been on a raid with Bloody Bill, and rode north with a portion of gold marked for the Golden Circle. Desperate to find a safe location to hide the gold, it was buried there at Fort Blue River.

"Born in 1840, Bloody Bill Anderson was the most notorious guerrilla leader in the Civil War. In 1863, Quantrill and 400 Confederates attacked Fort Baxter, manned by the famed Buffalo Soldiers, who defeated the Raiders. Bloody Bill wanted to attack the fort a second time, but Quantrill took half of his men to Texas, while Bloody Bill led his men to Nebraska. Bloody Bill hid a trove of gold there at Fort Blue River. In 1863, when Quantrill's Raiders killed 150 men and boys in Lawrence, Kansas, Jessie James was part of that brutal raid. In 1865, the Civil War ended, and the Knights of the Golden Circle enlisted the help of the notorious outlaw, Jesse James. The James Gang carried out a string of robberies from Iowa to Texas. During the Minnesota bank robbery in 1876, Jesse broke his ankle and recovered at his mother's farm in Rulo, Nebraska. It was during this time that Jessie hid gold at Robber's Cave.

"In Wyoming, engaged in the Indian Wars, Wild Bill and Bill Cody served as Custer's scouts along with Bloody Knife, a Sioux scout for the 7th Cavalry. In 1864, Bloody Knife met a band of Confederate prisoners in a war camp. It was there he came across Wild Bill, posing as a Confederate yet spying for the Union. Wild Bill told Bloody Knife of the gold buried at Fort Blue River. When Bloody Knife told Custer about it, the wily Colonel made plans to confiscate that gold.

"In 1873, Custer awarded Bloody Knife a silver medal with his name inscribed on it. Custer's penchant for these medals led to a set of bronze arrowheads being engraved with the faces of Buffalo Bill, Wild Bill, and Custer on them. Setting his sights on the cache of gold belonging to the Golden Circle, Custer, a Freemason, knew about the engineering feats that the Circle used to safe-guard their gold. So, he hired his own engineers to travel to Fort Blue River to create a vault that could only be opened by inserting the three arrowheads into its lock device. Custer planned to send the other two to Wild Bill and Buffalo Bill with an invite to meet at the end of the Plains War, when they would use the medallions to open the vault.

"In 1874, Custer and the 7th Cavalry, trespassing in the Black Hills, started a gold rush which enraged the Sioux. It was this trespassing into their sacred land, that led to Custer's death at the Little Big Horn in 1877. There, Bloody Knife was shot in the head and killed. His deeds were remembered in song, and he became one of the most famous scouts of the US army. In 1876, Wild Bill was killed at Deadwood, and in regards to the gold at Fort Blue River, only Buffalo Bill remained alive.

"Several months after the battle of the Little Big Horn, Crazy Horse was killed at Fort Robinson, Nebraska. It is Crazy Horse's father, who was actually the 2nd Crazy Horse in their family line, and yet he lived far past the age of his son into his late 80's. Early in his life, this second Crazy Horse had a vision of an owl who told him that he would rename himself, Worm, to step aside for the sake of his son. Jesse Lee, the Indian agent, whom Worm trusted, aided Worm in burying his son in the Black Hills. To thank Lee, Worm gave him the three arrowheads he'd taken from Custer's body at the Little Big Horn. Worm valued tokens of power ever since his son received a black stone from a medicine man. This sacred stone protected Crazy Horse from bullets. In his eyes, the bronze arrowheads were tokens of power.

"In 1885, a Lakota war band attacked Fort Blue River. Henry McGinn the First would have died in the attack, but for a company of Buffalo Soldiers stationed there. McGinn fled, watching the fort burn to the ground. He lived at Beatrice for years after and McGinn's son became Sentinel of Rivermoon.

"In 1889, Buffalo Bill, belonging to the Platte Valley Lodge in North Platte, became a Knight Templar and received his degree in the Scottish Rite. It was then that fellow Mason, Jesse Lee, gave him the three arrowheads and the letter Custer had written, instructing him to use the arrowheads to open the vault. And yet, Cody determined it was gold that had been the downfall of so many others. His own adventures started when at age 12 he set out for the gold fields. Custer trespassed into the Black Hills in search of gold. Bloody Bill and Jesse James had been killed in their quests for gold. And Wild Bill had been shot dead as he played cards, drawn to Deadwood in search of gold. Cody served the Union during the War, but his loyalties ended when he began his Wild West tours. He put the medallions aside, storing them in a trunk.

"In 1903, a river boat captain attended Cody's show at North Platte. Samuel Clemens hailed from Hannibal, Missouri, and by then was well-known for being a writer. After the show, Cody shared with Clemens the tale of the gold buried in the vault beneath the ruins of Fort Blue River. Cody gave Clemens a leather pouch containing the three arrowheads. Clemens thought the tale a tragic one, and when he shared it with his friend and fellow boat captain, Amos Hawkins from Beatrice, he impressed upon him the power of gold fever.

"Sam and Amos spoke often of the gold buried beneath the ruins of the fort, but the bronze medallions ended up as mere pocket-watch fobs passed down to Amos's son, Amos.

"And time will tell if they remain that way to the end of days."

Chapter Twenty-One

A thunderous pounding came from Gran B's front door. Badger and Cooper erupted with fierce barks. I helped Gran B out of her rocker and she went over to the door. She had barely opened it, when Ty came barging through, a pistol aimed directly at her face. "Time for all the monkey business to end! Rebecca, hand over that ledger! Mary Kay and Kat, head out to my patrol car!"

He latched onto Gran by the collar of her robe. Mary Kay took Kat by one hand, and the two of them hurried out to the front porch. Badger and Cooper were confused by Ty's aggression, and Dec grabbed onto their collars to prevent them from getting shot by Ty.

Ty shoved Gran back toward her rocker. He jabbed with his pistol at the *River Kings* book she'd placed on the end table beside her rocker. "Is this the ledger?" he growled. "Give it to me!"

Gran followed his directions, handing him the book. "Take it. But don't take the girls, Tyler. Leave them out of this."

Ty gave a wicked laugh. "Chris, go tell Henry to meet me out at Rivermoon. Tell him to bring that map, and once we've settled up out there, I'll let Mary Kay and Kat go."

"Why," Richard said, "don't you go and get him over at his house?"

"Ghost," Ty growled. "While Mac and Noah are out searching for me, that Indian has set himself up to watch over Henry out front of his house. One of you is going to sneak up to the back door. Tell Henry where to meet me. I need Henry to open that vault! Or Mary Kay and her baby will be destined for the cemetery just outside of town!"

"Tyler?" Gran B said, softly. "Just how lost are you, son?"

Big Ty raised his pistol, aiming it at Gran's chest. "No!" I said, stepping up between his raised gun and Gran B. A second later, Richard slid around in front of me. He shoved that pistol aside. "How dare you point a gun at my grandmother and my brother!"

Ty slammed his gun upside Richard's head, knocking him back into me. In trying to stop his fall, I threw both hands up, dropping those arrowheads. They made solid clunking sounds as they struck Gran's wooden floor. Richard and I fell down, the arrowheads scattering on the floor before us. Having no clue what they were, Ty kicked at them with his booted feet, sending them sliding past us across the floor.

He then wheeled around and left through the front door.

Terrified of what Big Ty might do to his sister and his girl friend, Chris was determined to sneak past Ghost to get to Henry. The second Chris left, Richard ordered me to retrieve the map. Dec and I left Gran's place together. I ran for home, while he ran for the courthouse to tell his dad about Ty taking the girls as hostages. As we ran off, Cooper followed him and Badger followed me, both dogs as loyal as ever.

We got back to Gran's place ten minutes later, both of us colliding with one another. We stumbled and fell, landing in a tangle of arms, legs, and dogs. Snorting in disgust at our clumsiness, Richard snatched the map out of my grasp. "I'm not waiting for Chris and Henry. They'll just waste more time arguing over whether to retrieve that gold. I've had this talk before. This time, I am doing things my way!"

Richard rolled up the map and took off running away from Gran B's place, leaving Dec and I alone on the porch.

Dec said, "Dad and Noah are down in Pawnee City. The sheriff down there called about a mountain lion killing a cow out in a farmer's field. Gracie down at the courthouse said Dad and his posse left heavily armed and headed on a cougar hunt! We won't get no help from them!"

I stared into the shadows beyond the porch. "Mountain lion? Pawnee City? Why, that's only 40 miles from here."

Dec zipped up his parka. "Let's leave the dogs with Gran. Then lets go get us a boat. Let's rescue the girls from big dumb and ugly Ty. I'm all for getting Kat and Mary Kay out of this mess, and leaving the dogs here is smart. No telling what would happen if Badger and Cooper had a run-in with this Chupacabra."

The front screen door swung open and Gran B stepped out into the frosty air. "Yes, boys, leave your dogs here with me, but take this along with you if you dare to step foot on that island, Jessie."

I accepted the umbrella she handed me. "A Rainy Day Gun?" I asked, carefully examining the umbrella. "How many of these did Dad make?"

"This is the first one," Gran said. "Your dad made sure the Matron of this family was taken care of. There's been many spooky nights when I heard unfamiliar sounds that woke me. I've always felt safer taking this umbrella with me when I went to investigate."

She ushered the two dogs inside her house. "I wish you could just let Mac deal with Tyler, but I know circumstances don't allow for that. I heard Dec talking about that cougar down in Pawnee City."

Gran handed me a small leather pouch. "The arrowheads," she said. "Chris and Richard forgot them. If you find this vault, it will be you who have the keys to open it."

I tucked the pouch into a pocket of my insulated jacket, then turned to give Gran one last hug. But she was already gone, leaving a mere vapor trail behind her as she stepped back into her warm, inviting home.

Dec led me over to Ella Street and into the car port on the side of his house. There sat Mac's hunting and fishing mobile. A four-wheel drive Toyota truck, with a seventeen-foot aluminum canoe strapped to its roof. During the first six blocks of our drive down to Court Street, Dec had not quite worked out the timing of stepping on the clutch, then letting it out to shift. He was grinding those gears each time he shifted. "Relax, Hawk," he said. "If you're worried about cops pulling us over, the town cops are miles from here on a mountain lion hunt. Once I get these gears sorted, I'll be driving like a champ at the Indy 500!"

Those nine miles down to East Locust Road were the scariest ever. After fish-tailing at every corner he turned, swerving toward the ditch each time he took his eyes off the road, and his sudden braking to keep us from jack-rabbiting over steep hills, Dec finally drove us through an iron gateway. He killed the engine, turned off the headlights. We sat there for long moments staring at the still black waters surrounding Rivermoon three-hundred yards ahead of us.

After unloading the canoe, we drug it to the edge of the steep shoreline. I returned to the truck to retrieve the umbrella gun. As I rejoined Dec, I checked to make sure it was loaded. Satisfied to find a shell in its single chamber, I flicked the safety off. Slightly mesmerized by the silver radiance shimmering on the water's surface, Dec said, "You know those currents could suck a boy under. Maybe pull him down to the muddy bottom where the eels and the leeches lurk."

Scanning the island three-hundred yards ahead of us, Dec said, "I read up on this place. In the 1800's, river pirates had a fort there. Indians slaughtered them all one night, leaving their ghosts to wander."

Snow started to fall. Mist rose from the waters separating us from Rivermoon. Through the flurries, we could see dim lights on the island. Nebraska winters can be blizzard-like. We were likely in for a fierce winter storm. Using long, slender fingers to feather back strands of his blond hair, Dec narrowed his eyes. He scanned the distant island, watching for something to move. Finally, we launched the canoe, sliding it into the waters beyond the shore. Suddenly, we both looked up to see a black creature swoop down toward us, its long, slender wings blocking out the moonlit sky. An angry hiss came from the bat-like thing, followed by a gurgling noise and a solid *Thunk!* as something dropped into the center of the canoe. "Gawd!" Dec gasped. "It just tried to crap on us!"

Glancing at the black creature winging away from us, I used my paddle to remove the foul smelling object from the floor of the canoe. "Sick!" Dec said. "Would an owl do such a thing? Do owls even poop in flight?"

I flicked the smelly turd into the water. We watched the winged thing melting into the shadows of Rivermoon. "Owls have feathers. That thing had leathery wings, and a thin body like a monkey."

I said, "Yeah, but monkeys don't fly."

Dec muttered, "Well, this one sure did!"

Our canoe shot through the dark waters like a shark zeroing in on its prey. Dec dug his paddle into the water and pulled a full stroke. Seated in the bow of the aluminum canoe, he kept his gaze fixed on the island ahead of us. He dipped his paddle once. Twice. Three more times. But he lost control, and the currents sent the canoe shooting toward the southern tip of the island. At a rather swift clip. Pointing back at the rapidly shrinking shore behind us, I said, "Slow us down some, Dec!"

Dec drove his paddle deep into the dark, swirling water, then turned it sideways in an attempt to slow our forward momentum. His desperate dipping motions did little, however, to decrease our speed. We were now heading straight for the rocky shore of the island less than ten yards ahead of us. Growling in frustration, Dec yanked his paddle out of the water, allowing the current to take us where it wanted.

A loud hiss came from the flurries above us, and the monkey creature burst from the specks of white and dropped down toward the canoe.

"Shoot it!" Dec cried, gesturing at the umbrella gun in the bottom of the canoe. Snatching up the flechette, I raised it and slid my finger into the trigger guard. The winged creature came crashing into me, scrabbling to get a hold of the umbrella. It forced the gun down and hot lead spat from the muzzle of the umbrella and punched a hole in the bottom of the canoe. White water shot up into the air, spraying me with a chilly burst. The winged monkey actually snickered before flying away.

We smashed into the island with a loud crunch. An eerie *Screeeechhh!* followed as the aluminum craft scraped against the rocky shoreline. Dec flipped over the bow, and landed in a pile of brush. I was catapulted high into the air. I flailed crazily with my arms and propelled myself forward, managing to land on dry ground. Dazed from our collision, we both watched the canoe shoot away through the churning water. It then capsized, filling up with water. And down it sank. Its stern bobbed up and down like the nose of a drowning man poking up for one last breath. It was then gone. Down where the leeches and eels lurk.

Chapter Twenty-Two

Moving away from the dark water, we discovered a trail snaking its way into a small forest of cottonwood trees ten yards from the water. We traveled thirty feet down the trail winding between the cottonwoods, when Dec tripped and fell over a bulky shape on the ground. Scrambling back up, he peered down at what appeared to be a dead man sprawled there on the path. "A guard," he said. "Or he *was* a security guard. Uniform. Badge. Gun belt. Gun's gone."

"What could have done that?" I asked. "Looks like he's been mauled by a grizzly. Only there ain't no grizzlies here in Nebraska, but there is a cougar down near Pawnee City."

Looking off into the trees, I froze. Dec shot to his feet. A shadow detached itself from the shadows beneath the cottonwoods. Then slid back into the undergrowth. There for a second. But now gone. Hidden once more in shadows. An eerie voice startled us, and we looked down at the dead security guard. At first, we thought maybe the poor guy hadn't been dead, that he was now weakly calling to us for help. But when we heard the voice a second time, there was a crackle in its tone.

"Walkie-talkie!" I said, pointing down at the man's belt. After long, low hiss, Kat's voice came from its small speaker: "Base to Rover Three. Come in, Three. Do you copy? Rover Three, do you copy? Brady? They're loose! Ty opened all of their cages! They've gone on a rampage!"

Dec kneeled down, reaching for the walkie-talkie. "What are you doing?" I whispered. "You want to let Ty know we're coming?"

Dec said, "Maybe they're not holding her hostage, if they are letting her use the walkie-talkie."

He reached down and removed the walkie-talkie from the guard's belt. "Base to Rover Three!" Kat squawked. "Brady, get to the tower! Lock yourself in! They're not alone! Mock is leading them! He's already tried breaking in here, but we've sealed the doors!"

We stared down at the walkie-talkie in Dec's grasp. He pressed the orange button on the walkie-talkie. "Hello?" he said.

Kat's voice came out of the walkie-talkie: "Declan?"

Pressing on the button, Dec said, "Me and Hawk crashed our canoe on the north end of the island, coming out here to rescue you! We found a dead guard on the trail!"

Kat said, "Brady is dead? You are in danger. You need to get yourself quickly off of Rivermoon!"

Dec responded, "Our canoe sank."

Dec and I exchanged glances. We waited. It took several seconds, but finally Kat asked, "Can you swim back to the far shore?"

Considering her suggestion, I turned and looked back down the trail, peering at the river barely visible between the giant cottonwood trees. It must have been at least ten yards away. Even if we bolted and ran toward the river, I had the feeling we would not make it.

I then saw it move. A dark figure slithered between the cottonwoods at the head of the trail. It shifted ever so slowly, keeping to the shadows, moonlight reflecting from its yellow eyes. The thing then vanished. Either it ducked down and scurried through the thick undergrowth. Or it had slid up against one of the trees and was hidden there. Watching us. Waiting to see what we intended to do. Wanting us to make a run for the river. It would then pounce on us.

Dec said, "It's in the tree! That winged monkey-thing!"

The creature clung to the upper branch of a tree thirty feet away. As it slithered around behind the thick branch, shafts of moonlight grazed portions of its body. The tip of a leathery wing. The long claws of one paw. The shiny dome of its small head. Bright lemony eyes. Never did we see the entire body, but it certainly looked like a monkey with wings.

Dec raised the walkie-talkie to his lips. "Whatever killed this guard, it's here now, cutting off our path to the river. Some creepy, slithery thing with wings, that stands about as tall as a five-year-old kid!"

"Is he alone?" Kat asked, her voice sounding distant.

Dec said, "*Him*? Do you know what this thing is, Kat?"

"His name is Mock," Kat said. "More than likely he'll bring the others and set them on you. Is he alone?"

Dec and I scanned the trees on either side of the trail. We looked at each other. "We don't know," Dec said. "It's really dark out here. What do you mean by *others*? Others like him?"

Kat said, "If that's Officer Brady you found out there, then he should have weapons on him. A pistol and a tazer. Check him."

Dec said, "His pistol's been taken. Tazer's gone too."

Kat responded, "Arm yourselves. If Mock sets the band of rhesus on you, you need a stick to keep them at arm's length. The rhesus will go for your face! They go for the face because clawing out the eyes of an enemy is a good way to blind one."

Dec spoke into the walkie-talkie. "So how do we get to this tower? And better yet, where's Ty? Is he still holding you hostage?"

Kat said, "Ty and Sal were attacked by Mock and a gang of baboons. They locked themselves in a bunker sixty yards from the control room, which is where Mary Kay and I are hiding. The control room is about a hundred yards in from the front gate. We became separated from Ty when Richard, Chris, and Henry showed up. Now those three are holed up in the tunnels, hiding from the marauding mob of mad monkeys. Keep to the trail you're on. Fifty yards ahead of you the trail forks. You'll come out of the trees and see the tower forty yards in front of you. Don't run. You'll want to. But don't. Walk straight to the tower. If anything gets in your way, use your sticks and protect your faces."

The walkie-talkie went silent.

"Anything else?" Dec pressed the button and asked.

We waited. We nervously scanned the trees, the trail, the high branches where the winged Mock creature had been. Still, we waited.

"Yes," Kat finally said. "There are chips implanted in the Nigerian squirrel monkeys. I've been watching their movements on a scanner. They're heading toward you. Don't panic. They're not moving fast, but they are moving. So get to the tower."

She paused and quickly added, "Oh, and one more thing. Shut off the walkie-talkie. If not, they'll hear us communicating and be drawn to you out of curiosity. Good-luck."

We moved down the trail, weaving our way beneath the cottonwoods. I'd caught a glimpse of Mock sailing away through the branches when we left the clearing behind us. Dec had the feeling the bug-eyed, winged creature had been watching us, waiting for us to try to make our escape. We armed ourselves with long, thick sticks as Kat had told us, but if indeed, Mock had murdered an armed security guard, then we figured the creature could dispatch us whenever it chose to.

Dec skidded to a halt just past the bend in the trail Kat had told us about. We still had some ground to cover before we even reached the edge of the tree line ahead of us. "Something just moved," I said. "I saw something shoot across the trail and scurry into those bushes."

Swinging his stick up and placing one end of it over his shoulder, Dec said, "I'll go clear us a path if I need to."

Several moments of silent and stealthy walking brought us to a bend in the trail. Between the trees ahead of us, we spotted a circle of light that marked the end of the trail. We heard a thrashing in the bushes some distance behind us. It was followed by the solid pounding of bare feet pattering on the ground. A moment later, a small, shadowy shape skittered onto the trail, thirty feet behind us. Then two more appeared. Then more than a dozen small squirrel monkeys formed a cluster in the center of the trail. Five of the spindly figures crouched down and sat staring at us, their luminescent eyes slowly blinking. Two of the little beasts charged.

I startled the entire band of monkeys by running directly at them. I swung my stick like a baseball bat at the two charging down the trail. Striking the first one with my stick, I lifted it completely off of its feet. The creature screeched and went flying end over end, squirting brown fluids behind him. It landed somewhere in the darkness beyond the trail, and a cluster of dark shapes scattered and shot away between the trees.

Dec ran up to me and said, "Sleeping Jesus! That was cool, Hawk!"

I said, "I hope I didn't kill any of them! What if they want revenge?"

Dec searched the darkness, knowing full well the band of monkeys was out there watching us. "Come on. Let's go find that tower."

The moment we turned and started down the trail, we heard crackling, snapping, and thrashing in the undergrowth on both sides of us.

It was obvious we were being followed. Maybe even herded down the trail. Shadowy shapes darted between the boles of the cottonwoods. Dark scrawny, shapes skittering on all fours, moving so fast they were mere blurs. Blurred monkey shapes with gleaming yellow eyes.

We came out of the trees, discovering an open field. The tall, white tower of an ancient lighthouse stood at the end of this field. Kat had told us it was one hundred and twenty yards from the tree line. But huddled there at the opening between the trees, we knew it was definitely too far for a quick run. A haven for certain, but just too far away.

We heard the small creatures scampering through the undergrowth. It was hard to tell if the mad little beasts were behind us. Or if they were crouched down on either side of us. Watching us. Waiting to break from cover and launch an attack. Dec whispered, "Oh, no! There's a big bastard coming toward the field! Look, he's climbing over that fence!"

Two-hundred yards to our right, a high chain-link fence bordered the south side of the field. A large, dark shape moved agilely up the opposite side of the fence. And then another dozen shot out of the darkness. Until at least twenty of the creatures were plastered against the fence, clawing their way up and scrabbling over the top. They silently clambered down to the field, forming a small mob. All of the large monkeys were peering directly at us kneeling there between the trees.

"Rhesus," I said. "The ones Kat said to keep away from our faces."

Dec slowly stood up. The entire band of rhesus reacted at once, crouching on all fours and staring menacingly at us. The moment I stood up to join Dec, three of the larger males hooted and took three pouncing steps forward. Then stopped, letting out sharp, angry barks.

"We'll move to our left," Dec said quietly. "We'll just move over to the shoreline, fifty feet to our left, and travel along the edge of the water. That way, they can only come at us from one side. Let's just head for that shoreline. If they attack us, we should just take our chances in the water. I doubt if they'll swim out after us."

Chapter Twenty-Three

A flurry of movement came from the trees behind us. We wheeled around, expecting to be under attack by the smaller squirrel monkeys. A pattering of bare feet on the hard-packed dirt trail filled our ears. We could see only blurred shadows weaving in and out of the brush and between the trees. The sudden noise agitated the band of rhesus on the south side of the field. They were all standing up now, some on all fours, others up on their hind legs, craning their necks and peering hard at the trees around us. One of the males let out a sharp, commanding bark that instantly brought a stillness back to the wooded grove. He barked twice, gruffly. He then leaped forward in long, graceful bounds. And stopped sixty feet from us. "He gets any closer," Dec said, "I'll charge him and scare him back."

"No!" I whispered. "If we show any aggression, these big guys will come at us in a swarm! Let's just stick to your water plan."

The lone rhesus male curiously watched us move out of the trees. The big male stayed crouched on all fours, his body tense, his nose pointed upward, his eyes unblinking. Four other large males sprang forward, joining the lone male. All five of the beasts let out a startled screech when the woods in front of them came alive with a flurry of small, dark bodies bursting between the trees. The rhesus monkeys wheeled away from the small squirrel monkeys, scattering in a panic.

Thankful for the distraction, Dec and I moved to the rocky shore of the island fifty feet away from the trees. We were still nearly sixty feet shy of the tower, but so far nothing had pursued us. We looked across the field to see a few stragglers skittering out of the woods as if they were being chased. We then saw the winged shape gliding out of the trees, swooping down toward the fleeing squirrel monkeys. Mock.

Diving down, he scooped up an unfortunate little monkey in his claws. The smaller animal screeched horribly, then fell silent as Mock sank his talons into its body. Twisting about in mid-air, Mock tossed the dead monkey down into the swarm of rhesus and squirrel monkeys.

Chaos then broke out. The rhesus attacked the advancing mob of squirrel monkeys, tearing into them with fangs and claws. Small dark bodies flew through the air in all directions. The majority of the smaller monkeys swerved swiftly away from the grappling paws of the larger primates. The rhesus hooted in frustration as an explosion of squirrel monkeys wheeled around and headed back to the trees.

Mock plummeted down and herded the retreating monkeys back and away from the trees. Sickened by the merciless killing, tears blurred my vision. Despite Kat's warning that we should walk to the tower, we couldn't stick to that plan. Not after what we had just witnessed. Mock was dangerous. If he rallied the troops, we knew that getting inside the tower was imperative. The sooner the better. We ran.

Thirty feet from the lighthouse door, something small and dark blocked our path. "Sweet Jesus!" Dec gasped, going from a dead run to a bone-rattling skid. We faced the thing that now stood between us and the tower. "A squirrel monkey," I said.

It was a skinny little thing, the black fur around his small eyes making it seem like he was wearing a mask. He simply sat there, looking up at us with no hostility in his intense gaze. The monkey then turned away and retreated down the path leading to the tower. Halfway to the lighthouse door, he scooped up a ring of keys. The metal ring was at least six inches in diameter and held dozens of keys. The keys jangled noisily as the small monkey lifted the ring above his head and shook it, looking like an athlete holding up a prized trophy.

"Okay, squirt," Dec said, "you're either for us or against us."

We started walking toward the monkey. He stood there upright before us, holding the key ring above his head, watching us curiously. A shadow passed over us. We looked up to see Mock flying down at us. He spat, spraying us with hot saliva. Passing completely over us, Mock latched onto the ring of keys the small monkey held. Fiercely beating his wings, the flying monkey rose up, but the little guy gave a savage howl, tugged on the key ring, pulling Mock out of the air. Fierce growling erupted from both creatures, and a wild tug-o-war ensued. The tiny monkey jerked down hard. Mock's wings flapped up and down, causing him to rise. But the monkey hauled him back down. Caught off guard, and still attached to the metal ring by his paws, Mock slammed into the ground with a loud thud. Before he could recover, a chimpanzee darted out of the open doorway of the tower. The big chimp latched onto the key ring, gently removing it from the smaller monkey's grip. He then rolled his shoulders and swung Mock over his head. Only to slam him back down in the middle of the path.

"Oscar!" Dec whispered. "How did he get out here?"

Mock snarled, launching into a furious fighting frenzy. Springing up, he released the ring and attacked the chimp. His long, sharp talons raked bloody gashes in the big primate's chest. Oscar dropped to the ground and lay there, stunned. Mock practically danced around him in glee, hissing and cackling. Rather than fight back, the poor chimp seemed only interested now in holding onto the keys. He no longer wanted to fight. Hunching down there on the trail, he held the keys against his bleeding chest as Mock closed in on him.

Crack! echoed through the night air as Dec's stick slammed down between Mock's wings and shoulders. He swung again, striking the creature on the head. Mock reeled to one side and dropped to the ground. Dec raised the stick above his head, then froze as Mock ever so slowly turned his head and peered up at him with a human-like sneer. A low hiss escaped from between his lips. Screaming in rage, his putrid breath burst from between his jagged rows of teeth and invaded our nostrils. White, foamy froth dribbled down his chin. He grunted. And received an answer from the rhesus band coming across the field. Dec and I looked behind us to see the rhesus monkeys charging toward us. More than a dozen of the large rhesus monkeys had worked themselves into a frenzy. Once they closed with us, they would savagely attack us. Biting. Gouging. Ripping. Tearing. And plucking our eyes out.

A strange sound suddenly came from behind us. It sounded like insects had flown directly into a bug zapper. We glanced back to see the black-masked squirrel dart away from the open door of the tower behind us.

The tazer the tiny monkey held in its fore paws crackled and sent brilliant bursts of blue light arcing between the metal prongs of the weapon. And as the band of rhesus closed with him, he shoved it into the face of the first monkey in line. A loud, crisp ***Zap!*** echoed through the air as the metal prongs connected with the larger primate's face. It lurched backwards, as if it had been struck by an invisible force. The other monkeys reacted at once. Screeching in fear, they scattered.

The squirrel monkey chittered in triumph. He was so intent on watching the rhesus flee that he didn't see Mock sweeping in behind him, thrusting both fists before him. The force of the blow was so powerful the squirrel monkey was sent somersaulting through the air. He lost his grip on the tazer, then landed ten feet away. A low moan escaped from his tiny lips as he collapsed beside the open tower door. Mock wheeled and sped back to pick up the tazer. He would have had it, too. If not for the sudden appearance of yet another squirrel monkey springing out of the open doorway of the tower. Black and tan fur covered its tiny body, but its snow-white face appeared to be glowing. Mock had just latched onto the weapon when the squirrel monkey grabbed onto it and tore it from his grasp.

Mock took to the air, rising above the buzzing tazer. Hovering there with slow, ponderous flaps of his long wings, he sent out a high-pitched wail. As if under hypnotic command, the entire band of monkeys fixed hostile gazes on us. Slowly, they all peered up at Mock. At once, the rhesus came up on all fours and started to advance.

Oscar provided a brief distraction as he ambled toward the tower. The moment Mock turned his attention on the wounded chimp, the rhesus on the field skidded to a stop, hunkering down in confusion. "He's controlling them," Dec said. "It's some kind of mind thing!"

Thirty feet lay between us and the relative safety of the tower. But with Mock blocking our path, thirty feet seemed too far. Mock steadily pumped his wings and cried out to the rhesus. The entire company of monkeys glared hatefully at us, preparing to charge. "Oh God!" Dec hissed. "We ain't gonna make it, Hawk!"

Dec then made a mad dash toward the white-faced squirrel monkey. The tiny monkey let out a startled yelp, dropped the tazer, and scampered inside the tower. Dec scooped up the tazer. His finger grazed the trigger and a burst of blue light sizzled between the metal prongs. Mock barked a command at the rhesus. I looked on in disbelief as Dec risked the few brief seconds we had to pick up the black-faced squirrel monkey sprawled in front of the open door. A moment later, the howling horde of rhesus swarmed all over us. We went down beneath the snarling, growling, hooting mass of furry bodies. I closed my eyes and waited for sharp fangs to pierce my flesh. I felt the hot breath of our attackers explode into my face. I gagged on the putrid stench, then instinctively reacted. Surging to my feet, I plucked the tazer out of Dec's grasp and struck anything resembling monkey. The crackles, pops, and furious buzzes of the weapon were followed by a bizarre mixture of howls and shrieks. Howling and screeching, the big monkeys scattered in all directions. "Yahh!" I yelled. "You damned smelly apes!"

I smirked triumphantly and pulled the tazer's trigger.

And nothing happened.

I pulled it again. A slight pop erupted between the metal prongs, but then fizzled and vanished, leaving a blue spark hanging in the air. Mock let out an airy huff that sounded like mocking laughter. I heaved the tazer at him, striking him hard in the chest. Still cradling the limp body of the squirrel monkey against his chest, Dec slipped inside the tower, when Mock swooped down in front of me, cutting me off.

Oscar came barreling into Mock and sent him flailing through the air. The big chimp would have continued his attack on the winged creature, but I reached out and latched onto his shoulder. "No, Oscar. There are too many of them. Get inside the tower."

Oscar offered me a thoughtful look. He softly hooted and scampered inside the tower. I sprang forward and leaped in after him, pulling the door closed behind us.

Chapter Twenty-Four

I locked the door by sliding its metal lock bar into place. A loud, furious pounding came from the other side of the thick metal door. It shook and rattled, but remained firmly in place as the infuriated Mock struck it over and over.

His thunderous pounding was followed by a long pall of silence. Dec and I stood there straining to hear any sounds coming from the other side of the door. But the eery silence continued. I looked around us. We stood in a twenty-by-twenty foot room that appeared to be a guard house. There was a desk in one corner of the room and several metal cabinets situated along one wall. "I wonder," Dec said, gently placing the limp body of the monkey beside the door, "if this is the only way in. There's probably a door or a window at the top of the tower. Hopefully, its locked and he can't get in that way. But who knows?"

He pointed to the left of the spiral stairway where another set of steps vanished into the darkness below. "These go down. So there could be a tunnel down there with another opening."

"Poor guy," I said, pointing across the room at Oscar slumped against the wall. The big chimp sat there, staring at us, holding his keys, bright red blood welling up from the deep gashes in his chest.

Dec said, "Who knows what Mock could be carrying. Venom? Poison? Rabies? Could be Mock is a vampire. Now that he's infected Oscar maybe he'll turn into some sort of evil beast, too."

We both jumped in alarm when the black-faced squirrel monkey opened his eyes and sat up. He peered curiously up at us, blinking repeatedly. I kneeled so as not to seem intimidating. Though I wanted to reach out and pet the dazed creature, I knew that any attempt to connect with the monkey might be perceived as a threat. I said, "How you feeling? You saved us out there. So don't be afraid. We're not going to hurt you."

Dec grinned. "Look at him. He doesn't seem to be freaking out that we're this close to him. He's just sitting there. Looking like he doesn't know where the hell he's at. He's probably in shock."

I continued talking softly to him, keeping my distance and not making direct eye contact. A moment later, the white-faced monkey scampered out from behind the desk, dragging a pistol behind her. The little creature boldly moved toward us and dropped the gun at our feet. "Whoa!" Dec said, kneeling down to scoop up the pistol. "At last! Something we can blow that Mock away with!"

Dec opened the cylinder of the pistol and inspected it. "Fully loaded! It's a six-shooter. I think this pistol and that tazer belonged to the guard we found mauled on the trail. Remember? Kat mentioned that Officer Brady should have a gun and a tazer on him? Well, I bet these little guys took them from him after he was attacked."

Dec smiled, pointing down at the white-faced monkey watching us. "Only one is a *guy*. The masked bandit is a boy. Snow-white is a girl!"

I smiled for the first time since we'd crashed on the island. "Oh," I said, sheepishly. "Sorry if I've offended you, my lady."

I made a slight bow in her direction, and to my astonishment, the tiny, white-faced monkey imitated my bow, complete with a flourish of one tiny paw. I experimentally raised two fingers on my right hand and gave her the peace sign. We both gasped out loud when she raised one tiny paw and stuck up two of her slender fingers in the exact same gesture. "Damn!" I said. "Someone must have trained her."

Oscar hunkered down in the corner and softly moaned. Hearing his distress, the female monkey scampered over to the badly bleeding chimp. "No," Dec said, "you don't want to bother him, little girl. He's been hurt pretty bad. He might not want you invading his space."

I, too, became a little worried about how the large chimp might react to the squirrel monkey as she planted herself directly in front of Oscar and gently placed her two tiny forepaws on his ragged, bloody wounds. "No!" I whispered, fearfully. "You don't want to do that! Please!"

"Shhhh!" echoed through the room, and Dec and I looked down in amazement at the black-faced squirrel monkey. The little guy held one finger to his puckered lips, making the universal sign for silence. "Shhh!" came from between his tiny lips once more.

"No," Dec muttered, staring down at the masked monkey in disbelief. "No way in hell is he trying to tell us to shut up!"

The black-masked squirrel monkey peered up at us, then nodded his head. He lifted one little paw and pointed across the room at the other two primates. Oscar suddenly slumped to the floor as a radiant glow of blue light erupted from the outstretched fingertips of the little, white-faced squirrel monkey. The nimbus of shimmering blue light flowed from the tiny hands of the female monkey and actually soaked into the jagged, bloody wounds of the chimp. Brief seconds later, the radiance slowly vanished, leaving behind a faint white glow on the completely healed lacerations on Oscar's chest.

"Sweet Jesus!" cried Dec. Nodding silently, I continued to stare at the four slight marks that remained on Oscar's chest; the only evidence that he had indeed taken four serious wounds from Mock. I whispered in sudden awe, "This is like way too cool, Dec!"

The white-faced monkey scampered over and held her little black paws up toward Dec. He peered down at her and said, "Holy Jesus! She's got powers! Strange powers, like an angel or super hero!"

The tiny monkey lifted her white face, her shiny, black eyes fixed earnestly on both us. She chittered excitedly and held up her hands as if she wanted us to reach out and touch her, as if she were preparing to give us a high five. Dec carefully placed his right forefinger in the center of her upraised left forepaw. She grinned, showing her white teeth. She hopped forward, placing herself directly in front of me. "Touch her," Dec said. "Just reach down, Hawk. She's not going to bite you."

"I'm not afraid of her," I said, placing the entire palm of my right hand flat against both of her upraised paws. "I just wish you could talk so you could explain how and what you did. No offense, little girl, but this blue light thing is sorta creeping me out!"

She chittered once more, then held up her arms like a child who wished to be picked up. "This is just weird," I whispered, but I gently used both hands to scoop her up and hold her in my arms. The squirrel monkey showed no fear or panic, and soon she curled up against my chest, placed her face against my interlocking arms and closed her eyes. "I'll be go to hell! She has to be someone's pet, Dec. Someone's treated her really kind to remove her fear like this. Hell, even my own cat won't let me hold her like that!"

The black-masked male monkey hopped over in front of us, pawing at Dec's pant leg. "Are you feeling left out, little guy?" Dec asked.

Surprisingly, the masked fellow shook his head from side to side and pointed at the walkie-talkie attached to Dec's belt. "Kat?" I said. "Is that right, little guy?"

The monkey nodded.

Dec flicked on the walkie-talkie and summoned Kat.

You made it to the tower?" Kat asked, sounding relieved. "Yes," Dec replied. "We had trouble from Mock, but unexpected help from Oscar and two squirrel monkeys."

"Oscar?" Kat said. "He's really a decent fellow. This research center used to be his home before he came to live in Beatrice."

"Well," Dec said, "Oscar and Mock sure weren't on friendly terms. Mock tore him up pretty bad, but there's something you should know."

He clicked off, waiting for her to respond.

"Yes?" she said, her voice fading with an abrupt click!

I said, "Don't say anything about the monkey-power thing. It might freak her out. We need her to tell us how to get out of this mess. Not think we're two nut-jobs!"

"You still there?" Kat asked. "What did you want to tell me?"

Dec said, "Is Ty still trapped? And Richard and Chris? I mean, how soon before you can send a rescue party out to get us out here? Call in to town so Gracie could alert my dad we're in trouble."

"Winter winds," Kat said, "took out the telephone lines. Getting you safely to the command center where I am, is not going to be a walk in the park. There is no cavalry. Officer Brady was the only security staff on duty tonight. If Mock killed Brady, then that only leaves Ty."

I said, "You'll freak her out if you tell her about the monkey mojo."

Dec depressed the button on the walkie-talkie and said, "Kat? These two squirrel monkeys. You got names for them?"

"Bandit," Kat said, "is the male, because of the markings on his face. The female is Miracle, because she's able to do some extraordinary things. Are Oscar, Bandit, and Miracle inside the tower with you?"

"Yes," Dec said. "Is there another way in here? Can Mock sneak up on us? Because I think we have Officer Brady's pistol. The pistol is fully loaded, but we used up the tazer."

"There is a tunnel," Kat said, "beneath the tower. But so far, its entrance remains sealed. I see nothing on my monitor indicating that its locked entryway has been breached. The stairs in front of you, lead up to the tower's outside observation deck. An alarm would sound if Mock tried breaking through that door."

Kat fell silent for long moments before saying, "If you have another encounter with Mock, don't shoot him unless you have a clear head shot. Any wounds to his body, will just send him into a frenzy."

Dec muttered, "A clear head-shot? Good God, we're just kids, not some expert marksmen from a SWAT team! This is a nine millimeter. Not as powerful as a .357, but still it's one powerful gun."

Staring down at the pistol in his hand, he raised the walkie-talkie and said, "Are you saying that this Mock can't be stopped by slugs from this gun unless we put them straight into his head?"

Kat said, "Yes. And there's one more thing . . . Mock is not the worst thing loose out here. His name is Wraith, and he leads a pack of baboons. Thanks to some wacko scientist he infected the troop of baboons with a virus that makes them go crazy. If Mock sets them on you, you will not survive an attack by Wraith and his mad mob."

Before we could respond to Kat's new information, a rumbling noise came from somewhere outside the lighthouse tower. Kat said, "There's a boat heading toward the island! I can see it on my monitor! It's going to dock to the north of the tower you're in!"

Chapter Twenty-Five

I followed behind Dec, aware that all three monkeys were curiously watching us climb the spiral stairway. We were halfway up the stairs when Miracle leaped up, waving her tiny hands, gesturing for us to come back down. "It's okay," I told her. "Help has arrived."

She became even more agitated, springing up the four steps and clawing desperately at my pant leg. "Shh!" I urged her as I bent down and scooped her up. I proceeded up the remaining steps, Miracle cradled in my arms. "Dec?" I said. "Once you unlock that door, open it slowly."

Grunting with the effort to unlatch the metal bar keeping the door secured, Dec said, "Before I open this, I'm cocking this pistol. If Mock tries to ambush me, I'll put a lead slug into his ugly face!"

Pulling back the hammer, Dec reached for the handle of the metal door with his free hand. The rusty metal screeched horribly as the door swung outward. He stepped back, giving himself room to fire if he needed to. But the only thing that came through the open door was the rumble of the boat as it pulled up to the dock to the north of the tower. We stepped out onto the platform just beyond the open door. Miracle squirmed in my grasp, for her vision was much better than ours. We then saw gray shapes drifting through the falling snow near the docks.

"Baboons!" Dec said, staring at the bulky forms of the thick-limbed monkeys. I, too, peered hard at the cantering troop of baboons sneaking up to the hedges lining the far end of the dock. There the shaggy-maned beasts stopped, silently looking on as the boat glided in to the docking bay. Mock appeared in the sky above the troop of baboons, hovering there in the air, glaring down at the intruder docking his boat.

"They mean to ambush him," I told Dec.

"Yeah," Dec whispered. "We've got to warn him."

Dec waited impatiently as the driver of the boat finally killed the engine. He then raised the pistol in the air and fired off one round. The loud ***Bang!*** caused the man now standing on the dock to peer up at the tower thirty yards away.

Dec shouted, "Get back in your boat! Get off the island! There's a whole mob of baboons waiting to attack you just beyond the dock!"

Rock, the thug from New Orleans, moved awkwardly as he slid across the slippery dock. "What are you boys doing out here?" he shouted.

He pushed his way though the bushes, unaware of how close he was to brushing up against the gray bulky shapes hidden there amidst the shrubbery. Dec yelled back, "Move back to the boat! Now!"

Miracle let out a high-pitched screech as she saw Mock swoop down and lash out Rock's head. He ducked, then stumbled and drew his pistol as Mock made another aerial assault. The pistol boomed and bucked in his fist, and in the brilliant flash of the muzzle, dozens of glowing yellow eyes appeared in the bushes beside him. Rock was halfway to the boat, when baboons emerged from the bushes behind him. He glanced back once. Twice. And on his third terrified glance behind him, he ran directly into Mock coming down in front of him. Mock broke into a frenzied fury of striking, tearing, and gouging. Rock toppled over, throwing his hands up, trying to ward off the attacks.

Once he was down, the entire troop of baboons were savage in their attack, using their razor-sharp canines to rip flesh and tear runnels in the big thug. He rose up once in a last desperate effort to reach the boat, but he was engulfed in a mad swarm of crazed baboons who mobbed him under and continued to bite and claw at him until he quit moving.

At the top of the tower, Miracle let out a whisper of sound that caused us to look down at her. She peered up at us, a sad look in her little dark eyes. She shook her head from side to side, then fiercely jabbed her fingers toward the dock. We gazed past the dock, peering hard at the river beyond. There was another boat pulling up alongside the island. It was a rather large, sleek craft, complete with a nylon-covered cabin. Bright lights were shining from several locations, aft, stern, and in the middle of the boat's deck. One of these lights became a steady beam of frosty yellow light that zeroed in on the dock and Rock's boat parked there. The big boat steadily moved in beside the empty boat at the wooden dock. At once, Mock dropped down into the fog and joined the troop of baboons mingling there along the borders of the hedges lining the dock. Another ambush was being planned. Before we could shout out a warning to whoever was attempting to come ashore in the big boat, I saw the huge, bulky form of a white-furred baboon stepping from the fog beside the dock. As he bounded forward, the other baboons scattered out of his way, terrified of this larger beast. The thick, muscular creature showed his four-inch long canines, looking very much like a vampire.

"Wraith," Dec said, "that Kat warned us about."

And that's when I saw Ghost Running Thunder making his way across the dock. He fired off two rounds, and the front-line formation parted before him. Ghost hurtled forward and ran from the dock, breaking through the hedges. He came fleeing across the wide open field directly toward the tower.

Dec raised the pistol in a two-handed grip. Took careful aim. And fired. The hot lead slug sank directly into the center of Wraith's forehead. The sudden impact threw the baboon backward and sent him sprawling on his back there on the dock.

Miracle chittered anxiously, and we watched in stunned amazement as there on the dock, Wraith slowly sat up. He shook his long white mane from side to side, gave an explosive grunt, then angrily spat the lead slug out into the palm of his upraised right paw. He glared up at Dec, his soft snarl turning into a steady growl.

Dec raised the pistol, yet before he could squeeze off a shot, he froze, his eyes glazing over. The strange creature on the dock had some powerful form of mind control. I had read about it in Science Digest, a mind control program, *Project Monarch*, started at Offut Air force base in Omaha, though it was originally created by the Third Reich in Germany during Hitler's reign. It had to do with sending thoughts into a person's brain and forcing them to bend to someone's will.

I lifted Miracle to my left shoulder, and as she perched there, I reached over and snatched the pistol out of Dec's grasp. I had just raised it when Wraith blasted me with a barrage of hurtful accusations: **Say, Little Indian Boy, so afraid that you have a Bad Seed in your family, that* *you would do anything to outshine that outlaw brothers of yours! The youngest son of the clan, and you've taken a long, serious look at the misdeeds of your brother, and you are forever fearful that now, you, too, are locked on a course of self-destruction, doomed to be a failure! You can't understand why your brother wants to be like John Dillinger! And yet, are you any different from the likes of him? Aren't you infected? Burning with a virus? Plagued by a Bad Seed. you filthy little slug!*

I stood there, tears filling my eyes as the truth of Wraith's words hit me with all the force of an oncoming freight train. I could deny that I'd often had such thoughts about Richard, that I struggled trying to deny who I really was; ashamed of who I was, and trying to change and never go down the roads he had so wrongly traveled. But I couldn't. Wraith was right, I, too, had a Bad Seed in me. *Might as well kill yourself now,* Wraith sent through his mind-link. *Put that gun to your head and blow your twisted brain matter into the night wind!*

I thumbed back the hammer on the gun. I raised it and placed the muzzle against my right temple. I started to squeeze the trigger.

Miracle clambered around from my left shoulder and bounced over to my right, using her tiny hands to push the gun away. **Blam!** the shot blazed bright red out of the muzzle, and the lead slug passed harmlessly into the night sky. Blinking rapidly, I stammered, "God accepts me for who I am. He designed me before I was even born . . ."

Wraith laughed loudly. His thoughts came at me like fiery spears: *El Shadi? Pathetic title for a God who created this universe! Man gave God so many lame names. Allah to the Muslims. Krishna to Eastern Indians. Wakan Tanka to the Lakota. Yahweh to the Hebrews. King of Kings to Catholics and Christians. Yeshua? Prince of Peace? Lion of Judah? What about Odin, God of Thunder and Fire? What about Baal and Moloch, deities who asked a godly price for obedience? Child sacrifices were the ultimate gift a man could offer up to gods! Silly Indian Boy, you still think God wants to save you?*

I glanced over at Dec. But he was still out of it. He had not heard any of the wicked things Wraith had spouted. Did not as yet know that

I was such a bad person. Before I could respond to this, a sudden noise from below the tower caused me to look in that direction. There, thirty feet below the lighthouse platform, Ghost was heading toward the door. He kept glancing back over his shoulder to check on the baboons milling about the dock. He had his pistol in one hand. Shaking my head to clear it of Wraith's thoughts, I guided Dec back through the door, closing it behind us. Miracle sprang from my shoulder and landed on Dec's left shoulder two steps below me. Dec gave a startled yelp, and as Miracle gently stroked his left cheek, the mind control used by Wraith suddenly vanished. Dec asked, "What happened out there? My mind went blank and all I heard was hissing that came from a thousand cobras!"

The sudden pounding below us gave Dec a start. "Who is that?"

"Ghost," I said. "We'd better hurry and let him in."

Oscar had already opened the door by the time we reached the bottom of the tower. He actually reached out and hugged Ghost as he stumbled in through the door. Having just seen the brutal and vicious attacks out there on the dock, Ghost froze in Oscar's embrace. Dec hastily pulled the door closed and slipped the locking latch into place. Miracle scrambled down off his shoulder and she joined Bandit, curiously watching Oscar doling out affection to the big Lakota. "What in hell is going on out here?" Ghost asked, slipping the gun into his shoulder holster.

I said, "What are you doing here, Ghost? You after that gold?"

Ghost sights fixed on me. "I came here, only because your grandmother tracked me down and told me you two badly needed my help. She told me Sheriff Mac is in Pawnee City on a cat hunt, and that Tyler had actually kidnaped the two girls in order to get Henry out here to find that cache of gold. Gran B firmly believes Rivermoon is cursed because of that gold hidden here by White Soldiers. She asked me to help you rescue the girls and return you safely home."

Chapter Twenty-Six

Boom! Boom! came from beyond the metal door of the tower. Dec and I flinched at the sudden sound. Ghost placed his hand on the butt of his holstered pistol. Oscar, Bandit, and Miracle all three hissed in alarm and fear at what stood beyond that door.

Open this door, Wraith sent through a mind link. *Oscar? Oscar?*

The big chimp rose up from his place on the floor, dropping the ring of keys beside him. Miracle and Bandit scampered in front of him, trying to prevent him from moving forward. But the chimp brushed them aside and reached up to the door handle. "No, Oscar!" Dec said, causing the chimp to glance back at him, curiously. "Oscar?" I said. "Don't open the door. Don't let that creature in. We're your friends. Not him."

But it did little good. Wraith had triggered off the response he wanted in the chimp, and just as Oscar unlatched the door, he hooted excitedly as a strange, violet light began to glow from the pocket inside my coat. The leather pouch Gran B had given me gave off an eery purple light that bathed the room in its brilliant glow. I reached down inside my coat, clasping the pouch that held the arrowheads. I drew it out as the door swung open and Wraith stepped up to the opening. Suddenly, the pouch was shredded by a burst of light and the arrowheads in my hand crackled with some unseen power and purple beams shot upward, directly into the pale face of Wraith. "Arrrr!" he screamed in agony, his face smoldering. The baboon stumbled back and staggered away from the tower, his hands shooting to his face as smoke began to roil from his cheeks. He howled, then vanished into the mist beyond the tower.

I lowered the arrowheads, and Dec peered down at the faintly glowing medallions. "They are like some kind of holy symbol. Like a silver cross to ward off vampires. But how in hell did you activate them?"

I whispered in awe, "I think they reacted to Wraith."

"Cool," Dec said, closing and locking the door.

Ghost didn't appear to be too surprised by the mysterious arrowheads. He said, "Holy Symbols. You boys have probably heard of them in those spooky *Dracula* stories. But I've always been curious if it is the silver they are made of, or because they've been blessed by some holy man that results in repulsing vampires. Keep them close, Hawk. The All Father has just gifted you with a potent weapon to vanquish evil."

I shook my head, then blew a breath upward to part my bangs and keep them from falling down into my eyes. I slid the arrowheads into my pocket. Ghost gave me a thoughtful look. "I've dabbled in workings of the Otherworld. I have a connection with the Unseen realm, and I believe you are destined to become a Thunder Dreamer, Hawk."

Ghost looked down at Bandit and Miracle who had sidled up to his legs and proceeded to climb up his tall, lean frame to plant themselves directly on his shoulders. "Friendly little things," he said as Bandit and Miracle patted his cheeks, then settled down to perch on his broad shoulders. *Trust him,* Miracle sent her thoughts my way. *He speaks truth. He means the best for you, for he is a Red Road Warrior.*

I blinked twice in sudden surprise. "Did you hear that, Ghost?"

He gave me a confused look. "Never mind," I said, peering in disbelief at the white-faced squirrel monkey.

Ghost said, "I came to small town Beatrice as a bounty hunter, sent here by the private investigator I work for, but I am also a Ghost Hunter, determined to find and challenge ghosts and demons who have strayed in here from the Otherworld. And that Wraith character has himself a demon hitching a ride with him. One that badly needs to be dispelled. Have you ever watched *Dark Shadows*? The TV series features ghosts, werewolves, zombies, monsters, witches, warlocks, time travel, and a parallel universe. Barnabas Collins? Quentin Collins? It's like *Creature Feature* in the middle of the day. In the book, *Fairies, Fate, and Fantasy* tales come to life. Myths. Legends. Greek Gods. Irish Champions. Viking Sagas. Dragon Hoards. Pirate Maps. Giants. Leprechauns. Banshees. Arthur. His Knights. The Round Table. Magic Rings. All real, not just words in a book. For the quest ahead of you two, the movie and the book are right up your alley. If we get out of this, perhaps you should give them a spin."

While Oscar walked up to me, taking my hand and seating himself beside me, Dec called Kat on the walkie talkie. He excitedly told her all that had taken place, including the arrival of Ghost and my use of the holy symbol on Wraith.

Kat said, "Climb down to the tunnel below you. Follow the four blocks of corridor that lead here to the control center. You should be safe. Now, get yourself here, and we'll see what we can do about rescuing Chris and Richard. I'd like us all to get off of Rivermoon before Ty and Sal come out of the bunker they are hiding in."

Dec clicked off the walkie and clipped it back on his belt. With Ghost leading the way, we descended the spiral stairway down to the entrance to the tunnels below. We moved forward into the tunnel, and found the 6 by 4-foot corridor dry and warm, despite the fact that it was carved out of river rock beneath the surface of the island. We moved at a rather fast clip, the dim lights in the ceiling above us giving off enough of a glow to illuminate the passage. As we walked, Oscar continued to hold my hand. Bandit and Miracle hunkered down on Ghost's shoulders, and Dec brought up the rear, checking behind us to make sure we weren't being followed by whatever else was down there in those dark depths.

When we reached the end of that first section, we came to a four-way intersection. The tunnel continued straight ahead, but on either side of us, twin corridors stretched away into total blackness. Cold air came from the left side, leading off in the direction of the river. Warm, musty air flowed out of the right hand corridor. And then something large and dark moved ten feet down the shadowy corridor. I yelped when I saw the massive, hairy creature shamble forward out of the darkness.

Dec raised the pistol and froze. "Big Foot?"

"Mountain Gorilla," Ghost said, drawing his own gun.

Oscar let out an angry hiss and furiously pounded his chest. The gorilla glanced down at the agitated chimp and bared his fangs. Oscar literally went ape there in the center of the corridor. He hurtled forward, springing up on the creature. His charge was delivered with such force, that he sent the large gorilla staggering into the wall behind him.

"Move!" Ghost said. "Give Oscar room to retreat if he has to!"

Taking one last look at Oscar pitting himself against the larger gorilla, we ran to a second section of tunnel branching off to our right. Running in the lead, I reached another door and wheeled around to focus on the corridor behind us. I sighed in relief when the big chimp rounded the corner thirty feet back, the gorilla in hot pursuit. "Come on!" yelled Dec, sticking the gun in the waist band of his jeans. "There's a door up ahead!"

I propelled myself forward and ran past him, directly up to the closed metal door. Reaching down to the handle, I opened it, revealing another corridor. Dim lights above illuminated the passage. Ghost slipped through the doorway past me, but Dec turned and took his place beside me. "Come on, Oscar!" he hollered.

Oscar put on a renewed burst of speed, gaining enough ground to pass us and dart down the continuing corridor. **Wham!** echoed through the tunnel as both Dec and I slammed the metal door closed. And **Bam!** came a moment later as the ape struck the door. "There!" Dec said as he slid a locking bar into place, barring and securing the door. "That should keep him out!"

But the moment he said this, there came a furious pounding on the door, and we watched as dents and creases appeared in the center of the metal door.

Chapter Twenty-Seven

We could see a metal door standing before us down at the end of a long corridor. We had about sixty feet to go before we reached it and the safety of the other side. I said, "If any place on this island is safe, it has to be the command center where Kat has been speaking to us from. It sounds as if she and Mary Kay are locked securely behind this door ahead of us."

Oscar ran a little ways ahead of us. Bandit and Miracle scampered ahead of us and ran to catch up to the big chimp. They were almost to the door when the large gorilla emerged from a side passage, stepping directly into Oscar's path. The chimp didn't hesitate. He simply lowered his head and charged. The collision of the two primate bodies could be heard all the way down the corridor. Oscar and the gorilla went down in a tangle of arms and legs. When they came back up, they were locked in fierce combat, clawing at each other's throats. Ghost moved up behind us. He gently pressed us back against the wall behind us as Mary Kay Long Soldier stepped out of a recessed alcove, a tazer in hand. She stepped out around us and bravely approached the two struggling creatures fighting in the middle of the corridor. "Samson!" she cried. "Allow me to sort this out, Big Brother!"

Surprisingly, the gorilla broke off his attack. Mary Kay thrust her crackling tazer out before her. *Zazapp!* echoed down the corridor as she lashed out at Oscar with the crackling tazer. Oscar looked at the green-glowing tazer with slight alarm. "No, Oscar!" she said, firmly.

There was a slight muffled crackle, and Mary Kay flipped the switch on her tazer and the luminous green light went out with an airy *poof!* Oscar showed Samson his teeth one last time, then settled down on the floor beside Mary Kay, a subdued look in his eyes.

"Ah," she said, "good boy, Samson. Nice Big Brother."

Samson held out his left forearm to reveal the nasty gash Oscar had left. Mary Kay gestured down at Miracle, softly saying, "Here, Little Lady, could you do something about Samson's arm?"

Miracle scampered over to Mary Kay. The monkey clambered up her leg and perched on her shoulder. Mary Kay then addressed Samson, "Come here, let Miracle make your arm all better, Big Brother."

As a brilliant blue glow emanated from Miracle's outstretched fingers, Samson's deep gash was completely healed, leaving only a trace of a scar on his forearm. Mary Kay patted him on one cheek, then instructed Samson and Oscar to follow her the rest of the way down the corridor and into the command center. Samson and Oscar entered the large room, where they seated themselves in deep cushioned chairs situated before a row of monitors, their fight evidently forgotten.

After making sure all members of our little party had exited the tunnel, Kat closed and locked the thick metal door giving us some sense of security now that we had reached our goal. Dec and I stared at her, curious that she seemed to be in charge there on Rivermoon. She brushed back the long locks of her black hair with a flick of one wrist. "Just whose insane idea was it to venture out here to rescue us? With Wraith prowling the island, we now have a real problem of getting out of here."

Kat gestured at the six large monitors on the wall above rows of buttons, dials, and switches. Dec, Ghost, and I looked over Kat's shoulders to peer up at the active screens. On one, the white-furred Wraith and the winged form of Mock stood peering over the heads of the pack of baboons as they gathered before a large brick building.

"Inside of that warehouse," Kat said, "are Chris, Richard, and King Henry. Ty confronted them when they got here to take us home. Mock attacked all of them. Ty and Sal got cut off from the rest of them, taking shelter in a barracks building to hide from the wild mob of monkeys."

Ghost tapped one of the monitors with his fingers. "What are those monkeys doing?"

We all looked to the monitors and could see Mock leading one troop of baboons off to the north toward a large bunker in the distance. Wraith and his own troop were searching the brick building before them, looking for a way to get inside. "If that is where your brother and King Henry are holed up at," Ghost said, "do these tunnels lead out there?"

Kat gestured to the door across from us. "The corridor beyond that door will lead there. But if Mock or Wraith get into the tunnels . . ."

"Yes," Ghost said, "But maybe instead of hiding in here from them, perhaps we need to attack them. If we do nothing, then sooner or later, they are going to get past the doors out there where your brother is."

Kat studied him for long moments. She then looked at the gun holstered beneath Ghost's arm. "We don't have a weapon," she said, "that will work against them."

"I think," Ghost said, "you're underestimating the weapons we do have. I'm thinking Samson and Oscar sure put up one hell of a catfight!"

Leaving the girls in the command center, Dec, Ghost, and I entered the corridor that would lead to Chris and my brother. We closed the door behind us and proceeded down the shadowy tunnel, dim red lights in the ceiling illuminated the corridor. Dec had slipped the pistol into his jeans, while I had settled the arrowheads into the inner pocket of my parka. For the moment, it didn't look like we would need weapons to defend ourselves. We followed Ghost for another hundred feet, when we heard a loud commotion up ahead of us. The sound of shouting was coming through another metal door at the end of the corridor we were in. It sounded like King Henry, but I could hear my brother's voice mixed in with Chris's. Richard and Chris were shouting in some sort of distress, while King Henry was cackling with glee.

Ghost opened the door and we were all bathed in a bright yellow light coming from the chamber beyond. It was more well-lit than the tunnel we were in, having several light bulbs hanging down from the ceiling at the center of what looked like a sandstone cave rather than the cement walls that were man-made. This chamber appeared to be a natural cave connected to a series of underground passageways, for we could see three cavern-like openings leading out of the chamber.

King Henry stood before one of these passages, his laughter echoing down the dark tunnel ahead of him. We heard Richard cry out, "Snakes!"

Henry sounded like a mad witch, cackling and carrying on, seemingly amused by their plight. "Told you silly fools not to venture down there, didn't I? Told you my job as a Sentinel didn't allow access into that part of the caves! You reap what you sow, boyos! Reap what you sow!"

Walking up behind Henry, Ghost said, "Quiet down there, fellow."

Henry wheeled around, surprised to find the three of us standing behind him. King Henry's brow wrinkled as he said, "Big Ty had those two hooligans escort me out here. Once they did, they all four wanted to use my map to find that treasure. Then, the monkeys attacked us, and we all got separated. The boys and I got locked in down here. Don't know what happened to Ty. But the boys demanded that I lead them to the cache of gold that belongs to the ghosts of the Knights—"

"Help!" Richard shouted, his voice sounding as if it came from down the tunnel. "We're in a chamber full of snakes! We climbed on a ledge, but we can't get past this many snakes without getting bit!"

Ghost started forward, cautiously approaching a bend in the corridor. Dec and I followed him, leaving King Henry standing there. Ghost slapped his palms against our chests, stopping us from falling forward into the large chamber before us. We looked on in horror as the entire expanse of the cave floor shifted as hundreds of snakes writhed about on the floor. The chamber was dimly lit by a series of overhead light bulbs dangling from cords from the ceiling. From the opening where we stood, we could see across the chamber where Chris and Richard were perched on a rock ledge six feet from the snake-covered floor.

Ghost said, "Looks like someone set an elaborate trap for would-be treasure hunters. This speaks of human intervention." He glanced back at King Henry twenty feet behind us.

Henry said, "I'm in charge of the snake room out here on Rivermoon. Dead-end lies beyond this chamber. The decoy lies down this right hand tunnel behind us. A small pile of gold bars. Twelve in all. But nothing compared to the mother lode! It is sealed in a separate chamber that needs keys to open it. Ty would have stumbled upon this first pile and mistakenly believed they'd located the original gold hidden out here.

I created this decoy as a precaution. It was a slight of hand gesture that would keep the gold diggers away from the real treasure."

Richard cried , "When I get out of here, Henry, I'm gonna rip your head off!" Chris reached out, trying to stop Richard, but my brother had already stepped down into the chamber. He froze, however, when several of the snakes began rattling. "Get back up here!" Chris cried.

Several of the snakes struck out at him, and Richard wheeled back around and climbed back up onto the ledge like a scalded monkey. "What the hell you expect us to do? Stay up here forever?"

"No," Ghost said. "Just stay put. I've got an idea."

Chapter Twenty-Eight

Ten minutes later, Dec and I joined Ghost as he led us out of the tunnels. He'd outlined his plan with Mary Kay, risking a trip outside to gather what he called his "secret weapon." We followed him. I kept my hand closed around the arrowheads in the pocket of my parka, prepared to activate the holy symbols. Dec grasped the butt of the pistol in a two-fisted grip. Lumbering ahead of us, Samson and Oscar served as our forward guards. Mary Kay softly talked to them as they led the way through the blustery snowfall. "Big Brother," she whispered, "going to protect us if we run into Wraith or Mock, right?"

Trudging through the snow in front of me, Ghost glanced back to see how the ape and the chimp reacted to her words. I didn't know if Ghost expected the two of them to take on the entire mob of baboons, but I did know the gorilla and chimp made me feel a little safer as we left the tunnels.

Searching through the torrents of snow, Ghost found what he'd been looking for within five minutes of us stepping out onto the island. He produced a large Bowie knife from somewhere beneath his jacket, and bending down before a row of bushes, he quickly hacked them off near their roots. Within minutes, he had a stack of the bushes piled up at our feet. Dec whispered, "What kind of bushes are these?"

Slipping his knife back into its sheath beneath his jacket, Ghost said, "Marijuana. People smoke it to get high."

Static from the walkie-talkie in Mary Kay's hand startled all of us. It was Kat from her place before the monitors in the control room. She'd been keeping an eye on the entire island in case she needed to warn us of approaching danger. "Did you guys see that?" she asked. "Mock just flew over your heads! He knows you are out there! Get back inside!"

The torrents of fiercely falling snow made it hard to see anything beyond ten feet. It was as if white blankets had been thrown in front of us. Behind us. Above us. And in any direction we tried to see. Ghost tucked the bushes beneath his one arm and made his way to the doorway leading back into the tunnels. Dec and I fell in behind him, craning our necks to detect movement out there in snowfall. Mary Kay stayed on our heels, flanked by Samson and Oscar trampling through the snow behind her. Ghost suddenly stopped ahead of us. "Wraith!" Mary Kay harshly whispered as she huddled between the gorilla and the chimp. "He's between us and the door!"

And there, forming a crescent before us, were an entire troop of baboons. Wraith stood at their center, opening wide his jaws, revealing four-inch fangs. Samson bolted and ran directly at the baboon troop. Oscar stayed right behind him, hooting up a storm. A second later, they all collided and a sudden *thwacking* sound erupted into the air as gorilla and chimp ran smack dab into the bulky bodies of the startled baboons.

Wraith lurched forward, his sharp fangs grazing Samson's chest. But the gorilla was in full-blown attack mode and there was little Wraith could do to stop his momentum. Samson swung him around, spinning on his heels and lifting the enraged baboon off the ground. At the end of his sudden whirl, Samson released Wraith and sent him flying through the falling snow and sailing out into the black waters surrounding the island. Wraith plunged down into the icy cold water, and the baboons scatted. Oscar lit into them, erupting into a whirlwind of fangs and claws. Ghost's strategy to combine the fighting skills of the gorilla and chimp had worked. The two plowed their way through the stragglers and forced an opening for us. Dec opened the door and Ghost carried the bundle of marijuana bushes inside the tunnel beyond. Mary Kay followed next. Samson and Oscar lurched forward and into the tunnel. Dec turned to me. "Come on, Hawk!" he cried.

I peered through the falling snow to see Wraith paddling back to the shoreline, a strange glow coming from his red eyes. I could feel prickles inside my head as he sent out waves of furious hatred my way. *Stop!* he sent into my head. *Stop and don't go in there, Child!*

I stood frozen.

Fortunately, Dec caught onto what was happening. He darted away from the open door, reaching my side even as Wraith scrambled up and out of the water and sprang back onto the island. The enraged baboon came on then, moving with all speed to reach us. While I stood there still as a statue, Dec reached into my inside pocket of my parka and withdrew the arrowheads I had stashed in there. A loud buzz exploded from the medallions and a surge of purple lightning streaked from the metal symbols, striking Wraith in the middle of his chest. The white-furred baboon suddenly jerked upward as tentacles of violet lines of crackling power spread across his upper body. The moment the lightning streaked from the holy symbols, I was freed from Wraith's mind lock.

Dec stood before me, thrusting the arrowheads into my outstretched hands. I slipped the arrowheads back inside the inner pocket of my parka, amazed to see a strange glow illuminating the entire front of my coat.

I thought, *How did I summon power? I once read Bram Stoker's Dracula. Vampires scared off by crosses. Silver bullets defeating werewolves. All just make-believe. But suddenly, I have reason to believe that make-believe might very well be based on facts!*

As I stood there in the middle of a Nebraska snow storm, I was baffled, and yet knowing I was on the edge of learning something that I thought impossible, was in fact, real. Wraith let out an angry growl from out in the snow flurries. As in answer to his growl, there came the flapping of Mock's wings.

"Come on, Hawk!" Dec whispered. "Let's get back inside the tunnel!"

I was quick to follow him.

And he closed the door behind us with a loud *Clang!*

As Dec and I stood at the entrance to the cavern filled with snakes, we set our sights on Ghost ahead of us. The big Lakota was using a lighter to set on fire the last of his stack of marijuana plants. He had already tossed a good portion of them into the chamber. There, the bushy plants burned and smoldered, sending clouds of smoke drifting out into the chamber. "Try not to breathe too deeply," Ghost called to Richard and Chris seated thirty yards away on the ledge. "Cover your faces!"

The shifting clouds of smoke stayed low to the floor, leaving only slight tendrils to curl up and reach them as they sat there on the ledge, their arms thrown across their faces as Ghost suggested they do. "My God!" Richard said. "You're trying to get those snakes stoned!"

In response, Ghost chuckled. "I figured if I could, they might turn lethargic enough for you boys to get yourselves past them."

Dec and I had never tried smoking marijuana. We'd heard about it in DARE class at school, but we really didn't know what Ghost was trying to accomplish. However, it seemed to amuse Richard and after nearly ten minutes of cloud cover there in the chamber, he peered down at the comatose snakes and laughed, "Should have said No, you slimy fools! Now look at you! Stoned out of your little gourds!"

Ghost's plan worked. Those snakes didn't move as Richard and Chris slowly tip-toed their way across that chamber. Once, Chris had to stop and inch his way past the head of a snake facing him, and Richard used the edge of his boot to nudge a lethargic snake out of his path. But within minutes, both of them made it safely through the chamber and reached the tunnel where we stood waiting. Chris collapsed on the floor of the tunnel. Richard charged down the tunnel to deal out his wrath on Henry.

"Hold on!" Ghost said, hooking one arm across Richard's chest. "Save your anger! You're gonna need it to get off of this island!"

Richard struggled to break free, but Ghost was far stronger than him. He said, "How could you let us walk into a trap of snakes, Henry?"

Henry sniggered, "I am the Sentinel of Rivermoon! Guardian of the Gold! Champion and Knight Protector of the Golden Circle Gold! Would you all like to see where it's been hidden all of these years?"

We followed King Henry down a winding tunnel of sandstone. It was definitely not man-made, for it had no cinder blocks forming its walls. It was part of a cave system that had more than likely been there long before Fort Blue River had been built above it. It was old and snaked its way past two intersections before ending in a twenty-by-twenty foot room. There in the center of the chamber was a stack of gold bars. Twelve of them, all a foot-long and three inches wide and two inches thick.

Henry tried to keep Richard and Chris from picking any of them up, but they weren't having it. Swatting Henry's hands aside, both of them snatched up a bar apiece and stood there hefting the heavy suckers above their heads. "How much is this worth, King Henry?" Richard asked.

Henry said, "This gold minted in the early 1800's is valued at five-hundred thousand. It was first brought to Fort Blue River by my ancestor, Henry the First, who rode here, pursued by the law when he broke off from Bloody Bill after robbing a train carrying this gold. Henry ran into a war party of Sioux here in Nebraska. He took refuge here at the fort, and other Knights Gallant brought more and more gold to be stored here. These twelve bars are only the decoys. The real treasure is sealed behind that wall in front of us. It needs keys to make it open, on account of some Yankee engineers who hid a treasure in there before abandoning the fort. I've been Sentinel all these years to twelve bars, serving as decoys, but I've never seen what lies behind this door. Knights held council on it. Some wanted to blow the wall off of this chamber. Others wanted to dig another tunnel into it. Either way, the river would seep into this chamber. Whoever designed it was a tricky sum bitch."

Richard said, "How long has that treasure been sealed in there?"

"Since 1876," Henry said. "Engineers serving the Confederates, determined it can only be safely opened using three specific keys. Once these keys are inserted in the locking mechanism, it will magically open."

Richard stared at him in disgust. "You're telling us the Knights have known this great amount of treasure has been hidden away down here for over one hundred years and no one has tried to claim it?"

Henry shrugged. "Many have tried to replicate the three keys, but once they've been inserted into the lock, a pin inside the mechanism shatters the metal replicas all to pieces. Before Custer was killed at the Little Big Horn, he had them created by a talented jeweler, another damned Yankee. They were bronze arrowheads shaped to fit snug in that lock, and soft enough that those striking pins would not shatter them, but more like hold them in place, so they could be slid deeper inside the device on the door in order to open it."

And then it dawned on Richard, just exactly what he'd seen back at Gran B's when Big Ty had sent him careening into me and caused me to drop those three arrowheads on Gran's floor. "Hawk?" he said.

He stepped forward and Dec stepped deliberately into his path. "Gran gave them to Hawk. She wanted Hawk to use them, not you, Richard."

Stirred to anger by Dec's boldness, Richard reached out to latch onto his shoulders, when Chris brushed Richard's hands aside. "If Gran gave them to Hawk, then that is the way she wanted it to be."

"Chris," Richard said through clenched teeth. "If you don't get out of my way, I'm gonna floor you!"

"No," Chris said. "You're not."

For some reason, Richard backed down. I was never sure who would win in a fight between the two, but at that moment, Richard turned back to the stack of gold bars. "Okay, Hawk, but if you tell us you left those arrowheads back at Gran's place, you're gonna spoil the moment!"

Chapter Twenty-Nine

Ghost studied the wall, finding the lock mechanism that Henry spoke of. Slipping his fingers into the three slots at the center of the device, he said, "So, by slipping the correct medallions into these slots the door will open?"

King Henry said, "In theory, that is how it is supposed to work."

I moved removed the three arrowheads from the pocket of my parka, closely studying the engravings of Custer, Wild Bill, and Buffalo Bill imprinted on them. Henry said, "It goes along with the story of the *River Kings* that I wrote. The story of how these three legends crossed paths, and how this gold got left here. Custer was a high level Mason, who knew about secret doorways. He had this lock mechanism designed, along with the medallions. Historically speaking, Wild Bill and Cody served as Custer's scouts. So, it is all quite possible."

I stepped up to the wall and slid each arrowhead into the slots designed to hold them. At once, a strange golden glow illuminated each medallion, sending a sparkling lemon haze up into my face. There was a loud *Click!* and a lime-green luminous light spread outward to create the seams of a door in the wall before us. Another loud *Click* filled the air and the door opened, revealing a dazzling silver light flooding the twenty-by-twenty foot chamber beyond. In one corner, in neat rows, gold bars were stacked. There were hundreds of them. Beside them were a dozen shelves lined with Mason jars filled with coins. Where I thought there would be excited gasps of surprise there was only stunned silence.

We spent the next ten examining the treasure find of the century. We all knew that this was a monumentally important discovery. King Henry finally said, "My estimate of the gold and coins is over twenty-million dollars. The gold was amassed through dozens of train and bank robberies, all conducted by Knights Gallant, who came here after heists to deposit in this particular cache."

I stopped beside one of the shelves as I saw a leather shirt adorned with Native beadwork and two war clubs. Henry said, "The Indian relics came from the Oglala Lakota medicine man, Black Elk. He came from a long line of medicine men. At age nine, he had a visit by the Thunder-Beings. He saw a great tree that symbolized the life of the earth. He saw that the sacred hoop of our people was one of many hoops that made one circle. At age 12, Black Elk was at the Little Bighorn. During his family's escape after the battle, his mother put a trio of puppies in the pony-trailer. As they fled, they kept falling out, and Black Elk kept stuffing them back into the pack to make sure the pups stayed safe. When he was older, he traveled to England with Buffalo Bill. When Bill set sail for the United States, Black Elk was left behind. When Bill came back to Paris, he gave Black Elk a ticket to return to Pine Ridge. In 1890, Black Elk fought at Wounded Knee, rescuing some of Spotted Elk's people. In 1903, he became a Catholic. In 1930, he spoke with John Niehardt, telling him of the sacred pipe handed down to the People of the Seven Council Fires by Buffalo Calf Woman. In recent days, the Catholic Diocese designated Black Elk as a Servant of God, because of his work to share the Gospel with Natives."

I asked, "Why did a holy man of the Lakota leave these relics here?"

Henry said, "According to Henry the First, Black Elk was taking them to the Red Cloud Agency. They were stolen by Henry at gun point, while Black Elk was sent on his way. Those two war clubs belonged to Crazy Horse and Chief Gall. During the battle at the Little Big Horn, Crazy Horse and Chief Gall resorted to their war clubs because they ran out of bullets. Shirt Wearers were special counselors of the Lakota, among them, Crazy Horse, American Horse, and Sword. Ghost Dance shirts are sacred to the Lakota, who believed the shirt would protect them from bullets of the white man. In 1891, one Ghost Shirt was sold to a museum by a member of Buffalo Bill's Show. A survivor of Wounded Knee asked that it be returned. In a gesture of good will, the Ghost Shirt was returned to Pine Ridge. This is a Ghost Shirt."

I asked, "Could Crazy Horse have killed Custer with this club?"

Shaking his head, Ghost said, "No, Crazy Horse did not kill Custer. Gall led a frontal assault, while Crazy Horse led a flanking attack. In the heat of the battle, it was Buffalo Calf Road Woman, a 15-year-old Cheyenne girl, who knocked Custer out of his saddle with her long bow. White Bull, nephew of Sitting Bull, shot him in the chest and Custer remounted and rode away to Last Stand Hill. There, he was found with a bullet hole in his chest and one bullet hole in his left temple, supporting rumors that he shot himself, rather than be tortured by his enemies."

Ghost removed a leather backpack from the shelf and stuffed the Ghost Shirt and the two war clubs into it, then settled the pack on my back. It felt good that he trusted me with the ancient relics, and it felt right that we were taking them out of the vault and off the island.

He closed the door to the treasure room and handed me back the three arrowheads. "Right now," Ghost said, "all the gold in the world is not going to save us from what is lurking out there on this island."

He leaned back against the door to the chamber, folding his arms across his broad chest. He was daring Richard and Chris to challenge him. When neither did, Ghost said, "Good choice. Now, let's head to my boat docked out there near that light house. It's far too dangerous to stay out here."

"What about the decoy cache?" Chris asked. "You've gotta admit, it is tempting, Ghost. Let us just take two bars of that gold. Then maybe see later, if these Knights might be generous enough to pay us a finder's fee since Hawk holds the only keys that open this door."

Ghost said, "Let's involve Sheriff Mac in this deal. A finder's fee is a long-shot, but for now, it all stays here. You can't be carting that gold to the boat. You might have to run for your lives. Leave it. It stays."

Back at the command center, it took us only ten minutes to plan our course back through the tunnel that led to the tower. From there, Ghost planned to lead the way to his boat at the dock and make good on our escape from Rivermoon.

Mary Kay demanded we take Oscar and Samson along with us. She said, "Wraith will want revenge. There are thirty baboons in Wraith's troop, and even as strong as Samson is, it would be a heck of a way to repay him for his loyalty."

Ghost said, "Okay, but if they balk at riding in my boat, we leave them behind. I need to get all of you off this island."

As Kat studied the monitors, trying to determine where all the monkeys were out there in the still raging snowstorm, Richard said, "We need to arm ourselves if we hope to make it to that boat dock. You have your pistol and knife, Ghost, and we have nothing to fight with."

Richard spotted the pistol jammed into the waistband of Dec's jeans. "Hey, give me that gun, Declan. I'm a much better shot than you, you little squirrel."

Stubbornly, Dec said, "No. I found it. I keep it."

Richard shoved Kat and Mary Kay out of his way to get to Dec.

"Wait!" I said, reaching into my pocket and pulling out the bronze arrowheads. "If we want to deal with Wraith, then these are the best weapon! Let Ghost wield them. He would have the best chance of taking Wraith or Mock out with these holy symbols!"

Richard snatched the arrowheads out of my hand. He jingled the medallions in my face. "Holy symbols? You mean, like a cross used against a vampire? What has my little brother been smoking?"

I wished that the strange purple light would flare to life as he juggled those arrowheads around. I wanted to show him exactly what those symbols were capable of. I said, "Make fun all you want, Richard, but that is the best weapon we have!"

Ten minutes later, we stood at the open doorway of the tower. Madly falling torrents of snow fell outside, making it really hard to see anything beyond. Wraith or Mock could have been standing within a foot of that door, and none of us could see them for all the white snow coming down in furious patterns. Ghost took the lead, yet the strange light stored inside the arrowheads did not come to life as he held them in his hand. Dec said, "It only flares to life if there is danger. We must be safe."

Keeping his eyes on the arrowheads in his palm, Ghost moved out, passing silently through the falling snow. Samson and Oscar fanned out on either side of him, with Mary Kay and Kat staying close behind them. Henry, Chris, and Richard remained two steps behind them, and Dec and I took up the rearguard. Bandit and Miracle hitched a ride with me, both little squirrel monkeys seated at the top of the leather pack attached to my shoulders.

We came up over the rise, and though we could not see the dock still some hundred feet in front of us, we knew we were halfway to our goal. Samson growled and Oscar hooted, when two large yellow lights illuminated the snowy shrubbery surrounding the ramp that led to the dock. We all realized there was a Jeep partially hidden there in the snowy shrubs, and barely visible beyond the yellow halo of light, Big Ty stood up in the Jeep, aiming a pistol at us. "You're not leaving without the gold we came here to find. I figured you'd slink away on one of these boats. I've seen the savagery of the baboons. I know how dangerous they are. All of you turn around and head back inside the tower. Unless you want to rouse the monkey mob, walk slowly!"

Before he started the Jeep, we turned and started running back to the tower. I had been at the back of the line, so I was the first one to come in sight of the open door of the lighthouse before us. Bandit, riding at my left shoulder, chittered softly in my ear. I then saw why.

Wraith stood before the open door.

Frantically searching the grounds around him, my heart thudded inside my chest for I expected to see a troop of baboons backing him. From behind me, I heard the Jeep barreling up out of the gully and then Ghost shouting, "Don't shoot, you fool! You might hit Hawk!"

But as the Jeep came racing toward the lighthouse, bullets whizzed past me. Three of the slugs tore into Wraith's chest, knocking him backwards. The force of the impact sent him crashing into the metal door hanging ajar behind him. But he merely shook himself and clambered back to his feet. He sucked in a deep breath and gave a loud *Huff!* sending the slugs flying from the holes they had left in his chest. The hot lead slugs hissed as they fell in the snow in front of him.

Chapter Thirty

As I approached the door, I glanced back and saw Ghost swing a well-aimed fist and slam it into Sal as he stood there in the oncoming Jeep, armed with his pistol. The three arrowheads in his other hand came to life with a glitter of golden sparks. They sizzled as he dropped them in the snow beside him. Bandit sprang from my shoulders as I closed with Wraith. Reaching back over one shoulder, my hand closed on the war club that had once belonged to Crazy Horse. I withdrew it from the pack and swung it up and over my head. I brought it down hard on Wraith's head. At once, scintillating sparkles exploded from the war club and a multitude of dazzling fireflies flew in chaotic patterns through the air. Within seconds, an entire web of light beams encased the baboon, causing him to topple over and fall beside the door.

Ten feet from the door, Ty brought the Jeep to a grinding halt. Bandit darted past him as he sprang out of the dying Jeep. The monkey retrieved the sparkling arrowheads. He ran past Wraith, the medallions clinking together as he clambered back up my pant leg. He ended up perched on top of the backpack beside Miracle. Bandit let out a squeal as he saw the violet light bands encircling Wraith. "Big Medicine!" said Ty, gesturing at me with his pistol. "Big Medicine written about in your Grandma's book! I carried it out here with us, and I read the *River Kings*. And those arrowheads are the keys I need to open that secret vault!"

Ty shoved me inside the doorway of the tower. He came barging in behind me, forcing me forward and down the spiral stairs to the tunnels below. Pointing his gun at the two monkeys riding along on the backpack, Ty growled, "Take me to it, or I'll shoot me a squirrel monkey!"

I had no choice but to open the door leading to the underground tunnels beneath Rivermoon. We crossed the landing at the bottom of the stairs. Ty shoved me through the door leading into the tunnels. He then closed the door, shutting us off from the stairway.

I slid forward, using my free hand to steady myself by planting it on the nearby wall. In my other hand, I still held the war club, having no idea what powers could be summoned against Ty. His gun came up between us. I slid the war club back into the backpack, then peered up into Ty's furious gaze. I could see by the angry glare in his eyes that he was unhinged. It was hard telling what he was capable of in the state he was in, so I headed deeper into the tunnels. I could not remember how many intersections we had to pass to reach the control room, but as we came to the first one, I saw a flicker of movement in the shadows of the right hand corridor.

Behind me, Ty saw it too. He pointed his gun in that direction, but when no more movement came from those dark depths, he shrugged and lowered it. And moved on.

When we came to the next intersecting tunnel, I froze, certain this time that I saw a brief flash of white off in the darkness of the right hand tunnel. Perched on my shoulders, Bandit and Miracle saw, it, too. I could feel the tenseness in their little bodies as they stiffened and stared with some concern down that corridor. We reached the control center without any interference. Ty scanned the monitors at the middle of the room. He paused as the camera in the tower room relayed the attack taking place there. I inched my way up behind him. My heart leapt into my throat as I looked down at the monitor. Ghost, Samson, Chris, and Richard stood inside the open door of the tower as enraged baboons stormed in from outside. It was a rough and tumble brawl with Samson and Oscar tossing baboons back outside through the door. Behind them, Dec, Kat, Mary Kay, and Henry cowered on the landing of the stairway. I was relieved when Ghost rushed past the ape and the chimp, pulling the door closed and shutting the rampaging baboons off from the tower.

By the time we passed two more intersections, I knew we were being stalked by some unknown creature flittering through the tunnels running adjacent to the one we were in. Every time I turned to look, a flickering flash of bright white would flit into view, then vanish. When we at last came to the decoy chamber, Ty was spooked.

Standing before the twelve bars of gold stacked there in the center of the chamber, he asked, "Do you believe in ghosts? If God went through all the trouble of creating souls inside of so many millions of people, then how is it that a few got left behind when they died? That is the most popular theory on where ghosts come from: Souls who have lost their way. I heard demons are spirits without bodies, looking for a body to travel in. If a demon infiltrates a person's body and hitches a ride with them, it compels them to do evil things.

"I once read True Crime novels down at the library. Starkweather and the Omaha Sniper were evil people who left a dark stain on Nebraska. Starkweather and his teenage girlfriend Caril Fugate are the state's most well-known killers. In 1957, Starkweather killed a gas station attendant. Two months later, Starkweather killed Fugate's parents and sister before the couple set off on an eight-day killing spree that claimed seven more lives. He was executed in 1959. Caril Fugate claims she was not a willing participant in any of the murders. She's still serving time. Irish immigrant Frank Carter, the Omaha Sniper, in 1926, indiscriminately fired his gun into residential windows. Omahans were urged to keep their lights out at night since Carter was known to shoot people as they stood in their homes near lighted windows. Carter claimed to have taken 43 lives. He was a real nut job. I wonder what demon's hitched a ride with me?"

Tyler stood there for long moments, seriously thinking there was some sinister force manipulating him. And then the moment passed. "Hawk!" he snarled, a feral look in his eyes. "Get those arrowheads!"

Perched on my left shoulder, Bandit raised his tiny arm toward my face. As I reached back to take the medallions he had clenched in his fist, they began to glow. I remained silent as I slipped the three arrowheads into the slots of the lock mechanism. Slender shafts of golden light shot from the arrowheads and the door slowly opened. In his haste to get inside the chamber, Ty lurched directly into the path of a flash of white brilliance radiating from a small boy with tangles of white-blond hair charging past the trove. The boy, dressed in the uniform of a Union soldier, struck Ty with a frost-white bayonet attached to the end of his rifle. As the white blade passed into Ty's chest, streamers of lightning crawled like electric snakes down his chest. A puff of black smoke leaked out of his mouth. Gibbering like a fool, Ty ran down the corridor. Bandit and Miracle screeched in terror as the boy soldier turned to face us.

The little boy peered at me with piercing blue eyes. His rifle with the white bayonet flickered, then vanished with an airy *huff!* The boy whisked past me into the chamber where all the gold had been buried so long ago. He held up a battered, dusty ledger and drifted back out of the chamber and handed it to me. "You want me to read this?" I asked.

He nodded, his chin dipping down inside his blue jacket, his blond bangs obscuring his eyes. I looked down and I read out loud:

"The Boys' War, the hidden History of the Civil War: Bobbie Martin, youngest victim of the Lawrence Massacre, was ten. Most accounts state he was wearing a Union uniform, made from his father's uniform and carrying a musket and a bayonet. For perspective on the age of fighters it is estimated that 2,000,000 Federal soldiers were twenty-one. 1,000,000 were eighteen. 800,000 were seventeen. 200,000 were sixteen. 100,000 were fifteen. Three hundred were thirteen. Twenty-five were ten. There are numerous tales of buglers too small to climb into saddles unaided, who rode into battles. Most famous of these on the Union side was Johnny Clem, who became a drummer at eleven, and was soon lance sergeant. On the Confederate side, George Lamkin was eleven and severely wounded at Shiloh. T.D. Claiborne in 1861 became captain of the 18th Virginia that year, and was killed at seventeen. E.G. Baxter enlisted in the 7th Kentucky Cavalry at thirteen. John Tyler, twelve, fought with his regiment until the end, without a wound. T.G. Bean, thirteen, served as adjutant of the cadet corps taken into the Confederate armies. M.W. Jewett was a private at thirteen, serving at the siege of Petersburg."

I looked up from my reading and he looked me squarely in the eye.

In a soft whisper, he said, "I am Bobbie Martin, the youngest cadet killed in the Lawrence Massacre. 100 boys, training as cadets there, were also murdered by Quantrill's Raiders and Bloody Bill Anderson.

Most of Quantrill's guerrilla fighters who rode in the massacre were teenagers. The youngest, Riley Crawford, was 13 when his father was shot and his home burned by Union soldiers. Due to our town's rep as a center for Jayhawkers, who attacked plantations in Missouri, Lawrence was an anti-slavery stronghold. To crush support for Rebel guerillas, my Pa and his Jayhawkers burnt homes, raided farms, shot and killed Johnny Rebs. The raid on Lawrence, according to the butchers who sacked our town, was to avenge the wrongs done their families. At the beginning of the attack, Quantrill shouted, 'This is revenge for the Confederates hung by the neck until dead in Missouri!'

"At 5 a.m. when the roosters crowed in Lawrence on April 21st, 1863, 450 Rebels rode in. For four hours, they burned buildings and looted our banks. Due to revenge being a reason for the attack, Quantrill came with lists of men to be killed and buildings to be burned. John Speer, the owner of the newspaper, was on the list. When the first shots rang out, Mr. Speer instructed his sons to hide in the nearby church, but on the way there, Bryce and Miles were captured by Bloody Bill and executed, each with a pistol shot to the head.

"Mr. Speer's youngest son, 15-year-old Billy was captured a few minutes later by Rebel boys. I would have been shot had I not ducked behind a water trough. The second those Johnny Rebs had seen my uniform, the coat of a Yankee, they would have shot me on sight. Billy gave them a fake name, and they released him. Billy nabbed me from behind the water trough and we ran then together. It was a wild run, for Bloody Bill and the boys riding with him were howling like wolves as they murdered entire groups of boys who actually threw their hands in the air. They murdered a father in a field with his son. They shot a defenseless man in his sick bed. They killed an injured man being held by his pleading wife. They also tied a pair of men together with ropes and shoved them into a burning building where they roasted to death.

"After slaughtering over 150 men and boys, the raiders rode out of town. The raid was a bloody, brutal execution. Quantrill's order to kill young boys was a shameful act. His raid into Lawrence, left helpless women and children on his own side to bear the vengeance inspired by that raid. The Lawrence massacre was followed by swift retribution in the border warfare upon the innocent and helpless. Quantrill left Kansas with the loss of one man. The Union troops followed him and visited vengeance on all western Missouri. Unarmed old men and boys were shot down, and homes were burned, and helpless women and children turned out just before the winter. After the attack, Quantrill led his men south to Texas for the winter. Quantrill himself was killed in Kentucky, with only a few riders left. Among those who remained by his side were Frank James and his younger brother, Jesse."

Bobbie paused once more, a distant look coming to his blue eyes. "We never did make it to the church to hide. Instead, we picked up rifles from the looted hardware store. By the time we got to the street, Bloody Bill and the last of the raiders were racing away through a cloud of gun smoke. I didn't even see the rider take aim at me with his pistol and fire. All I felt was a terrific punch to the middle of my chest. It knocked me clean off my feet. I heard Billy fire his rifle. The last thing I saw were tears running down Billy's cheeks as he said, 'Got him for you, Bobbie. I sent him to see Jesus with a hole in his head!'"

Chapter Thirty-One

"That man killed me," Bobbie said, slipping a finger through the perfectly round hole in the breast of his Yankee jacket. "He ruined my Pa's old uniform, too. My Ma cut up his old jacket and sewed it to fit me, just until I passed my tests as a cadet from the academy."

Bobbie continued to slide his finger into the hole of his jacket. "After I got shot, I chased after those raiders. Though it took me a few days to come to grips with it, I finally accepted the fact that I was a ghost. I rode the wind like a swift falcon, following Quantrill's Raiders. Those kids who rode with him were scared. They knew they'd done our boys dirty. They panicked as Union companies scoured the land to find them. Bloody Bill and Quantrill both agreed to escape swift Union judgement, they had to split up. Quantrill took half of his raiders down into Texas, while Bloody Bill rode north into Nebraska with his band of mean-spirited boy soldiers. I followed them here to this island.

"Bloody Bill wanted to claim the trove hidden here, but he could not open this vault, for he did not have the proper keys. When he and his band of boys rode out, I tried to follow them, but I could not leave. Something was here. Something that came here long ago. It was evil. It came across the ocean from darkest Africa. It sailed here on a slaver ship, basking on the suffering of the slaves chained to the oars. It has stopped me from leaving here each time I tried. A monkey thing, all white with long sharp fangs and it sends thoughts inside my head. This island is a soul trap. Souls of many who have passed, cannot leave. The demon claims we're his collection. There are others like me trapped here. We've tried to get past his guard, but he stops us each time by sending a horde of phantoms after us."

Bobbie snapped his fingers, and his rifle once more appeared in his hands. "That man that was holding a gun on you? He's got a red demon inside him. It's a lesser demon and my bayonet wounded it."

He spun his rifle around, causing his glowing bayonet to flicker with bright flashes. He then mustered up the skills he must have learned back at the academy, spinning the rifle, slanting it left, slanting it right, and ending his maneuver with a flourish that sent bright sparkles flickering through the shadows of the corridor. Holding his rifle by his side, he saluted me crisply. "I think you were destined to come here."

Bobbie gestured then at the backpack I wore upon my back. "The moment I came down this tunnel toward you, something came alive in that pack you wear. It has been glowing with a strange, greenish light all the time I have been sharing my story with you."

"War clubs," I said, "belonging to Crazy Horse and Gall, war chiefs of the Lakota, who once rode the plains of Nebraska. My name is Jessie Hawkins. My friends call me Hawk. My grandmother is full-blooded Lakota, and she would approve of me freeing you from this island."

Bobbie pointed over my shoulder. "We have been bound here for the past one-hundred years. It is long past time that we all move on."

Still perched on the backpack, Bandit and Miracle let out tiny shrieks as a small group of ghostly figures appeared together in the tunnel behind us. They resembled reflections in a large glass window, so faint were their outlines. Three were soldiers, wearing the blue jackets of the Union. Three were a motley band of river pirates. Two were Pawnee warriors, for they wore their hair shaved on both sides with long manes down the center. And the last one was a young girl of the Lakota, her hair long and silky. Her eyes were bright, though she remained silent.

"We came here," Bobbie said, "for different reasons. I came stalking Bloody Bill. Privates Jeffery and Granger came in search of the gold. The French pirates, Jacques, Louie, and Francois came to retrieve the treasure. Lame Beaver and Tall Bear were their Pawnee scouts. And the shy girl? She is Bright Calf, a descendant of Chief Red Cloud. She and a war party came here in search of an item called the Ghost Shirt. When they arrived on Rivermoon, the French pirates killed them. Before each of their souls could drift clear of the island, Wraith and his phantoms sealed them in behind the boundary and confined them here ever since."

I looked at the young girl. "I have the Ghost Shirt in my pack. If I survive, I will take it to my Grandmother. She is also Lakota, and related to Red Cloud, as well. She will know what to do with it. She will see it returned to your people. Rest assured."

Bright Calf offered me a slight smile, but said nothing to me as I returned my gaze to Bobbie. "Retrieve your arrowheads, Hawk," he said, pointing to the lock mechanism on the vault door. "Their magic will aid you in the coming battle against demons and darkness."

I quickly scooped the medallions out of the slots and slipped them into the pocket of my parka. The door closed slowly of its own accord, once more locking the gold inside the vault. I led the small party of ghosts back down the corridor. Bandit and Miracle were still alarmed at the sight of the apparitions, but I spoke to the two softly and settled them down as we walked through the tunnels beneath Rivermoon. When we reached the spiral stairway leading up to the landing inside the tower, I listened for any signs of a struggle above. It was silent. I heard nothing.

I was just preparing to remove the war clubs from the pack, when I heard Bandit screech. Big Ty came rushing up behind me, latching onto my shoulders, and shoving me out of his path. Ty flung the door open, darted up the stairs, and muttering like a mad man, he bolted and ran outside into the furiously falling snow.

As I reached the top of the stairs, I was fiercely embraced by Dec. He couldn't talk, for if he did, I knew he would start crying. Kat also hugged me and said, "Great to see you, Hawk!"

Chris stepped up behind her, ruffling my hair with one hand. "Speaking of Ty, he just left here, the hounds of hell nipping at his heels!"

The Gypsy kid then looked from me to the faint images of the ghosts drifting up the stairs behind me. "Sweet Jesus in Heaven!" he said.

I said, "Souls of those trapped here for a very long time by a demon named Wraith. I need to destroy him to set them all free."

Richard looked away from the snowfall outside the tower. "So, is it Hawk the Demon Slayer? Best give me those war clubs, little brother, before you hurt yourself with them."

He crossed the chamber to relieve me of the war clubs. Bobbie Martin flickered in between us. "No," he said, his frosty bayonet aimed at Richard's chest. "It is to be him who challenges the demon. Not you. Too much darkness in your soul. It will get in your way. He is attuned to the thunder. He is aligned with the lightning and the wind."

Skidding to a stop there in the center of the chamber, Richard withdrew his outstretched hands, his eyes fixed on the white bayonet inches from his chest. "What trick are you pulling, Hawk?" he snapped.

Ghost stepped away from the far wall of the circular room. "No trick, Richard. Trapped souls are these. Where there is treasure, there are curses attached to the hoards in their hidden locations. Oak Island in Nova Scotia, where Templars long ago buried treasure. Robber's Cave, where the James/Younger gang hid their stolen loot. Saddle Ridge, where Black Bart hid his stolen gold. Each cache sets off its own mineral deposit into the ether, attracting dark entities to it. Many have died in their quest to wrest those caches away from not only earthly Sentinels watching over them, but supernatural guardians who have used these caches as bait for their soul traps, so that they may feed."

Bobbie said, "Templar Knights came here long ago, a remnant of the company who sailed to Oak Island. They traveled inland exploring, mapping, finding places to hide their own treasures. They were chased across the Great Plains by a large pack of wolves. They made a stand at the island fortress and killed many of them. When the Templars left, the souls of the wolves were trapped here. One each year have been sacrificed in order to quench the thirst of Wraith's phantoms. I fear we are next. Our souls, too, will be devoured by these phantoms."

I asked, "Wolves have souls?"

Bobbie said, "Haven't you ever owned a dog?"

"Badger, yes," I said. "He's a great dog."

"A great dog," Bobbie said, "meaning you know of his love for you, right? A dog with no soul could do very little in exchanging love and loyalty for his master. A dog has to have a soul to perform his task as a faithful companion, there would be no meaning otherwise. And so, the gray wolf who the dog actually hails from, has a most noble soul that shines like star light on a cold winter night. The silver souls of the wolves, whose pack has dwindled down to six remaining beasts."

It was the sound of Tyler starting the boat at the dock that alarmed Ghost. "If that fool leaves us with the smaller boat," he said, already heading for the door, "we won't be able to all leave this island!"

The long blade of his Bowie knife glowed with a faint blue light the moment he drew it from the sheath beneath his coat. What magic it contained I had no idea. Earlier he had claimed to be a Ghost Hunter, determined to challenge ghosts and demons who have strayed in here from the Otherworld. That luminous blue knife of his became a beacon for the rest of us to follow as we raced through the falling snow to reach the dock. We met no opposition as we came within sight of the hedgerow marking the dock in the distance. Beyond those bushes, the shadowy form of Ty steered the small boat away from the dock, heading across the dark water to the far shore. The torrents of snow made it hard to see him, but it was the fiercely falling snow that prevented the baboon troop from spotting us as we approached the dock.

Samson and Oscar flanked Ghost as he ran in the lead, his shimmering knife held before him. Richard, Chris, and Mary Kay stayed in a tight group behind the gorilla and the chimp. Close on their heels, King Henry, Dec, and Kat frantically turned their heads left to right, fearful that we were about to be attacked at any second. The ghosts of Rivermoon and I brought up the rear. Bandit and Miracle perched on top of the backpack, both little monkeys peering over my shoulders as I ran.

It was Bobbie coming up behind me who brought our formation skidding to a halt as he cried, "Birch, the alpha male of the silver wolves!"

And out of the snow flurries in front of us, there appeared a huge, phosphorous wolf, with green eyes shining so brightly, Ghost actually used his free hand to shield his eyes from the glare. Birch snarled as he eyed the glowing blue blade in Ghost's grasp. The ghost wolf was joined by five other wolves coming up on either side of him. Any fear I had was immediately replaced by a calmness, for the souls of the wolves were very beautiful. The way in which the torrents of snow passed through them was eerie, but these silver wolves were a marvel to behold.

Birch growled at Ghost with his long Bowie knife held between him and the wolf pack, *Lower the pretty blue blade, Lakota. It might do harm to a demon, but it could not do damage to the souls of the dead. The one with the potent weapons is the young cub standing behind all of you. And though I don't doubt the power that emanates from the war clubs he carries, I question his skill as a warrior to wield them.*

I froze as Wraith and his horde of red-eyed phantoms suddenly appeared in the snow flurries between us and the dock. I felt my knees go weak, my stomach churning, and I woodenly reached back over my shoulder, brushing Bandit and Miracle aside as I withdrew the war clubs of the two Lakota war chiefs.

Even as Wraith locked eyes with me, knowing exactly why I had come there, I heard:

The drum beat of a council fire.

I heard the song of an Oglala Lakota war chief.

I felt the breezes of a summer wind stirring the embers of a fire.

I saw those fiery sparks stirred to a bright, crackling blaze.

I saw lighting in a winter evening sky.

I heard thunder as the sun painted the sky red on a summer morning.

I heard the galloping hooves of the buffalo racing across the plains.

I heard the whinnies of stallions carrying warriors to the hunt.

The flap of an owl's wing.

The cry of an eagle.

The high scree of a redtail hawk cutting through the sky.

The roar of a grizzly bear rising at dawn.

The snort of a buck racing through dark trees.

Slowly, but most deliberately, I raised the war clubs of Crazy Horse and Gall. I held my head high and said, "I am the kin of hawks, falcons, and eagles! I am the brother of bear, buffalo, and the wolf! I am a Thunder Dreamer and I bring you the storm!"

Chapter Thirty-Two

Wraith howled and his horde of gray-skinned, man-shaped phantoms broke into a run. They lunged at me, claws extended, fangs exposed, preparing to rip me to shreds. Instead of stepping back to brace for their assault, I sprang forward, taking the fight to them. To utterly decimate these demons from the Otherworld.

Seconds before closing with the swarm of howling enemies, I saw a vision of warriors seated round a council fire. Sitting Bull. Red Cloud. Gall. American Horse. Afraid of his Horses. Spotted Tail. Touch the Clouds. Hump. Worm. Crazy Horse. It was his fierce grin that sent me into fighting frenzy that completely overwhelmed my many enemies. There is a certain rhythm one builds when attacking with war clubs. It has the grace of a hawk in flight. The swiftness of a falcon strike. The brutality of a bear attack. The preciseness of a cougar's slashing claws. The power of a raging buffalo. And once started, the constant strikes cannot break that rhythm as one club pulled me through to the next attack, with all things working in proper order. Stance of the feet. Roll of the shoulders. Swinging arms. All used in harmony to keep those war clubs moving.

I caught one demon beneath its chin, lifting it off of its feet, the war club erupting with bright flashes of rainbow-colored light. I clubbed another one over the head, spilling a spray of gray matter that sizzled as it struck the snow-covered ground. I became a brutal whirlwind of violence and power that sent the luminous war clubs plowing into dozens of demons. I dealt out blow after blow, dealing out death to the horde of enemies trying to bring me down. The snowy ground around me was soon littered with the transparent forms of demons that burst into ebony motes that vanished in the wind as I extinguished them with the medicine of the war clubs. Until . . . only Wraith remained.

Bad seed! he sent spiraling into my mind. *Weak blood! Corrupted spirit! Look at your brother! Look at your own dad!* he said, dealing out words that would tear and rip away my self-esteem. *You will follow *in their footsteps! Drunken rages! Criminal behavior! Nasty nature! For it's in your blood! In your family! Deep within your soul!*

And then in a kaleidoscope of images, Wraith sent me a collage of gruesome depictions of his history with a string of thought pulses: *I've feasted on the hearts of African kings and queens! I've devoured the souls of lions and hyaenas! I've slain bull elephants! I've led bloodthirsty slavers on the hunt for captives all across the savannahs of Africa! I have been a king! I am an instrument of murder and mayhem and the cause of countless sufferings! I am a doorway to death! I am a portal to darkest evils!*

I was staggered by the images he tossed into my mind and I saw:

A black-skinned Shaman seated at the center of a boma constructed of thorny brambles. The old, white-haired witch doctor sent black smoke from his fire to connect with the lone baboon surrounded by a pride of lions outside his boma. Thin tendrils of the rippling smoke slid up into the nostrils of the baboon, and he evolved into a strange hybrid of baboon and great ape. Instead of being killed by the lions, the creature that was Wraith ripped the lions limb from limb. In the nearby boma, the Shaman laughed with glee, then cried in alarm as the creature took notice of him. Wraith turned into a spirit-creature alive and backlit with streamers of crackling fire. Ethereal as the smoke from the Shaman's fire, the flaming spirit of Wraith slipped over the walls made of sharp thorns, and attacked the old witch doctor, turning him into a pile of blackened ashes. Wraith cackled with laughter. He then flew off and over the nearby trees, his red eyes fixed on a village in the distance. In seconds, he was within the walls of the village, his rage unleashed as he feasted on the souls of the terror-filled villagers.

Those images let me know that before me stood a creature of malice that my young mind could barely understand. I knew that its long years of roaming the earth had to be brought to an end. Why the Fates had chosen me to perform this task I had no clue. Why it came down to me, knowing so little of my own heritage as a Lakota boy was beyond me. How those two war clubs had come to be in my hand, was mind boggling. But I knew in my heart that I was taking the path of a Red Road warrior. I had no great desire to make a name for myself, for I considered myself to be a mere dust mote in comparison to the greats like Sitting Bull, Red Cloud, Black Elk, and Crazy Horse. In the scheme of all things Native, I was an insignificant being who held little worth.

Wraith's thoughts slithered into my mind: *Silly Indian Boy, you think Wakan Tanka chose you for this task? El Shadi? Allah? Krishna? Yahweh? Yeshua? You still think you are a Thunder Dreamer?*

All things hung in the balance then. Wraith began to bulk up, preparing to battle against me. *Strike now!* said Birch as he ran up beside Wraith.

As Wraith turned to deal out death to the silver form of Birch, I brought the war club of Crazy Horse up and over my head. Swinging it down with all my might, I did not stop. I could not stop, for once I launched myself into the battle, I let loose with all the strength stored in my soul. And I beat and pummeled Wraith over a dozen times before the death blow sent his dark, twisted soul spiraling up and out of his form. His red-eyed gaze locked on me in sudden disbelief, his smoky spirit hung there for several seconds. Dropping both war clubs, I reached into my pocket and drew out the three arrowheads. At once, three violet streams of light shot from the medallions. The phosphorus purple light beams transformed into three ethereal eagles, who clamped their talons around Wraith and flew him away to the Otherworld, ending his haunting in this world forever. As the piercing screes of the eagles echoed from some distance away, I dropped to my knees beside Birch.

Thank-you, Thunder Dreamer, the wolf said, then vanished in a burst of rainbow-colored sparkles.

Ghost rushed to my side, latching onto me and holding me up as I staggered dizzily, the arrowheads falling from my hands. Kat and Dec came next, both of them reaching out to steady me. "You did it, Hawk!" Dec said, keeping his voice low, for fear it would attract whatever else might be out there in the furiously falling snow. Surrounded by the three of them, I looked over Ghost's broad shoulder to see Bobbie Martin's small band of ghosts winking out one-by-one as their souls took to the ethereal plane. The Lakota girl offered me an earnest gaze. "She," Bobbie said, "asks that your grandmother gets the Ghost Shirt."

I opened my mouth to assure the ghost of the girl that I would see that Gran B took possession of the shirt, but she had already disappeared.

"Thank-you," Bobbie said, offering me a fierce grin. "I hear my ma and pa calling me. Best be on my way! Bye, Hawk!"

And with that, Bobbie Martin, the youngest cadet killed during the Lawrence Massacre in 1863 by Quantrill's Raiders, faded from sight.

Ghost gathered up the two war clubs and stuffed them into the pack on my back. He then scooped up the three arrowheads, slipping them into the pocket of his parka. He looked past me through the torrents of snowfall to the barely visible gully in front of the tower. "There's a mob gathering out there! Let's get to the boat!"

All of us ran and clambered aboard the larger boat at the dock. Mary Kay carried Bandit and Miracle in the crook of each arm, and Richard and Chris made sure Samson and Oscar made it inside the boat. I sighed in relief the moment Ghost started the boat's engine. Only Dec and I saw the gruesome sight behind us as we crouched in the stern of the boat. Back on the dock, Sal broke through the bushes and ran directly into the mad mob of monkeys. As Ghost drove us away from the island, Mock swooped down and struck Sal, and the baboons swarmed him under. Mock glared at Dec and I, then flew into a swirl of snow flurries, vanishing into the whiteness coming down from the skies.

Ghost drove us back to town in Mac's hunting truck. We carted Samson and Oscar out to Catlin's Junkyard, where Chris cleared out a space for them in their old barn, kept warm by the wood stove inside it. We left Chris, Kat, and Richard there to watch over the gorilla and the chimp. Next we dropped Mary Kay, Bandit, and Miracle off at Gracie Long Soldier's house. As Ghost drove Dec and I home, Dec asked, "How do we explain this to my dad?"

Ghost simply rolled his eyes and said, "Working on that."

Chapter Thirty-Three

That next morning, Ghost sat Dec and I down before Gran B's wood stove to prep us for the talk we were destined to have with Mac about our trip to Rivermoon.

Gran B said, "Winged monkeys? Ghosts of long, lost boys? Demons from the wilds of Africa? If you boys start that kind of talk, someone is going to recommend an evaluation on you out at the State Home. As far as a bizarre turn of events that had no real explanation, another tale with a supernatural twist comes from Pine Ridge. In 1895, there were dozens of brutal attacks made on herds of cattle. The cowboys up that way swore these savage attacks were done by a vampire, who killed the cows and tore them apart with his bare hands. Some saw him lapping the blood of his victim like a dog lapping water. Jack Lewis, a cowboy at Pine Ridge, herding cattle one evening, wandered away from his companions. The vampire knocked him to the ground, clawing at his throat. During the struggle, Jack drew his pistol and fired off a shot. The gunfire brought the other cowboys, and several of them pursued it on horseback, but the beast escaped, leaving Jack torn about the face and neck by a frothing man trying to bite his throat.

"There are a lot of weird things in Nebraska's history. On June 6, 1884, some cowboys were herding cattle in Dundy County, when they saw a flaming object crash to the earth. When the cowboys approached it, they saw a bubbling liquid on the ground around the wreckage. Scraps of machinery were strewn all about. They rode back to the ranch, prepared to return the following day after the heat died down. Overnight, people who lived nearby saw a bright glow coming from the crash site. The cowboys came back the next morning to find the main piece was sixty feet long and ten feet in diameter. But that afternoon, a storm struck. It lasted for 30 minutes, ending as suddenly as it had begun. And when the onlookers were able to see the crash site: The mysterious wreckage was gone! This story from Nebraska seems to predate every other UFO sighting reported in newspapers at the time."

Gran B held up the three medallions. "I think we should share the story of these with Mac or Richard and Chris will venture back out there to retrieve those gold bars stacked before the closed vault when those vicious monkeys are removed from the island. Ghost is taking the war clubs and the Ghost Shirt to the curator of Indian Affairs in Bismark, North Dakota this afternoon. There are Natives there who would be glad to receive these valuable relics. The ledger of Black Hawk is legitimate. The images he drew in there are authentic. Ghost will also see that Indian Affairs receive this rare book. But as to the *River Kings?*

"Although the claim is it is a story by Samuel Clemens, it is a story Henry fabricated. But there are parts and pieces of the story that are true, other parts made up. Your great grandfather and Clemens were steam boat captains. They met Buffalo Bill at his Wild West Show in North Platte in 1910. It was at nearby Rock Creek Station that Buffalo Bill met Wild Bill, and he and Wild Bill did serve as scouts for Custer. But as to why the medallions actually opened that vault? Perhaps, some Freemason sent an engineer here to design the intricate lock mechanism described in the *River Kings* story. And as to Henry being a Sentinel? I never knew how close to the truth he was when he wrote this story."

Sheriff Mac and his hunting party returned from Pawnee City later that afternoon. Noah, Hiney Scrabble, Mose Hadley, and Lawrence Shank had seen the huge paw prints of the cougar stalking cattle down that way, but not one of them had seen hide nor hair of the mountain cat, for he was as elusive as a ghost. They called the lion Houdini, for despite their best efforts to track it down, it had escaped into the bluffs down near Pawnee City. Mac met with King Henry a few minutes before Ghost escorted us into the office and told him about Ty kidnaping Kat and Mary Kay. Dec added bits and pieces of the story. He glossed over the part about how he drove us out to the island in Mac's hunting truck. But when he got to the part about how I had fired off my dad's umbrella gun and put that hole in the canoe, Dec sheepishly admitted that we'd stolen another boat. He knew if Judge Neely heard about this, he would sentence us boys to probation for sure. He finished his story, including the gruesome manner in which Sal and Rock had been savagely mauled by the baboons.

Mac said, "Ty needs to be arrested. I'm looking forward to placing the handcuffs on Ty myself!"

Noah said, "What if some of those monkeys find their way off of that island and wander into town? Hiney, Mose, Lawrence and I could take our guns out there to take care of them."

Mac said, "We're not going to start shooting monkeys. They deserve better than to be shot in order to subdue them."

"What about Samson?" Dec asked his dad.

"And Miracle and Bandit?" I asked Mac.

At first, Mac looked confused, until Dec said, "The gorilla and those two little squirrel monkeys May Kay has at her house."

Nodding, Mac said, "We'll have to see about them. We can't keep a gorilla penned up here the rest of his life. It would be cruel. And squirrel monkeys? I imagine those men who ran things out there on that island will probably demand that Mary Kay turn them over to them."

Dec groaned and said, "Let's hope not. They are both special."

Two more weeks passed. Still, Tyler was not found. There were rumors he was seen wandering around town after dark, but each time someone called Mac and Noah to have him arrested, Ty was gone by the time either of them arrived on the scene. It made it spooky for town residents at night. To have a creeper like Big Ty roaming like a lack-wit down our sidewalks was unsettling. Ty was a menace even in his right mind, but to hear rumors of this terrible snickering he was heard doing as he prowled our dark streets, it was downright crazy to think our former deputy had gone that far off the rails.

And the worst part of it was that Big Ty was armed with his pistol. Ty had always been a bully with a badge, actually harassing some townsfolk so much that they had feared he might snap one day. And not one of them doubted he would use his gun on them. Some townies spoke of that in hushed whispers. Dec and I kept a close eye on Badger and Cooper for fear that Ty might shoot them just to be cruel.

And I could not forget the dressing down my dad gave Ty the last time he'd confronted him over him taking our dogs. I could not be sure my dad was safe, especially when he was up a tree doing his trimming work. It just seemed like a convenient place for Ty to take advantage of if he spotted my dad high up in a tree with no way to defend himself.

Chapter Thirty-Four

Mac picked Dec and I up from school on a Friday afternoon. He gave us bottles of *Nehi* orange soda to drink as he drove us to the courthouse. He kept the conversation low-key, saying, "I contacted the research group that recklessly abandoned it, leaving such a dangerous element to roam loose on Rivermoon. They cleaned up the mess they left behind. They are using tranq guns on the monkeys that need to be rounded up out there. But even if they tranq all them, some of those creatures infected with viruses need to be disposed of. By the end of the week, Samson will be transported to the Henry Doorly Zoo in Omaha. Henry paid Harv Brindle ten dollars to buy Oscar from him. Mose built an enclosure out at his dairy farm where Oscar can roam. He's living in his old barn, where he has full room to sleep in. He actually agreed to adopt Oscar. Oscar is going to have a big home to live in instead of that old cage on the side of Harv Brindle's tree."

Dec said, "Oscar may outlive all of us. Did you ever hear of Cheetah? He was the chimp who acted in the Tarzan movies. Why, Cheetah outlived Tarzan, Jane, Boy, Numa the lion and Tantar the elephant, dying at the age of 95. We may have Oscar around for a good long time."

Mac glanced at us in his rearview mirror. "The monkeys have all been removed by the group who leased Henry's island. They were transported to several zoos in Kansas. Samson is going to like his new home at the zoo in Omaha, as he has girl friends to keep him company. But I don't want you boys to venture back out to that island. One of the vets in charge of the monkeys placed a quarantine on the island due to residual contagion, meaning one can breathe in some virus. Besides, the group that has claims on that gold out there is sending a hazardous material team here this weekend to retrieve it from that vault you discovered."

"The group?" I asked. "Rebels who belong to this secret society?"

Mac said, "Silas Vance prefers Sons of Liberty. He's involved in charitable work as opposed to the divisive goals of the original Knights. He wants that gold to finance a Children's Hospital that they own. It is ironic that rebels who fought for slavery switched their goals to help sick kids. If Henry goes to trial for the murder of Jon Kennedy, he is convinced he's going to be found guilty. Therefore, he made Gracie his power of attorney. Rivermoon can only be accessed with her consent. She knows how that gold got there. She knows these knights robbed and stole to finance their southern cause. But if these Sons of Liberty claim their motives are different from when they first started their crusade and they want to use that fortune for a hospital for children, Gracie may not have to deal with them at all.

"Due to extenuating circumstances, the judge asked for a hearing to determine if Henry's plea for self-defense applied due to the fact he shot and killed Jon Kennedy because he'd abducted Mary Kay. If those facts are presented in court, there won't be one juror to find Henry guilty of murder. Folks will consider Henry a hero for attempting to rescue his god-daughter from a very evil man. Drugging her to abduct her was bad, but with Mary Kay being pregnant, it makes Jon Kennedy sound like a monster. Andy wants to establish exactly what it was Henry knew before he shot and killed Jon Kennedy. For that, he needs you boys to testify about the shooting you witnessed."

Dec and I exchanged puzzled looks. So far, only Ty had come close to figuring we were perched up there in our tree house on the day of the shooting. Mac had never questioned us about skipping school, and now we both wondered how Andy Tate knew we'd seen anything?

As we approached the courthouse, Andy stepped outside, dressed in a fancy three-piece suit, every hair on his head slicked back and held in place by that magical elixir known as *Brylcream*. Mac and Andy led us down the hallway to Judge Neely's chambers. At the head of the table in the judge's chambers, sat Judge Neely, his walrus-like white mustache billowing like a ship's sail as he huffed and puffed. Andy, resembling Gregory Peck, sat down at Neely's right. Before him was a folder he tapped with his fingers as he waited to proceed. Behind him, at a smaller table, sat Gracie Long Soldier, who smiled at Dec and I as Mac seated us at the table.

Judge Neely swore us in on a Holy Bible. I think, by the shrewd look he shot at Mac, he wanted him to leave the room, but Mac moved to the end of the table and sat down, ignoring the angry look he offered him. Although it was an informal hearing, Judge Neely still hammered his wooden gavel on the table in order to make it seem formal. "Your first witness, Mr. Tate? State her name for the record."

"Mary Kay Long Soldier, your Honor," Andy said, gesturing at Mary Kay as she entered the room. She smiled at Dec and I, which settled us down some as we were both nervous about testifying, not knowing if we were there to clear Henry or if our words would send him to trial. Andy swore her in. He then sat her down directly across from us at the table. With a slight tap of his gavel, Neely said, "Proceed, Mr. Tate."

Andy opened the folder on the table in front of him. "First exhibit will confirm the abduction, the medicating, and establish the fact that the deceased was armed and dangerous and presented a menace to society, namely Mary Kay Long Soldier."

All of us seated at the table studied the 8 by 10 photos Andy displayed. The first showed Jon Kennedy forcing Mary Kay at gun point to walk toward his Chevy. The second showed Jon planting his pistol beneath Mary Kay's chin as she stood before the open trunk. The third photo showed Kennedy stabbing a hypodermic needle in her left shoulder. The fourth showed him forcing her into the trunk. "These," Andy said, "establish the viciousness that Miss Long Soldier was subjected to."

He quickly slid several more large black and white photos on the table. The first showed Henry McGinn stopped in his new Pontiac beside the Stop sign on Elk Street. The second showed Jon Kennedy ramming the nose of his Chevy into the trunk of the Pontiac. The third showed Henry climbing out of his car, his large caliber pistol in hand.

Andy slid five more photos out to the middle of the table. The images were slightly blurry, but they showed the struggle between Henry and Jon fighting over the gun. The last photo depicted Jon Kennedy with a bullet hole in the center of his chest. Andy said, "The streets of Elk and Eighth, empty. The vacant lot adjacent to the shooting, empty. The front lawn of the Hawkins' house, empty. The parking lot of the Baptist church across the street, empty. It would appear there were no witnesses to the actual shooting."

Andy slapped his last photo down on the table. It clearly showed Dec and I peering out through the wide, open window of our tree fort. "May I now present," Andy asked, "my second witness, your Honor?"

I nearly fell out of my chair when Andy said, "Amos Hawkins?"

Dad walked into the judge's chambers, cleaning his wire-rimmed glasses. Looking like handsome Robert Taylor, even dressed as he was in his tree-trimming overhauls, he walked over to Mac, saying, "Is this the circus you warned me about? Well, let it be known, I don't much approve of anyone in this court using my boy to determine the guilt or the innocence of Henry McGinn."

"All I need you to do, Amos," Andy said, "is confirm that this is Declan Connors and Jessie Hawkins inside this tree house on Elk Street."

Dad glanced down at the photo and said, "That's my son. But it don't prove what day it was, does it?"

"Why, yes, it does," Andy said, trying not to gloat. He reached down and tapped the picture. "See that there? It's a time stamp, noting it was taken at 12:30 on November 22nd. Modern cameras are equipped with that timing device. And since this was taken with a high-tech camera, it certainly showed the time stamp, your Honor."

Neely studied the photo, then asked, "Does this imply that the two boys were truant from school when this was taken? Miscreants do not make good witnesses, Tate. Who should I be scolding here? The lawyer using two hooky players as witnesses for his client? Or the fathers of the truant youths?"

Dad said, "The assassination of President Kennedy rattled my cage that day, Judge. I spotted the two boys climbing up into their tree house around 11 that morning. I meant to confront them, but my own weakness for nostalgic notions took me down memory lane. I remembered my own boyhood. Seeing those boys playing hooky brought a smile to my face, reminding me of Tom Sawyer and Huck Finn. I simply returned to my work shed. About that time, the news report came over the radio, John Kennedy had been shot. I stood there weeping for quite some time. I then heard the gun shot. But I never witnessed what the boys evidently did when Henry shot this other Jon Kennedy."

Judge Neely's thick mustache took on a life of its own as he ranted, "Sawyer and Finn were hooligans!"

"Your Honor?" Andy said. "Shall we return to the matter at hand?"

It was Mary Kay who actually reined in the judge. "I am wondering about something, Judge. Who took these pictures?"

Judge Neely stared hard at Andy, who said, "They were taken by a drone." He might as well said, "They were taken by a cotton candy machine," for everyone at the table had no idea what he was talking about. "Drone?" Judge Neely asked as confused as the rest of us.

"A camera," Andy said, "that can fly like a bird and take pictures of what is happening beneath it. A drone is like that flying contraption on Star Trek, and they had one on that one episode of Batman."

"Star Trek?" Neely asked. "Batman? Have you gone loony, Tate? Just who would have access to a gadget like that? And how on earth did you obtain such farfetched technology in order to present it in my courtroom? This is nutso, Tate, completely bonkers!"

Andy said, "I admit, your Honor, it is advanced technology, but the Star Fire Agency that leases Henry's island south of town had an invested interest in his dilemma with his abducted niece. Evidently, they've been using their airborne cameras for quite some time, flying them above our little town and—"

"Spying on its citizens?" Neely snapped. "How did it happen to be focused on Mary Kay on that particular day? And what sort of agency is this? I'm aware that scientific research was taking place on Rivermoon island, but if they recorded the abduction of Mary Kay, why didn't someone inform us of this earlier?"

Chapter Thirty-Five

Andy said, "Star Fire is an agency whose goal is discovering foreign viruses. Their research using monkeys seems inhumane, but if any of these viruses ever leaped over and chose us as their host, the United States would be doomed. Star Fire scientists have learned a lot through the use of monkeys. King Henry let their director know months ago of the theft of gold by Deputy Burke. Evidently, they had a camera tracking Mary Kay, but things spiraled so fast out of control that day, no one could prevent Henry from trying to rescue her. He not only saved her life, but the life of her unborn child."

Neely said, "Secret agency that spies on our citizens? Researchers playing with fire under our noses? And what is your end goal, Tate? You still want these boys to speak?"

There came a loud knock on the judge's chamber door. Silas Vance entered the room, followed by two large men with long, gray hair and salt and pepper beards. Silas moved to the head of the table and took hold of Judge Neely's left wrist. "Horace?" he said, in a southern drawl. "Correct me if I am wrong, but if I sent Caleb and Jacob here down to that house of yours on Lincoln Street, would they not find Klan robes and hoods that once belonged to your pappy?"

Judge Neely stared bug-eyed at the large man holding him by the wrist. "You can't barge into my chambers!" he cried. "This is—"

"This is," Silas said, "southern justice long overdue, Horace Neely! And this hearing is adjourned! You are no longer needed here!"

Judge Neely found himself latched onto by the other two burly men, who escorted him outside the chamber and on down the hallway, trailed by Andy. Silas walked over and closed the chamber door, then turned and fixed Mac in his lion-like gaze. He said, "You and I spoke years ago on this matter, Cormac. Henry McGinn was refusing to comply with my orders and could no longer be trusted to fulfill his vows. I cordially offered the Sentinel position to you. But you, being a man of lofty principals refused to take up the mantle, despite your southern roots.

You see nothing wrong with interracial marriages, or as in this case, interracial relationships? Because there was no marriage involved with this tragedy to take place in your small town, was there?"

Dec and I sat looked to Mac and Silas. Neither one of us had ever heard the term "interracial" before, so we had no clue what it even meant. Silas, a high ranking member of the Golden Circle Knights, had offered Mac the role as guardian over the hidden cache on Rivermoon because of something to do with where Mac's family had originally come from.

Gracie glared at Silas, offering him the worst case of snake-eyes I had ever seen. She looked directly at Dec and I seated across the table from her. "Poor boys. You have no idea what these men are taking about."

"Eighteen years ago," Silas said, "Grace had an affair with a man of color. When her husband found out about it, he wanted her to have an abortion. When Henry found out she was even considering it, he urged Grace to have the baby, even if that unborn child might suffer for being born the daughter of a Lakota mother and a black father. My grandpappy would be turning over in his grave at the disgusting notion that a colored man so much as touched this white woman. You, Cormac, should have carried out my orders back then, and charged this big, black buck with first degree rape."

Gracie said, "You should not have shown your hand so early, Silas. As power of attorney, I was more than willing to agree to giving access to your group to the island. Had you remained silent, instead of playing your hand here in Neely's chamber, the Sons of Liberty would have left here with your gold. But now, I see your true goal is to fuel the fires of your extreme hatred for the black race. And I won't relinquish one bar of all that gold on Rivermoon to a twisted soul like you. You and your Knights would just continue your crusade to Raise the Confederate Flag. All that gold shall remain sealed in that vault."

"Bravo, spoken like a true patriot," Silas said, grinning. "Now, let's get this hearing moving in the right direction! In 1956 before Mac was Sheriff here, there was a gruesome murder on a farm near here. Father, mother, and two daughters were killed and found in a bloody kitchen.

The London family tragedy plagued the law enforcement department in Beatrice. And the case went unsolved."

Silas reached inside his suit jacket and pulled out a sheet of paper. "Ever heard of selective investigation? When the investigators are so convinced they are on the right track, that they miss other clues. When investigators are so focused on motives that instigated the crime, they miss a piece of the puzzle. London producing fraudulent manuscripts of some very famous children's authors. All these years, investigators assumed the motive for the family tragedy was the theft of the works of these long-dead authors. The motive being money. But this murder was committed out of revenge. You see, Dr. London worked at the State Home, where he performed sterilization procedures on dozens of patients. 950 of these sterilization operations were performed out there. These doctors played god with so many troubled souls sent to the State Home. It is one thing to sterilize adults, and quite another to fix it so that an adolescent can never produce children."

Silas slid the paper down the table toward Mac. "Sterilize," he said, "is to perform surgery on male or female patients who are incapable of changing their deviant behavior, and so they can never produce another deviant just like them."

Mac looked down at the paper in front of him.

Silas said, "Roman Kowski. Clifford Loyd. Andrew Tate. And Henry McGinn. All four were boys when these surgeries were performed on them by Dr. London between 1940 and 1945. All four would have been adults in 1956. So, one of them wanting revenge for the sterilization by Dr. London during their stay at the State Home, murdered the entire London family. I came here today to clear Henry McGinn of both the London murders and the shooting of Jon Kennedy."

Mary Kay said, "But Henry has two daughters—"

"Adopted," Silas said. "He was sterilized in 1945, when as a youth he was sent there because of problem behaviors at home. In fact, it is his second stay out there that took place in December of 1956 that clears him of the murder. During the horrific events on that cold December day, when the London family was savagely slain in their farmhouse, Henry was confined to the State Home for an evaluation. He could not have been involved in the murders. My purpose in coming here, is to have Henry dismiss you, Grace Long Soldier, as his power of attorney. With Henry back in charge of his own affairs, we need not bother you with the retrieval of all of our gold. You've seen these photos of scenes captured by this drone camera. When shown to a jury, any prosecutor would have a difficult time getting them to convict Henry of the crime of murder. He would plead the defense of his god-daughter by eliminating the threat this Kennedy posed to her. Judge Neely will order this murder charge dismissed. Henry will resume his role as power of attorney. We can retrieve all of our gold from Rivermoon. And you, Sheriff Connors can make arrest a suspect. Besides, aren't you curious as to who removed the case file of the London murders from the evidence room?"

At this, Mac asked, "How do you know this, Silas?"

Silas gave a slight chuckle. "Secret Society stuff, Cormac. We move about in secret. Andy Tate worked hard for seven years to obtain a law degree. He could have ended up any where in the US, but he chose to return to his hometown of Beatrice. Perhaps, it was to steal that case file, so that he could never be prosecuted. Loyd became a bail bondsman, and where is his office located? Here in the courthouse. Pretty convenient. Both associated with the law, and using the law to cover their tracks. Prime candidates for the murder, wouldn't you say?"

Silas then said, "Caleb, bring in the monitor and the King."

Seconds later, King Henry was escorted into the judge's chambers by one of the burly men, who also carried a small television set and a leather satchel. Caleb sat them on the table in front of Silas, then pulled out a chair for Henry to sit in. He seated himself at the table when Silas slid a document in front of him and placed a fountain pen in Henry's hand. "Sign that, McGinn," Silas said, coldly.

"No, Uncle Henry!" Mary Kay said. "Do not sign that! They want their gold! We can't let them have it! And legally, Mom can stop them!"

Chapter Thirty-Six

"Let me show you something," Silas said. "Something that will help you make the right decision, Henry."

He picked up the remote control device Caleb had placed on the table next to the small TV, clicking on the device. All of us looked to the full color images that appeared on the screen of the televison situated on the table. It was an aerial view of Kowski's junkyard on the east side of town. There were rows and rows of junked cars on both sides of the dirt road leading to the yard's entrance. But instead of being parked side by side as Rome normally placed his old junkers, he had them stacked three high, creating a fortress around the junkyard. In the center where the gate sat, there were three cars sitting one on top of the other. In place of a movable gate, there was now an immovable wall.

"Someone," Silas said, "told him he was getting arrested. Here, let me show you what happened out there earlier today."

Silas worked the device in his hand, and on the screen appeared Mose Hadley driving his truck through the open gate of Kowski's junkyard. We watched the screen as Mose drove down the driveway and parked in front of Rome's house at the end of a car-made cul-de-sac. Rome stepped onto his porch. Mose climbed out of his truck and handed him a manilla envelope. The grizzly man opened the envelope, stood there a few minutes reading some paper he drew out of it. When he finished, Rome snatched up a baseball bat from his porch and hit Mose in the the head, dropping him like an ox on the dusty boards of his porch. On the screen, we watched as Rome used a grader and a bulldozer to move junked cars into place, creating a wall around his yard and his house. Images of Rome going to town on his make-shift fortress flashed past us in swift-moving scenery. The finishing touches were the three cars he placed in his gateway, blocking the entrance to his junkyard.

Silas reached inside the leather satchel before him. He drew out two items. "Now, to help remind these boys that they saw Jon Kennedy pull a gun on Henry McGinn, I had to have a little motivation."

Dec and I had tears in our eyes as we fixed our sights on the two leather collars Silas tossed on the table before us. A second later, there on the screen of the televison, Badger and Cooper appeared, tied to a wooden milk crate next to Rome's front porch. Mose was standing on this crate, his hands tied behind his back and a thick noose around his neck. The rope attached to the noose was tied to the thick branch of a giant cottonwood beside Rome's house. "A Hoot Owl tree," Silas said. "The treasure long removed by Klansmen some fifty years ago. But still, an appropriate place for that black buck to be strung up to."

Mac stood to his feet. But it was Gracie who snapped, "If any harm comes to Mose, I'll shoot you myself, Silas! You are a mean-hearted bastard!" She turned to face King Henry who was sitting there, blinking like an owl in bright daylight. "Sign the paper! Give this monster consent! And get them out of town as soon as possible!"

Henry hastily signed the paper. "Take your gold," he said, visibly shaken by seeing Mose with the noose around his neck, "and be gone, Silas Vance. I give you permission to venture out to my island and to leave with what you came for. The sooner you're gone, the better."

Silas studied the signature for several seconds. He then reached down into the satchel and withdrew a walkie-talkie. He switched it on and after a brief crackle filled the room, he spoke into it, saying, "Mister Kowski, this little theatrical number is over. Now, release the dogs. Get Hadley down from there. For the part you played, the guarantee of a good lawyer is in the works. Let's see if we can't get you acquitted of the London crimes."

We all followed Silas's gaze as it flickered toward the screen on the TV set. There on the screen, Rome came into view. He was holding another walkie-talkie. A loud crackle came from the one Silas held, and then Rome said, "Dogs are done gone. Chewed through the ropes and took off into the junkyard behind me. But Mose is another story, Mr. Vance. Is the Sheriff there? Can Mac hear me?"

Mac crossed the room and swiftly moved to the end of the table, where he snatched the walkie-talkie out of the big man's hand. Mac raised it to his lips and very firmly said, "Roman? Let Mose go. I'm coming over there. We can sort this out when I do!"

Mac turned and looked to the screen of the TV set. Rome stood on his porch, holding the walkie-talkie. He gestured at Mose who could be seen behind him, still standing on that milk crate, the noose tight around his neck. The walkie-talkie in Mac's hand crackled and Rome said, "No, Mac. You're not arresting me. I want a get away car delivered here in one hour, or Mose Hadley is gonna swing. When you come, Mac, bring along Tate and Loyd. They both need to tell you they were there that night. It was Andy's idea to kill London. It was his plan. Before I head on down to Mexico, you need to hear the entire story."

Rome reached down to the bench beside him and snatched up his lever action rifle. He worked the lever in plain sight of that drone catching his image, and shouldered his high-powered rifle. All of us sat back in our chairs instinctively as Rome fired his gun and shot that drone right out of the sky. The entire screen on the TV set turned pitch black.

Silas shook his head in disbelief. "I truly never meant for this to happen, Cormac. So sorry about this turn of events. I just wanted to make sure Henry gave us consent to take our gold."

Offering Silas an angry scowl, Mac headed down the hall to retrieve Noah. Dec and I followed close behind him. When we got to the sheriff's office, Mac was unlocking the gun cabinet as he explained Mose's predicament to Noah. He had just drawn out a high-powered rifle from the rack inside the cabinet, when Clifford Loyd came through the door, a pistol in his grasp. He cocked it with one thumb. "Put the rifle down, Mac," Loyd said. "Remove the pistol from your holster. And step into the first jail cell."

"Clifford?" Mac said. "This is not how to sort this out. This—"

"Shut up!" Loyd snapped. "Do as I say! Or I will shoot you!"

Noah followed Mac's lead as he removed his pistol from its holster. At gunpoint, Loyd led them into the first jail cell. Loyd kept the gun trained on Noah so that Mac didn't risk his life by doing anything rash. Once they were in the cell, Loyd turned to us. "Follow them," he said.

It was then that Gracie walked into the office, facing Loyd, staring directly down the barrel of his gun. "Leave the boys out of this, Cliff," she said, firmly. "They pose no threat to you. Leave them be."

Loyd snorted and said, "Mac? Close the cell door."

Mac closed the iron door with a loud clang. Loyd snatched up the ring of keys hanging by a nail on the nearby wall. Hastily, he sorted through the keys, finding the one for that particular cell. He shoved it into the lock mechanism, then used the butt of his gun to hammer the key into a misshapen form, jamming up the lock. Tossing the keys aside, he turned and left the sheriff's office at a run, his last words trailing behind him, "Stay put, Mac, and you won't get hurt! I'll deal with Rome!"

Mac rushed to the cell door and tried to open it, but it would not budge. It became obvious he and Noah were locked up. Gracie turned to us boys, saying, "Rome's a psycho! We need fire power! You heard him say if he didn't get a get-away car in one hour, he would hang Mose!"

"Firepower?" I said. "You mean Lawrence?"

"Damn right!" Gracie said. "Go and get him!"

In full-blown running deer-mode, Dec and I took off for the train yards a few blocks away. I lagged behind Dec as we came to the first set of tracks. I veered off and ran toward the Hadley place at the west end of the yards. Racing off toward Lawrence's train-house, Dec glanced back and shouted, "Where you going, Hawk?"

Continuing to run, I shouted back, "Getting a bulldozer to move those cars out of Sheriff Mac's way so he can get in that junkyard!"

Five minutes later, I rode Rosie down the road leading to Kowski's junkyard. I peered ahead of us to the gateway Rome had dozed into place. Rome stood just behind one of his cars, using it for cover as he aimed his rifle down at Loyd who stood before the impenetrable fortress.

I still wasn't sure if Rosie understood my hasty string of sentences I had rattled off to her in regards to Mose, or if she just sensed my own distress and was now determined to help me out. The second we came in sight of the car-castle in front of us, Rosie picked up speed and was running directly for the three stacked cars blocking off the yard at the end of the road. I felt my hair lifting off my shoulders and streaming out behind me as I clung to Rosie's collar. It felt like we were flying as that huge elephant worked herself up into a canter. As Rosie ran straight out for that solid line of cars before us, I noticed I was high enough off the ground to see completely over those cars blocking us from the junkyard. And I could clearly see Mose struggling to remain upright on that milk carton. It must be what Rosie saw, too, for she suddenly lifted her trunk and trumpeted a call to her master.

I had no idea what went through the mind of an elephant when it came to love and loyalty of the man who had taken care of her for the past twenty years, but if she was anything like Badger or Cooper, totally dedicated to Dec and I, then Rosie was in full-blown rescue mode.

Ahead of us, Rome, standing on that stack of cars, stared in disbelief at the enraged elephant coming straight for him and his car-obstruction. As he frantically pawed at the lever on his rifle, his eyes got big as silver dollars, for Rosie refused to stop. She ran me right up to the gateway of stacked cars, and rather than stop and use her trunk to lift them out of her path, she instead rammed the three cars with her head. Rome flew backwards, his arms flailing, his legs kicking, then landed on his back on the hard ground of his driveway, his rifle landing beside him. He cried out as Rosie toppled those three cars over, sending them hurtling down toward him sprawled on the ground inside the junkyard.

Snatching up his rifle, Rome scrambled out of the way before he was crushed. An explosion of dust flew up as those cars crashed to the ground, and for several seconds, Rome disappeared from my sight.

Rosie let out another trumpeting call with her raised trunk, she then barged her way past the cars and ran full-tilt up the driveway of the junkyard, her sights fixed on Mose struggling to stay upright on that milk crate. Rosie was desperate to save Mose from swinging from that cottonwood tree. I had no idea that my words would penetrate her elephant brain and yet, I coaxed her to slow down as we approached Mose attached to that tree by the noose around his neck. Skidding to a halt beside Rome's porch, Rosie practically slid into Mose, standing there held upright by the rope and struggling to breathe.

"Hupp, Rosie!" Mose gasped. "Hupp! Hupp, girl!"

Rosie snaked her trunk around Mose's legs, and gently lifted him up and off that milk crate. Seated there between her neck and back, I peered down at Mose now sucking in air. His eyes locked with mine and he hoarsely whispered, "Thanks, Hawk! Thanks!"

"What do I gotta do," I said, clinging to Rosie's collar, "to get you down from there, Mose?"

As he opened his mouth to respond, I saw Mose look past Rosie and open his eyes wide. "Sweet Jesus!" he gasped, his sights fixed on the entrance to Kowski's junkyard.

Clifford Loyd was there, armed with a pistol.

Chapter Thirty-Seven

I glanced back to see Lawrence Shank coming through the opening Rosie had created in those junked cars. He was dressed in a long, black duster. Black slacks. Black boots. Black vest. Black cowboy hat. Dust swirls rose up around him as he drew out his twin six-shooters. Having kept up with him all the way from the train yards, Dec ran up behind him, huffing and puffing, his hair plastered to his head from sweat running down his face. Loyd raised his pistol, but Lawrence made a flickering movement with the pistol in his left hand. It barked and spat a fiery ball of flame out of its muzzle, sending a lead slug slamming into Loyd's chest. From up on Rosie's back, I got all light-headed as I saw the bright red blood burst from Loyd's back. The bullet passed completely through him, and he fell to one side of Rome's driveway.

A loud gun shot came from somewhere in front of me and Rosie, and I turned my head to see Rome working his lever on his rifle. I glanced back again to see that he'd missed Lawrence, but Dec was scrambling behind several cars to take cover now that Rome was shooting at them.

Lawrence made one of those flickering movements with his right hand gun and he sent a lead slug directly into Rome's left shoulder. The impact of that slug sent the big man floundering back against his house, his shoulders making a solid thudding sound as he struck the white-washed boards. Rome slid down on his rump, leaving a crimson trail of blood on his house, while his rifle clattered at his feet.

I swooned, fighting to overcome the nausea I felt at the sight of so much blood. Beneath me, Rosie must have felt me struggling to remain upright as I clung to her collar, for she swung her trunk up and over her head even as I fell forward. Her trunk connected with my forehead, then blackness swept over me and I fell through empty air. I struck the ground so hard the wind exploded from my lungs. Dec lifted me up. "You okay, Hawk?" he said, his hands on my shoulders. I nodded, unable to breathe, let alone speak. "Don't do it," we both heard Lawrence telling Rome. "Leave it alone, Roman."

Sprawled there in Rosie's shadow, I looked up past her to see Rome holding his rifle. Although he was bleeding badly, he worked the lever on his rifle, ejecting a shell and sending a cartridge into the chamber of the big gun. I cringed when Rome raised his rifle and fired. That rifle of his was meant to take down deer at a good distance away. And there was only thirty-some feet between Rome and Lawrence, so when the bullet struck him, Lawrence actually flew back and off his feet, his pistols fallen to the ground beside him.

All that gunfire was too much for Rosie, and as she turned and fled, Rome levered another bullet into the chamber of his rifle. He leaned up against the side of his house, shouldering his gun, drawing a bead on Lawrence as he rose to his knees. I stared in disbelief that he was even alive after taking a shot like he had taken from that high-powered rifle. I was still sucking in air and unable to move, but Dec ran to his side and snatched up both pistols by their barrels and placed them into Lawrence's hands. "Ouch!" Dec cried. "Damn, those are hot!"

Rising up on both knees, Lawrence raised the two pistols and fired, sending angry hornets of hot lead flying. Rome stiffened as the first bullet struck him in the chest. A second slug grazed his brow. A third slug buried itself in his left arm. A fourth passed through his right hand, shattering the wooden stock of his rifle, leaving the butt in splinters. His fifth shot struck the propane tank fitted snugly beside Rome's house, igniting the fuel, sending a rip-roaring explosion of heat that knocked Rome completely off his feet. The power of that blast sent shrapnel flying toward Dec and I, and Lawrence suddenly sprang in front of us, taking the brunt of that flying metal in the center of his chest.

I saw him fall back for a second time, and then a loud creaking sound caused Dec and I to look up at Mose, who had been knocked off the milk carton by the force of the blast. And he was hanging and swinging round and round with that noose gone tight about his neck.

Dec sprang forward, wrapping his arms around Mose's legs, trying to raise him up so that he could draw a breath. But Mose was a big man, and Dec was struggling to even hold him up. I could see by the look on Mose's face that he was in serious trouble. I don't remember running over to Lawrence sprawled there on his back. Nor do I remember snatching up one of his pistols. But I do know that it took me long, agonizing seconds to cock the pistol, raise it up, and draw a bead on that length of rope tied to the branch of the cottonwood above Mose. My first shot missed. So, too, did my second. The third shot, however, was dead on, slicing through that thick rope and cutting it clean in two. Dec holding Mose up by his legs, grunted as the big black man tumbled down and took them both to the ground. I lowered the pistol and kneeled there, watching Rosie lumber past me and used her trunk to gently touch Mose on his sweat-drenched face. He grimaced a bit, still struggling to breathe. Dec scrambled back to his feet and he hastily freed Mose from that noose and slipped it over his head.

"That," I heard a voice say, "was a fine shot, Jessie."

I looked up to see Lawrence kneeling beside me, struggling to remove a green flak jacket from his upper body. Bits of smoldering metal were still embedded in the fabric of the jacket, and some bits had plastered Lawrence's arms. He grimaced as he withdrew a lock-blade knife from an inside pocket of his jacket. With a flick of his wrist, the blade snapped into place, and with the very tip, Lawrence picked smoldering pieces of metal out of his wounds, flicking them aside with soft curses.

It took him several seconds, and when he finished, he handed Dec the knife and said, "Cut those ropes binding Mose's wrist together."

Tears welled up in his eyes as Dec sawed at the rope tied so tightly around Mose's wrists. Guess he'd nearly been overcome by emotion that we came through the last several minutes alive. I fought back tears of my own as Cooper and Badger came running up from wherever they'd been hiding in the junkyard. Once he freed Mose, Dec dropped the knife and wrapped his arms around Cooper. I did the same to Badger, and for a few moments, we both made over our dogs with an outpouring of love and affection.

Lawrence holstered his pistols, then went to check on Rome sprawled out dead beside his porch. Staring down at him for several moments,

Lawrence silently nodded. He then walked toward the gate of the junkyard to check on Clifford Loyd. But he was no longer there. He had left the yards, leaving a trail of blood behind him.

Lawrence returned to us seated there on Rome's porch on either side of Mose. The dogs planted themselves at our feet, and Rosie stood in front of Mose, touching him with her trunk. Mose gestured at the flak jacket peppered with shrapnel. "Where did you get such a thing?"

"Lidice," Lawrence said. "On July 2nd, 1942, 82 children from Lidice, a small village in Czechoslovakia, were transported to an extermination camp and all 82 of those boys and girls were gassed. 82 children killed because of our attack on Reinhard Heydrich, a high-ranking German officer, regarded as the darkest figure in the Nazi army. Hitler called him the man with the iron heart, who helped organize Kristallnacht, a series of attacks against Jews throughout Germany before the Holocaust. Upon his arrival in Prague, Heydrich eliminated opposition to the Nazis by executing members of the Czech resistance. He started the Einsatzgruppen, the special task forces which murdered 2 million Jews, by mass shooting and gassing. His reign of terror ended in May 27th, 1942, when he was critically wounded in Prague. I was a part of the ambush team sent to kill Heydrich. He died from his injuries a week later. Nazi intelligence falsely linked the assassins to the village of Lidice. The village was razed; all men and boys over the age of 16 were shot, and all but a handful of the women and children were deported and killed in concentration camps.

"I visited the small village, blaming myself for their deaths due to my involvement with killing Heydrich. I took revenge for those children by shooting a Nazi, which is where I got the flak jacket from. I kept it as a keepsake from that horrible war, never knowing I would use it one day here in this shootout at Kowski's junkyard."

Lawrence paused, then said, "Back in 1940, I killed my wife and my daughter. The judge said, either prison or to war. I took the sentence to make sense out of what I did to my Lizzie and April. Because it was on account of that war that I killed them in the first place. During the

Holocaust, it wasn't just the Jews who suffered at the hands at the Nazis. The Gypsies were also persecuted. As early as 1937, Jews and Gypsies became targets for elimination by wandering groups of Einsatzgruppen. In 1941, over 30,000 German gypsies were deported to Poland. 5000 Austrian Gypsies were deported to the Chelmno death camp where they were all gassed. In France, thousands of Gypsies were shipped off to Dachau, Ravensbrück, and Buchenwald.

"500,000 Gypsies were murdered during the Holocaust. They named it the Devouring. It was this Devouring that consumed my wife's every waking moment. My wife was born into the Roma of Blue Springs. Our daughter so greatly resembled her mother, that she identified as Gypsy. My wife got it into her mind that the fate of the Gypsies in Germany would soon be the fate of the Gypsies of America, and rather than let the Nazis send my Lizzie and April to the death camps, I took matters into my own hand and relieved them of any future suffering.

"Most folks think I did the deed out of hatred. But I did the deed of out of love. The irony of it all, the judge sentenced me to the US Army, and the Army sent me to Prague, where I became part of the assassination team to take down Heydrich. And those children of Lidice paid the price for his death."

Chapter Thirty-Eight

Chris Catlin came barreling up Rome's driveway in his beater of a Ford truck. Kat sat on the passenger's side. Both had worried looks on their faces as they surveyed Kowski's junkyard. Chris parked the truck some distance from Rosie so as not to startle her, and before he had turned his engine off, Kat leapt out of the truck cab and came running to check on us. "How did you know," I asked, "we were here, Kat?"

Kat gently reached down, planted a warm hand beneath my chin, lifting it slightly. "You've got a welt on your forehead, Hawk. Sheriff Mac is on his way here. Gracie went and got Richard to pick the lock down at the jail. He managed to set Mac and Noah free. While Mac and Noah loaded their rifles, Chris and I slipped away from the courthouse to come and check on you two. Gracie told us you might be here. If you don't want to get into trouble, Dec, you best hop in the back of Chris's truck. Your dad is coming, and he looked mad as hell."

Dec started to rise, when Mose placed a hand on his knee, keeping him seated on the porch. "Calm yourselves, boys. Sheriff Mac has no reason to be riled at you. When I tell him how things played out here, he's likely to swear you in as deputies. You'd sure as hell make a better one than that knucklehead Ty Burke!"

A lone siren wailed in the distance.

Chris looked over at Rome's dead body, "Mac told us to stay clear of Kowski's. He's gonna be none too happy to see us here, Kat. Although he owes us one. If Richard hadn't taken lock-picking 101, he and Noah would still be locked in the can. Who shot Rome? Lawrence?"

"Of course it was Lawrence," Mose said. "But if not for the quick thinking of these two boys, I would have been hung by that lunatic. Hawk here is a crack-shot. Best shooter in this whole damned county!"

I started to flush red with embarrassment, when Mac came roaring through the gateway of the junkyard in his patrol car. Seated in the backseat, Hiney and Noah scanned the yards warily as Mac brought them skidding to a stop twenty feet from the porch. Mac shut down the engine and jumped out of the car, drawing his pistol. Noah followed behind him, armed with a .12 gauge shotgun. Hiney trailed behind the two, a wooden club in hand.

Mac ran to the dead body of Rome. "Where's Mose?" he hollered, almost in a panic.

"Right here, Sheriff," Mose said, standing up from his place on the porch. "You ran right past me, Sheriff Mac. I am safe and sound thanks to these two boys and the gunslinger there."

Mac retraced his steps, stopping at the porch. "Who shot Rome?"

"Me, Sheriff," Lawrence said. "I shot Loyd, too, just not bad enough."

Mac looked to the three cars that Rosie had bulldozed out of the way. He shook his head in disbelief, saying, "What are you and Hawk doing here, Declan? Do you realize you could have been killed in the hail of bullets that obviously flew around this yard?"

Before Dec could respond, Mose told the whole story, starting from when Rosie shoved the cars aside. He spoke of the gun fight. He talked about the exploding propane tank, and how he was left hanging by the rope. All eyes drifted over to me as he told them all about the shot I took to sever the rope. Mose ended with the part about Lawrence taking the brunt of that exploding tank in the center of his flak jacket. Mac studied the metal shards embedded in the jacket. He turned to Mose as he asked, "Why would Rome want to hang me, Sheriff? What did I ever do to him?"

Mac walked over, examining the abrasions created by the noose around Mose's neck. "It's a long story, Mose. Why don't you take a ride with Noah to the hospital and get that neck looked at? Lawrence, your arms are bleeding, so go along with them, please."

"Okay, Sheriff," Mose said. "But what about Rosie?"

Mac said, "Boys? Take Rosie home to the Hadley place. And then, both of you head for the Hawkins' house. I'll be working on this the rest of the night. Noah, I'll stay here at the crime scene. Give Hiney your shotgun before you leave."

As Noah drove Mose and Lawrence away, Chris followed behind his patrol car in his truck. Kat remained behind, saying, "I'll walk with Rosie and the boys, Mac. Someone needs to keep them out of mischief."

Mac smiled for the first time since entering Kowski's yards. "That might be a tougher task than you think, Katherine. These last few days, my son has a broken compass when it comes to common sense. Hiney? With Loyd and Ty still running loose, would you walk the boys and Rosie home?"

Hiney said, "Since my place be right down the tracks from Hadley's, it would be no bother at all. But, are you going to arrest Lawrence? He killed Rome. We know he needed killing, but . . ."

Shaking his head, Mac said, "How about I talk this over with Judge Neely tomorrow morning? We'll get this sorted in the morning."

We must have looked pretty strange walking down the middle of Elk Street on our way to the rail yards. Dec was seated behind me up on Rosie's neck, Kat and the dogs walked on one side of us, while Hiney walked on the other. The gawkers came out of their houses, having heard the shootout at Kowski's. All of them wanted to know what had happened. Some stood on their front porches, staring at us curiously, while others came out onto their front lawns and warily edged toward the street on account of Rosie. She didn't have a mean bone in her body, but many on-lookers were being as timid as mice around her, keeping their voices low and being sure they didn't make any sudden movements that might startle her. As we passed by Norm Bailey's house, Norm came out to the street and asked, "Was it Ty? Was it Deputy Burke doing all that shooting? I always said he was a bad apple."

I'd forgotten all about Ty running loose around town. It just didn't seem as dangerous now that I had witnessed a real-live shootout before my eyes. But I suppose the loon was at the forefront of every townies mind, beings he had not been arrested yet. "No," I told Norm, "it was Rome Kowski trying to hang Mose Hadley."

Norm looked confused. "Hang him? You mean with a rope?"

"Yes," Dec said, looking down from our high perch on Rosie's neck. "On account that Mose is black. Rome was one prejudiced sum bitch!"

Norm said, "That's on account that Rome's daddy was Klan. All of them Klansmen are riddled with hatred."

Dec glanced back at me, exchanging a curious look. "Klan?" he asked. "Rome was involved with the Klan?"

"Sure was," Norm said. "I know because he tried recruiting me. And you are right, Rome was a prejudiced sum bitch!"

I prodded Rosie with my knees, urging her to keep walking toward home. She picked up the pace, leaving Norm Bailey standing by his mail box, looking relieved that Rosie was moving away from him.

We reached the rail yards without further incident.

Chapter Thirty-Nine

Rosie took us for a wild ride as she ran for her corral to the west of the rail yards. I clung to her collar, and Dec clung to me. The dogs kept up with her, but Kat and Hiney were left in a cloud of dust as Rosie took off for her home. She ran into the enclosure Mose had built for her and stopped in her tracks, throwing Dec and I forward. We clumsily slid down from Rosie's neck. Dec went and closed the gate to her large pen. I removed her collar and rubbed her down with an old blanket. Rosie just stood there, basking in all the attention.

Glancing at Kat and Hiney still some ways down the Hadley's driveway, Dec quietly said, "I'm feeling might ashamed of myself, Hawk. Remember how King Henry said we'd never know who the ghosts were? He let on that my own dad might be inside the circle. I got all bothered by the fact Henry insinuated that there was secret society stuff going on here in town. And Henry planted a bad seed in my head, when he said that my dad actually knew about this gold already. According to Silas Vance, my dad did know about the gold on Rivermoon. Silas offered Mac the position of Sentinel, because Henry had gone off the rails. But, Dad refused the offer. Dad came from Georgia, and if he'd been alive during the Civil War, he and his family would have been Johnny Rebs. Silas wanted to recruit Dad into the Golden Circle. He said Dad was a man of lofty principals who refused to take up the mantle, despite his southern roots. And he wanted Dad to arrest the black man who got Gracie pregnant, but he refused."

I stopped rubbing Rosie and turned to him, saying, "So what? Does that change the way you feel about Mose or Mary Kay?"

"No," Dec said. "I'm not prejudiced. Before I see Mose as a black man, I see him first as just a man, and a good one at that. That's what I'm trying to say. All this time I was so afraid that my dad was involved with these Knights and I was afraid he was a bigot. I was wrong about that. I had nothing to fear. I'm ashamed that I thought so little of my dad, when he definitely stood up to a man like Silas Vance. My dad likes Mose a lot and he would never even consider arresting him for that interracial stuff. He wouldn't harm Mose in any way and the color of his skin don't matter to him. Or me."

Kat and Hiney approached Rosie's pen. "It looks like," Hiney said, "you boys and Rosie be friends. I doubt if anyone else but Mose could have got her to find her way home like you did. That's on account of the baths you give her in the Blue."

"Hoot! Hoot!" exploded into the air and the four of us looked up toward Mose's house, where Oscar sat in his new enclosure.

Dec and Kat ran to his steel pen and greeted the excited chimp. He was glad to see them and patted at their hands as they stuck them through the bars. I bid Rosie good-bye, then climbed over the fence to follow Hiney and the dogs over to Oscar's pen. He was excited to see me, too, and made smacking noises up and down my arm I extended through the bars so that I could hug him. His puckered lips tickled my arm.

"You're such a good boy," I said, rubbing his head.

Oscar puckered his lips at the sight of Hiney. When the big man walked up to the bars of his pen, Oscar latched onto one of Hiney's large hands. He then proceeded to kiss his arm. Hiney laughed, "He sure do like his new home. Mose good to him. Oscar deserves this after being locked in that cage on the side of a tree all these years."

Looking off to the west of the train yards, Kat said, "The sun will be down soon, we best head for your house, Hawk. I don't want to be out after dark with two lunatics running the streets."

Hiney hefted the shotgun over his right shoulder and said, "Any lunatics cross our path, ol' Hiney gonna send them to see Jesus."

By the time Hiney walked us to my house, darkness was falling fast. Dad invited our shotgun-toting escort inside for a cup of coffee, and as they went inside, we heard voices coming from over in the side lot. As we stealthily rounded the corner of my house, we looked to the fire pit beneath our tree fort. A blaze from the crackling fire illuminated the features of Chris and Richard as they carried on a heated argument. Mary Kay sat on a half log to one side of the fire.

Looking to the fire forty-some feet from my house, I was startled when Chris snapped, "What do you mean, it's your baby? How could you both betray me like that? My best friend and my girl friend went behind my back and now Mary Kay is pregnant with your child?"

As we stood there in the shadows, unnoticed by the three over beneath our tree fort, Kat peered hard through the shadows, tears glistening in her dark eyes. "Richard," she whispered, trying not to sob, "is the father of Mary Kay's child? This is going to tear my brother's heart apart."

The three of us stood there in the shadows, quietly listening. Mary Kay tried to comfort Chris by placing a hand on his arm. He pulled away from her and snarled, "Ever heard of the miracles of Richard Hawkins?"

Looking confused, Mary Kay asked, "Miracles?"

"Yes!" Chris said. "Richard claims they were all miracles. Me? I think God was simply looking out for a fool."

He paused then quoted, "'Like snow in summer or rain in harvest, so honor is not fitting for a fool. Like a sparrow in its flitting, like a swallow in its flying, a curse that is causeless does not alight. A whip for the horse, a bridle for the donkey, and a rod for the back of fools. Answer not a fool according to his folly, lest you be like him yourself. Answer a fool according to his folly, lest he be wise in his own eyes.' Proverbs 26:1-28."

He went on then to tell Mary Kay some stories about my brother that I had never heard before. "When he was just 9-years-old, Richard used to go around and steal the milk money of townies. He would set out long before the sun came up, venture up onto the porch of sleeping townies, and empty out their change they'd left in milk bottles for the Milkman to collect. He'd been working the streets up and down Elk and Ella for nearly two solid months, when he reached down to pick up a milk bottle and the porch light snapped on. Richard knocked over the bottle and it broke, scattering change all over the porch at his feet. Despite the fact a grumpy neighbor man had him dead to rights there in the glow of his porch light, Richard heard that money jangling and spotted a shiny silver dollar where that broken bottle had been. He reached down, snatched up that dollar coin piece, and darted past the astonished neighbor man who had tried to catch him.

"Gripping that silver dollar in his tightly clenched fist, Richard ran for another four blocks before coming to a stop to examine his take that morning. He'd gasped in pain and surprise, for in his haste to snag that silver dollar, he'd actually scooped up the entire bottom of that broken milk bottle, and it had left a perfect bloody circle of ragged flesh in the palm of his hand. The miracle according to him was he'd not got caught and despite the deep cut in his palm, he'd come away with a shiny silver dollar as a reward for his efforts.

"When Richard was 16, he got into a fight with his dad over stealing a car, and he ran away from home. He ended up hitch-hiking all the way from Nebraska to Chicago. There, he met the rich daughter of the Elgin Watch people. Her father had founded Elgin Watches and Richard hooked up with the girl, his sights set on all the money that company was worth. He got engaged to her, and in the weeks before their wedding, he met up with some real live thugs. Richard claimed he fell in with the likes of John Dillinger and Baby Face Nelson. Even if it was just a brag on his part, he did commit several jewelry heists by cutting through the roofs of buildings, managing to snag valuable gems and diamonds. When the cops questioned him about such thefts, he made a phone call to some of his high level thugs who got him out of going to the clink. To allow things to cool there in Chicago, Richard took to the back roads between Illinois and Indiana, to burglarize farm houses.

"The second big miracle of his life, according to him, was when he stumbled upon a wake for a military veteran who had died in the Korean war. As the man's family gathered inside the farm house parlor to mourn their loss, Richard broke into the trunk of the dead vet's car and stole his highly decorated uniform. He put it on, and for months, that uniform got him free meals at diners and all the gas he wanted at farm houses along his route.

"Wearing that uniform, he returned to Chicago to marry the Elgin watch girl. And right in the middle of that wedding, Feds came crashing through the church doors to arrest Richard for his previous burglaries. He was also brought up on charges of impersonating a highly-decorated soldier of the US military. He served two years in the Illinois state pen, and at the age of 18, returned to Beatrice. Not at all discouraged by his imprisonment, Richard went down to Marysville one night and stole a combine tractor, worth over ten-thousand dollars. He drove it up country roads and back to Beatrice, where he used a bulldozer to dig a hole big enough to bury that monster machine. He buried it in a farmer's field and this same farmer plowed into the exhaust pipe extending up from the buried combine. Richard was arrested and sat in jail for six months, while the city prosecutor was building a case against him. That was when the third big miracle in his life happened. That city prosecutor became our town's new public defender, and since he knew so much about Richard's case, he had to dismiss it. The stolen tractor case was dismissed and Richard walked free once more."

I felt hot tears in my eyes as Dec and Kat looked sideways at me to check my reaction to Chris's heated words. Kat reached out and patted me on my left cheek. "Chris is just mad," she whispered. "He's making stuff up to make your brother look bad."

I whispered, "You don't hear Richard denying any of it, do you?"

Chapter Forty

Richard simply grinned and said, "Gullible, Chris Catlin, you are so damned gullible. I made all that up, idiot child. Told you those stories to impress you, to make you think I was a big-time thug."

Chris looked at Mary Kay. "Is that what you want for your baby? A thug and a hood for a father? What a bright future you're gonna have."

Mary Kay softly said, "But I love you, Chris. Richard and I made a bad mistake. A terrible mistake. It happened a month after you and I were going together. A month before Richard—"

"And that makes it all right?" Chris asked, rage behind his words.

"No," Mary Kay said. "None of this is all right. He came to me just before being sent away. He was scared and desperate. He was getting sent to the State Home for his fourth time, and this time, someone was going to do something drastic about his behavior."

"Mary?" Richard said. "Enough. Chris doesn't need to know."

"Know what?" Chris snapped. "What don't I need to know?"

Mary Kay said, "It would help him to understand why it happened."

Richard growled, "So you can shame me?"

"There's no shame," Mary Kay said, "in what happened to you. It would make a difference to Chris to know I did not do it out of love, but instead, out of pity for you."

"Pity?" Richard said as he stood there facing them over the fire. "My acting out got me sent out there. The doctors told my mom I had severe behavior disorders. Doctors claimed this is where my rages come from. So, instead of fixing my rages, they fixed me!"

Although still fuming, Chris asked, "Fixed you? How?"

Mary Kay reached out to touch Chris's arm once more to try to calm him. "He knew it was coming. He knew the next time he was sent out there the doctor was going to force him to have the procedure done to him. So he could never—"

"So," Richard spat, "I could never produce a messed up kid like I am! They told me that mom and dad gave them permission, too! But they lied about that. Dad and mom did not know anything about it until it was over. So I was a raging bull of fury and I wanted to prove to everyone that I could still win! Leaving a kid behind was the only way I could do that! So I slept with Mary Kay in defiance of those doctors!"

Chris said, "So, a child is coming into this world, conceived not by love, but by pity and defiance? What a legacy! You gonna tell the kid that one day, Mary? You even gonna tell him who his real father is?"

Mary Kay said, "If you are still willing to take me as your wife, I thought you would be the father, Chris. But if you no longer love—"

"Love you?" Chris said, gritting his teeth. "I can't even trust you! I asked you over and over whose child it was, and you refused to tell me. But to know that my best friend slept with you drives a stake through my heart. Do you know what I should do?"

Richard and Mary Kay looked to him, the blaze from the fire illuminating his tear-streaked face. "I should distance myself from both of you. Never, ever cross your paths again."

Mary Kay pleaded, "Please don't say that, Chris. You know you don't mean that. If you could find it in your heart—"

"To what?" Chris snapped. "Forgive you? Forgive both of you? That is way too much forgiveness to ask of me, don't you think?"

He paused, blew out his breath, and shook back the long strands of his dark hair. "To what end? To go ahead and marry you? And what then? Every time your kid called me, 'Dad,' I would remember exactly who his real dad was. This deed you two did out of defiance and pity, would haunt me the rest of my days. And I've got a word for that, too! It is pathetic!"

Chris tucked his hands into his front pockets and walked off into the darkness, leaving Richard and Mary Kay watching him fade away.

Kat cried as Dec and I guided her around to my back porch. She was shaken up by this turn of events. She loved her brother a lot. She also liked Mary Kay a lot and had looked forward to being an aunt to her baby, but this news rattled her something fierce. When we stepped inside my house, Mom met us at the door, worried that Kat was sobbing. "She fell down," Dec said, sitting Kat down at our kitchen table.

"Oh, dear," Mom said, going to the kitchen sink to wet a wash cloth.

Dad came into the kitchen and retrieved three Kleenix tissues from a box on the counter. He walked over to the table and handed Kat the tissues. "Here, dear," he said, fumbling with them until she took them and blew her nose with one. Mom sat down beside her at the table, handing her the wet wash cloth. "Is it your knee that hurts?" she asked. "Do you want to roll your pant leg up to put this cold cloth on it?"

Kat shook her head. "No, no, that's okay. It just stings a lot."

All of us in the kitchen looked over to our back door as Richard came storming through it. He cut a path through the kitchen, heading down the hall to his room. *Wham!* He slammed his bedroom door closed, leaving Mom and Dad sharing puzzled frowns. "Well," Mom said, shifting her gaze over to me, "what do you suppose that's all about?"

I shrugged. There was no way I was going to be the one to tell them that they were soon to be grandparents to the child Mary Kay was carrying. Especially when my brother would beat the living hell out of me if I spouted off about his indiscretion with Mary Kay.

Time was rolling around to eight o'clock by the time the three of us left my house. Kat had decided to stay the night at Gran B's rather than head for home, where she would certainly run into Chris. She just didn't think she could keep quiet about the conversation we'd heard, and she wanted to give her brother time to think this dilemma through before she discussed any of it with him. Dec and I had just walked her to Gran's front porch when gun shots erupted from somewhere down the street. I immediately thought Chris had retrieved his pistol from Gran B's and was shooting my brother. Then we heard the sounds of thumping feet as someone ran past the house and down the street.

"That was Andy Tate," Kat said.

No sooner had Andy ran off into the shadows then Loyd came running down the street behind him, a smoking pistol clutched in his hand. He glanced over at us kids plastering ourselves against the front of Gran's house, but he kept running, taking another wild shot at Andy even as he ran. "None of our business," Kat said. "Best head inside and not get involved, right, Hawk?"

I turned to face her. "Why look at me? I've got more sense than to run after crazy Clifford Loyd with a gun, don't you think?"

Kat stopped Dec from leaving the porch, placing a hand on his chest. "Remember what Sheriff Mac said about you having a broken compass when it came to using common sense, Dec?"

Dec slowly looked down at her hand in the center of his chest. "And what? You're gonna become like Jiminy Cricket in those Disney films we see at school and become my conscious, singing, 'I'm no fool, no siree, I'm gonna live to be ninety-three?'"

Kat nodded. "Someone has to watch over you here lately."

I said, "Yeah, Dec, let's just go inside and tell Gran B the news about Mary Kay. Maybe she can be a peace-maker for all three of them.

"Yes," Dec said, "maybe. But Loyd and Tate are running toward the courthouse. What if they end up at my dad's office?"

Lightly shoving Kat's hand away from his chest, Dec took off running off the porch and down the street. Kat and I watched him slipping away fast into the darkness. I did an eye-roll and said, "So much for common sense, right?"

And as she fell in beside me to follow Dec down the street, she muttered, "Damn that kid!"

Chapter Forty-One

The three of us were winded by the time we reached the courthouse. Dec latched onto the flag pole to keep from falling down. Kat plopped herself down on the single wooden bench beside the sidewalk running up to the building, and I skidded to a stop on my knees, sliding five more feet in the slick grass.

All three of us froze when we saw Andy Tate standing at the main entrance doors, his hands in the air and pleading with Loyd not to shoot him. Loyd, his arm in a sling due to Lawrence's bullet he'd put in him earlier, pointed his gun in Andy's face.

"We can work this out," Andy said, "we don't have to go down for this, Clifford. There's a clear way out of this."

"No, there's not!" Loyd cried, placing the muzzle of his gun inches from Andy's face. "Rome removed that from the board. You were there that night, Tate. It was your idea. Your show."

Andy kept his hands above his head. "No one needs to know about any of that, Cliff. Rome is dead. We can lay the entire blame on him. Besides, it was him going psycho that sent this whole thing crashing off a cliff! If we stick to that story, Mac will not be able to place us at the scene of the murder. We will be free and clear. It was Rome who did the killing. It was Rome going crazy with the knife, not you or me."

Loyd cocked his pistol. "Inside, now!" he snarled.

Andy lowered his hands and turned to open the courthouse door. He stepped inside and Loyd followed behind him.

Still breathing heavily, Dec said, "Let's get to the catwalk!"

Kat and I reluctantly followed him over to the fire escape steps leading to the third floor of the courthouse. Dec had the window open before we reached the tops of the stairs, and he ushered us inside. Stealthily and quiet as nimble cats, we crawled out onto the catwalk overlooking the sheriff's office thirty-some feet below us.

Mac stood at his desk. Noah sat at his desk beside Mac's. Both were focused on Loyd and Andy standing on the other side of the counter.

Loyd trained his gun on Mose who appeared to have just walked into the reception area. "Mose," he ordered, "step around the counter with Mac and Noah. I've seen you go to town with those fists and I don't aim to get clobbered. Do as I say and I won't have to shoot you."

As Mose complied with his order, Mac said, "Cliff, you know you're bleeding, right? Let's get you over to the hospital."

"I'm okay, Mac," Loyd said, turning the gun back on Andy. "Lawrence shot me clean through my shoulder. I'm bleeding like a stuck pig, but I am on a mission here, it can't wait for no bullet hole to be plugged. I expect you know why Tate and I are here, right?"

Mac kept his arms folded before his chest. Although his pistol was holstered six inches from his hand, he really had no chance of drawing it with Loyd waving that pistol around. Noah, seated at his desk, was at more of a disadvantage, seeing that he would be fit to be tied to even get to his own gun. Loyd had both lawmen over a barrel.

"Tell them, Andy," Loyd said. "Tell them what happened that night back in 56. Tell them how it was your plan."

Andy stood there, clearly shaken by having that gun waved in his face. He looked worried, too, as if he knew how far Loyd had come unhinged. He just stood there, shaking his head and not saying anything.

Loyd was becoming increasingly more angry. "It was on account of what was done to us out there at the State Home, Mac. Do you know what Doc London did to us as boys?"

Mac said, "Yes, Cliff, I do. It was a terrible thing that happened to you. It was a tragic event. But the bigger tragedy was what happened to London's little girls who had nothing to do with what he did to you."

"It was Andy's idea," Loyd said. "Andy put the seed in our heads. It was Andy who stole those rare books. Tell them, Andy. Tell them how you whisked that box of manuscripts out of there. Rome took that prized dog. Only he didn't keep him, he sold him to breed more dogs with the bloodline of Bear. Tell them how we only meant to hurt the Doc, not his family. Tell them how crazy Rome went with that knife. And then there was blood, Sheriff Mac, lots and lots of blood."

Mac glanced over at Noah. They both looked at Mose as he said, "I assume you're talking of the London murder, Cliff, but what does any of that have to do with me? Why did Rome want to hang me?"

Loyd's gaze flickered over the counter to Mose. "Rome was Klan, Mose. He's had it in for you ever since you got Grace Long Soldier with child. That is a disgusting notion. You left Mary Kay without and a good and proper father all these years. Silas Vance ordered Rome to tie up that loose end. Hanging you was how he chose to end your sin. How to rectify an interracial relationship that was wrong from the get go. We can't abide blacks and whites coming together like that."

Despite the fact Loyd had a gun, Mose said, "Who died and made you God? What gives any man the right to judge Gracie and I for what we once had. Or didn't you think a black man could love, too? I would have married her back then, but too many people in this town wouldn't have understood that. So, I broke off my ties with Gracie, and yet I always stayed in touch with Mary Kay. She's a sweet girl and did not deserve to be abandoned by her father."

Loyd scoffed, "Still a sin, in my eyes. And so is what we done in 1956. Tate? You gonna admit your guilt?"

Andy lowered his hands and simply refused to meet Loyd's angry glare. "I'll take that as a no," Loyd said. He then spoke to Mac, saying, "The three of us, Rome, Andy, and me got to drinking one night. It was a winter night and we had to plow through deep snow to get to the London farmhouse. We'd been talking about the procedure Doc had performed on us. We were mad as hell about it. Andy just wanted to rob him of those rare books he was producing. Rome wanted to steal his prized dog. We all three thought that would be enough for the revenge we wanted to take on him. We never even mentioned his wife and daughters as we trudged through the snow up to his place.

"Once we broke into the farmhouse, Doc picked up an iron poker from the fireplace and he hit Rome in the head with it. Next thing you know, Rome pulled out a large hunting knife, and he began stabbing. He first drove his knife into Doc's chest. He then turned on Doc's wife, stabbing her, too. I admit Andy moved between Rome and those little girls out there, trying to cool him down some, but Rome was like a madman. He even slashed at Andy, forcing him to back off. He then stabbed those girls. All four of the London family was dead within the first two minutes of Rome's brutal and savage attack.

"Andy and I were shaken by Rome coming unhinged. While he went outside to the kennel to retrieve that dog, Andy packed those rare manuscripts into a wood box from beside the fireplace, and had me help him carry them to our car down the driveway by the road. We talked about turning Rome in for the bloody murders he committed, but Andy said we would be considered accessories since we went out there seeking revenge. So, we drove back to town and acted shocked like every one else when someone discovered the bodies and reported it the police. Rome took the dog down to Marysville, where he had it breed with another papered Staffordshire, and he ended up with several of Bear's pups, without no one being the wiser what happened to the dead doctor's prized dog. Andy kept those manuscripts. Get you a search warrant, Sheriff Mac. See if I ain't been telling it true."

Andy looked up at Mac, saying, "You will need probable cause to do that, Mac. You know that, don't you?"

Loyd snapped, "I just gave him probable cause by my confession."

"Oh," Andy said, "a crazed man holding the Sheriff and his deputy at gun point? That won't stand up in court. Anything Mac found in my house would be inadmissible in a courtroom. Besides, Judge Neely wouldn't grant a search warrant on that flimsy story of yours, Clifford. Your story is a lie. I had nothing to do with the London murder. I have not even associated with you or Rome for the past seven years. If Rome murdered the doctor and his family, he's dead. It is a closed case."

It was the wrong thing for Andy to say. I was surprised with Loyd holding a gun on him that he would be that stupid. He should have just played along until Loyd put that gun away. His talk about probable cause for a search warrant was not what Loyd wanted to hear. He lost it then. Swinging the gun up and over his head, he brought it crashing down on Andy's head, dropping him to the floor. Taking the pistol in a two-handed grip, Loyd pointed it down at Andy and was just using one thumb to cock it, when Sheriff Mac did something incredible.

Mac was fast, too. He looked like one of those quick-draw gunslingers of the Old West. He drew his pistol with greased lightning speed and fired. The bullet was dead on, too, for it passed through Loyd's two hands and shattered the butt he grasped. He cried out in pain, dropping the pistol and wringing his hands. Blood splattered everywhere in the reception area. On the counter. On the walls. All over Andy sprawled before the counter on the floor.

Mac then leaped over the counter and took Loyd out with one solid punch to his nose. And then, there was more blood. I started to feel woozy, and rather than pass out there on the catwalk and fall through thirty feet of space to land smack dab in the middle of the sheriff's office, I crawled my way back and off the catwalk.

Dec and Kat wormed their way behind me, and we exited the courthouse's third floor by going back down the fire escape.

Chapter Forty-Two

Dec talked about those manuscripts all the way back over to Gran B's house. He said, "To heck with search warrants. Let's just sneak into Andy's house, locate that box of manuscripts, and turn them over to my dad. You with me, Hawk?"

I shrugged, still feeling lightheaded from all the bright red blood I'd seen below me in the reception area.

Kat said, "Don't be stupid, Declan. You could interfere in your dad's investigation, and if you removed those scripts from Andy's house, you could get that evidence against him thrown out of court. Do you really want Andy to get by with murder?"

Dec replied, "Of course not, but these laws are stupid. Loyd confessed to the murder, telling Dad that he, Rome, and Andy were all involved in it. If we could whisk those manuscripts out of his house, that would be proof that Andy did steal them when those murders took place."

Kat said, "You really do have something wrong with your compass."

Dec and Kat argued about it all the way up to Gran B's front door. Miffed at Dec, Kat went inside, slamming the screen door behind her.

Dec turned to me. "Come on, Hawk. Let's go investigate. Andy will more than likely be hospitalized over night. His house is sitting there empty. We would get in and out without anyone knowing."

I said, "So, what if we did find those manuscripts in his house? Kat is right. We could get that valuable piece of evidence thrown out of court. What else would Mac have to tie Andy to the murder?"

He thought about that for maybe a minute before saying, "Okay, I won't cart them out of there, just prove that Andy has them."

"And what?" I asked. "Go and tell your dad that we broke into Andy's house? Tell him we saw them with our own eyes?"

Dec wheeled around on me, saying, "Are you chicken?"

"I'd rather be chicken," I said, "than a dead duck!"

We argued heatedly about it for a good thirty minutes. In the end, I agreed to go with him up to the back of Andy's house. He would sneak inside, while I stayed outside. I figured he was right about Andy staying the night at the hospital. Loyd had hit him pretty hard with that gun, and he was knocked out cold when we crab-crawled our way off of that catwalk. So the chances of Dec getting caught inside was slim. Even if Mac did get Judge Neely to grant him a search warrant, it would not be that quick. Certainly not this late at night. So the chances of Mac catching his son sneaking about inside Andy's house were slim as well.

The house was dark when we got to it over on Lincoln Street. Both front and back doors were locked, too. So were three of its windows. The fourth one we checked was slightly ajar, so Dec had me boost him up on the backside of the house to open the window.

He slipped inside within seconds, leaving me standing there sweating and fidgeting something fierce. As I craned my neck nearly out of place, looking this way and that for any nosey neighbors, I spied a step ladder leaning against the house. I decided to make Dec's exit from his investigative excursion a little easier by placing that step ladder beneath the window so he could more easily climb down when he came back out.

Five entire minutes passed. I paced back and forth below that window, my eyes shifting about in every direction. I must have looked like a wild-eyed Cheshire Cat as I searched the darkness for any sign we were about to be caught out.

Finally, my nerves got the better of me. "Dec?" I whispered.

I then climbed up the step ladder so I could see inside the window. "Dec? Come on, you've been in there long enough! Let's go!"

I squinted into the shadowy room and saw that it was a bedroom with a door thirty feet in front of me that led to a dark hallway. And then, I saw movement. Some one big and dark moved past the open door. It was way too big to be Dec. My heart nearly exploded when the large, dark figure moved back in front of the open door to the hallway, and gave me a wicked grin. Big Ty was in there with Dec.

I fell back and off the ladder, frantically thinking of what I should do. At first, I thought about running around to the front of the house, banging on the front door, and making a racket to hopefully not only alert Dec inside, but also to wake the neighbors. My eyes darted up to the open window, then over to the backdoor. That's when I saw a long-handled ax among other garden tools situated next to the house. But I actually shuddered when I imagined me having to deal a chopping blow to Ty in order to save Dec. I wasn't cut out for this kind of stuff. But I had to get Dec out of that house, and so I snatched up the ax.

Climbing up the ladder, I slipped inside Andy's house and into his bedroom, carrying the ax with me. It was pitch dark in there and I could barely see my way into the hallway, but then I heard voices coming from the end of the hallway in what must have been Andy's livingroom.

I heard Big Ty snicker and say, "Caught me a burglar, I did. What you doing snooping about Andy Tate's house, Declan Connors?"

Dec sounded scared as he said, "Solving a murder, Deputy Burke. See all this paperwork? These are manuscripts that Andy stole from Doctor London when Rome Kowski killed him and his family. Do you wanna be a hero? Get Sheriff Mac to take you back as his deputy?"

"Too late!" snapped Ty. "I've gone too far off the rails for that, kid!"

Dec asked, "You been hiding out here at Andy's all this time?"

Big Ty laughed wickedly. "Yep, been right under Mac's nose, not four blocks away from the courthouse. I've got plans, and they certainly don't include you. The Sheriff is gonna find his son dead, but I'll be long gone from here by then. Do you understand what I am saying? No hard feelings, but see that gold bar? Yep, that one on the mantle. I'm cashing that in to make good on my escape."

Dec managed to say, "This is one of those bars you stole from Robber's Cave? This is what you carted out of Jon Kennedy's car out at Catlin's, right?"

Ty laughed again. "Too bad you ain't ever gonna grow up. You would make a good detective, Declan. Maybe a better lawman than your self-righteous dad. But we'll never know now, will we?"

Dec said, "I swear I won't tell on you until your long gone from town. You just let me go and I will not say anything to anyone until you take that gold bar on down the highway. Sound like a plan, Ty?"

Ty growled, "Sounds like a load of BS to me. You're too much like your dad, always gotta be doing the right thing. Unlike me, your moral compass is fairly sound. That's why you gotta die."

By then, I had crept down the hallway and stood looking at both of them standing in front of Andy's fireplace. Neither of them had turned on any lights, so it was still shadowy and dark, which is why Ty did not see me. Dec did, however, and he took that moment to run. Wheeling around, he started for the front door. Ty was on him in a second, latching onto his arms and pinning him to the wall in front of them. Dec squirmed and fought to break free, but Ty was fiercely strong and held him firmly.

As I crossed the room, I had the sudden vision of Linus Rawlins in *How the West was Won* movie. Linus, played by Jimmy Stewart, was waylaid by some low-bred mountain men who stole his furs and threw him in a deep, dark cave to get rid of him. Only thing is, Jimmy Stewart survived and started his epic fight with those bad guys by throwing an ax and sticking it one guy's back. He finished the fight with them and in the end he got his furs back.

Before Ty heard me coming, I thought I had better toss that ax and bury it in his back. But just as I swung it up and over my head, to prepare for the throw, I cringed when I thought of how much damage that sharp ax would do to Ty. As much as I hated him, I could not bring myself to bury that ax in him. Instead, I twisted the ax around in my grasp and swung the back end of it at the back of Ty's head. Desperate to save Dec, I whacked him good, too. Ty let go of Dec, spun around toward me. He dropped to the floor on his knees, wobbled about for a second, then fell forward onto his face and chest. I dropped the ax.

Dec swallowed hard and said, "Look at what I found, Hawk. It is more than enough proof that Andy was involved in that murder."

He skirted around Ty's prone body and led me over to an alcove beside the fireplace. There inside a wooden box were a stack of papers, aged and yellowed by the years since they'd been typed upon. Dec said, "They are all there, too, just like Ghost mentioned, with the names of a bunch of authors like JRR Tolkien, Edgar Rice Burroughs, and even

Mark Twain. If Mac got these, he would have Andy dead to rights with enough evidence to convict him."

I was sweating and fidgeting quite a bit by then, and as I glanced back at Ty lying still on the floor, I said, "We can't take them, Dec."

Dec said, "Look at these photos and the papers that go with them. This proves Loyd's story about Doc London's prized dog was true."

I peered down at the stack of photos he spread on an end table beside the fireplace. My heart skipped a beat as I saw Badger, my own dog staring back at me in three of those photos. "It's Badger!" I said.

"No," Dec said. "It's Badger's sire. It looks just like him because this dog, Bear, is his dad! This paperwork proves his pure bloodline. You heard Ty say that Badger was a papered dog that day he took him over to Rome's place. Remember?"

"Leave them, Dec," I said. "We would be messing with evidence."

Dec stood there fuming and simmering, but he did not move to scoop up the photos or the papers. "Okay," Dec said. "I'll leave all this evidence behind, but I am taking that with us. We're gonna be rich!"

With that, he rushed to the fireplace, and with some effort, lifted the foot-long bar of what I assumed was pure gold. "Don't even bother to stop me, Hawk. We've got as much right to this as Ty. Remember what he said out to Catlins? Finders keepers, losers weepers!"

Taking one last look at Ty still unconscious on the floor, I followed Dec out through the back door. He was moving way too slow for my likes. I wanted him to just drop that heavy gold bar so we could both run far away from Andy's darkened house.

We made it to Andy's back alley, when we ran directly into a tall, dark figure who emerged from the cedar trees to one side of the alleyway.

Chapter Forty-Three

Ghost Running Thunder stood directly in our path. I dodged to one side. Dec, however, ran directly into his outstretched hands. He was so startled he let go of the gold bar as Ghost removed it from his grasp. Dec said, "That's ours, Ghost! But we found enough inside Andy's house to solve that murder you're investigating! So, let us have that gold, and we'll let you in on what we found! Deal?"

Shaking his head, Ghost lifted the bar out of Dec's grasping hands. "I don't make deals with burglars."

"All we were doing," Dec argued, "was snooping!"

Ghost raised the gold bar and rested one end of it on his shoulder. He studied the open window in Andy's house. I explained what had happened since he left town. I told him about the shootout between Rome and Lawrence, about Mose getting hung, and about Rosie bulldozing those cars out of the way. I then told him about Loyd forcing Andy into the sheriff's office at gunpoint, and about Loyd's confession. I told him about what we'd found in Andy's house. I also included that Ty had been hiding out in there all this time, and how I had thumped him with the ax. Dec pointed at the gold bar and said, "So, by all rights, that should be ours. How about we split it with you? Like seventy/thirty, with us getting the lion's share? Deal?"

"No deal," Ghost said. "Kat?"

Dec and I both looked to the row of fir trees as Kat silently slipped out between them. "She told me where I'd find you," Ghost told us. "She was pretty worried about you, saying you'd both lost your marbles by wanting to break into Andy Tate's house."

I smiled at her to let her know I wasn't mad at her for snitching on us, but Dec snorted, "When we split this gold, you're not getting a cent!"

"Quiet down," Ghost said. "I'm walking you boys home, then I've got to find a way to get a warrant to get inside that house, before someone whisks that stuff away. Now, march! While I come up with a workable plan. I don't want any of that evidence to vanish."

When we got back to my house, Ghost walked directly toward our tree fort. He gestured at the boards nailed to the side of our old oak tree. "Climb up and open that door, Declan."

"What for?" Dec asked, still peeved at him for taking that gold bar away from him. Ghost said, "You're wasting time. Make like a monkey and climb up there and open the door."

Muttering under his breath, Dec climbed the seven boards leading up to the door of our tree fort. The big Lakota climbed halfway up the boards behind him, and shoved that gold bar inside the open doorway. He leaped back down, gesturing for Dec to join us near the smoldering fire pit. Dec closed the door and nimbly climbed down to join us.

"I'll work a deal," Ghost said, "if you boys will promise to leave that gold alone for right now, I'll work out a finder's fee for you. But right now, I'm going to ask you to return to your homes and stay put."

Dec asked, "How much of a finder's fee? And what about all that stuff we found in Tate's house? What about Big Ty?"

Ghost snapped his fingers and pointed up at my house. "Go. Now. I'll deal with this my way. The less you know, the better."

Of course, we didn't stay put as Ghost had ordered us to do, for even Kat was curious when we told her what we had found inside of Andy's house. The three of us stuck to the shadows, and followed behind Ghost as he ran down the street some distance ahead of us.

As it happened, three Vandals came roaring up the street ahead of him and he skidded to a stop as they closed with him. We sidled up to a copse of cedars to watch them from about a hundred feet away. We couldn't hear what Ghost told them, but he was waving his hands around and seemed pretty determined to get them to do whatever he wanted them to. The second, they wheeled their bikes around and headed south, Ghost took off again, running toward the courthouse. Dec and Kat would have followed behind him, but I stopped them by saying, "We know where this is gonna end up at, so let's head over to Andy's!"

"Good idea, Hawk!" Kat gasped, out of breath from running.

So we made a B-line over to Lincoln Street and as we came to the alley behind Andy's house, we slid in between a copse of fir trees, and hunkered down with a good view of the back of Andy's dark house. Seconds later, the three Vandals pulled into the alley nearly thirty feet from us and shut down their Harleys. Two of the burly, shaggy-haired bikers ran to the back of the house and used the step ladder still leaning against it to climb in the window. The third guy stayed behind, smoking a cigarette and pacing back and forth beside the three bikes.

Long moments passed and we stood there peeking out between the thick branches to see Sheriff Mac and Noah pull up in their cruisers. They parked some distance down the alley. Noah climbed out and approached the Vandal beside the three Harleys. Mac walked directly to a large oak tree in the middle of Andy's backyard and there he stood, waiting and watching the back of the house.

"Thought I told you to stay put," Ghost whispered as he merged with the branches of the fir trees, slipping in behind us silently and without being seen by Noah or Mac. Kat looked sideways at him and Ghost whispered, "No need for a search warrant, when there is a burglary in progress. No time to get one either, so I did the next best thing. I sent those Vandals inside to deal with Ty and those manuscripts, then sent the Sheriff to arrest them when they come back out."

He gestured up toward that open back window as one of the bikers climbed out, using the step ladder to reach the ground. The big brute turned around then, and took the large wooden box the other biker handed him through the open window. Sheriff Mac approached the two bikers with his gun drawn. Next thing we knew Mac and Noah had their handcuffs out and they arrested the two Vandals who had entered into Andy's house. Noah led them over to his patrol car, while Mac kneeled down beside the box they had carried out of the house to examine its contents.

The three of us waited with Ghost, keenly watching Mac and Noah drive away. We waited several more minutes until that third Vandal kicked his Harley to life and rode away before emerging from those trees. "I'd like to be a mouse in the corner," Ghost said, "when Andy tries to explain his way out of this. Mac's gonna hit him with those stolen manuscripts, and Andy will have no room to wriggle out. You'll get no thanks for helping to solve this case as no one but me will know what you discovered by sneaking into that house. But I will remember what you did in the days ahead, and I will owe you one."

Ghost grinned. "There is still one bar of that gold still missing. If you want Silas Vance and his goons to leave your town, he won't do it until he has that last bar of gold. Any idea where it might be?"

Kat shrugged and said, "Mary Kay might know. She was involved in that whole twisted mess with Loyd, Big Ty, and that Kennedy fellow who abducted her."

And I just stood there, failing to meet Ghost's intense gaze as I recalled something that Loyd had said to Ty back when we were hiding in that bathroom at the hospital: *"These guys have been sent to deal with anyone who confiscated hidden gold caches. They've got a large network. Find out who got Mary Kay pregnant and you'll know who has that second stolen bar of gold."*

And I dreaded knowing that fact, for that meant I would have to confront my brother and convince him to cough up that last stolen bar of gold, without letting him know that I knew he was the father of Mary Kay's soon-to-be-born baby.

As Ghost walked us back to Gran B's place, he constantly searched the darkness around us, looking into shadows, peering in between houses, scanning the streets behind and before us. Once we reached Gran's front porch, he said, "Only thing that didn't work out so well is the arrest of that Deputy Burke. I assumed that when the Vandals entered Tate's house, there would be a confrontation. But evidently, Tyler must have left before they arrived. He's a loose cannon and one you kids best avoid."

Ghost then slipped away off the porch and as he faded into the darkness he called back, "Watch your topknot."

Dec laughed and responded, "Yep, and watch yourn!"

Chapter Forty-Four

Three days later, I worked up the nerve to confront Richard about that one last bar of gold. I begged Dec to come with, and though he was scared of my brother's fierce temper, he and our two dogs joined me as I entered my brother's bedroom. Richard sat there at his desk, working on a model airplane. He barely spared us a glance as he used a tube of glue to attach a wing to a bomber jet. "It's Curly and Moe," he said. "So where's Stooge number three?"

And that's when our front door bell rang.

A second later, we heard Noah talking to Mom: "A string of burglaries of weather vanes stolen from more than a dozen barns. We found them hidden in your husband's work shop. It sounds like a petty crime, but Mac had so many complaints from so many farmers, we had to pursue this. Is Richard home?"

The moment he said my brother's name, Richard opened his window and dove through the opening. Sheriff Mac was standing there at the back of our house waiting for him. Mac cuffed his hands behind his back and carted him away in his patrol car. Deeply disappointed that my brother had gotten himself in trouble again, I followed Dec and the dogs out to our fire pit beneath our tree fort.

While I sat on a half-log with Badger and Cooper on either side of me, Dec clambered up into our fort to see if Ghost had left that bar of gold up there. "It's gone," Dec muttered, sullenly. "So much for a finder's fee, even though we helped him solve those murders."

Squinting with the late afternoon sun shining in his eyes, he slammed the door to our fort closed and joined me beside the fire pit. Badger and Cooper let out soft growls as a black Cadillac parked in the street in front of my house. Silas Vance climbed out the car. We sat there watching the bear in his suit ambling over to our fire pit. "Afternoon, boys. I'd like to have a word with you two, if you don't object."

Of course, I wanted to object because I knew he'd been involved in Rome hanging Mose. I tried to muster up a mean look as Silas went through the motions of packing the bowl of his pipe with sweet-smelling *Captain Black*. When he finished, he struck a match and puffed on his long-stemmed pipe, blowing blue-gray smoke into the afternoon air. "Did you know your friend, Agent Running Thunder was the catalyst that stirred this whole thing up?"

"Not our friend," Dec said, still mad at Ghost for taking that gold.

Silas said, "When he came to town to do his snooping, the moment he put the word out that he had an interest in rare books, the London murder was destined to be solved. Roman, Loyd, and Andy started to react in light of the investigation Ghost opened up. Remember when Roman tried to drown those pups in the river? He was getting rid of the evidence that he'd stolen their sire. He was just getting ready to shoot their mama dog, too, when some biker club known as the Nine Poor Knights showed up here, asking about the Staffordshire. Any dog born from that mating is special. Even that one you got right there. Care to sell him to me, Jess Hawkins? I'll pay a pretty penny for him."

Dec blurted, "So, what? You can throw him into a dog fight?"

Silas took a long drag on his pipe. Blowing out three perfect smoke rings, he said, "No, I love my dogs. I have a whole collection of pure bred terriers at my ranch down south. I raise award-winning dogs to compete in competitions, no fighting involved."

I said, "Badger ain't for sale, Mr. Vance."

Silas said, "Okay, now as to my second reason for this meeting. Lots of chaos got stirred up by flushing that murderous trio out of their dens. Roman dead. Loyd and Andy Tate will be going to prison for being accessories to the London murder. Those manuscripts discovered will seal that deal as far as Judge Neely is concerned. The trial will go much more smoothly if the sheriff gets that file back. That file should be snuck back into that evidence room. ASAP."

I worked up the nerve to say, "How come a man like you loves dogs, but so bitterly hates a man like Mose?"

Silas gruffly said, "Ever read your Bible? Why, right there as bold as can be, Saint Paul wrote, *'Slaves obey your masters.'* The Union folk ignored that when they fought the Confederates during the Civil War. God made a lesser race to ours to serve us. The negroes—"

"We know," Dec said, "that Mose Hadley is a good man. Mose once boxed in the Olympics and won a lot of medals."

Silas said, "Yes, some blacks are of a violent nature. Our prisons are full of them darkies who just can't function in our society because of their savage nature. And then, to top it off, they lie with our women! The last thing we need is them to breed with our own and produce more little black rascals—"

"Mary Kay," I said, "is one of those rascals, Mr. Vance. She is the sweetest girl we know. It didn't go against her to have Mose for a father."

"Oh," Silas said, "she not only stole a bar of gold that doesn't belong to her, just like her mama, she got herself pregnant. Mark my words, boys, she's got a Bad Seed in her, just like her father."

I could tell Silas wasn't aware that it was my brother that got Mary Kay pregnant. It was on the tip of my tongue to rub it in his face how Richard had hidden that second gold bar so well that no one would find it until he was released from the State Home. But I didn't, for fear it would incriminate my brother.

Silas said, "Sons of Liberty have removed all that gold from Rivermoon. It will be put to use in good causes, namely several Children's hospitals scattered throughout these United States. Why, never let it be said that the Golden Circle has truly died."

He reached into his jacket and pulled out a small leather pouch. He tossed it over our fire pit. I caught it in both hands. "Agent Running Thunder allowed me to borrow those with the firm promise I would return them to you when I was finished using them, Jess."

I opened it and dumped the three bronze arrowheads out into my hand. I was a little surprised that Ghost had given them to Silas to open that vault and retrieve all that gold, but then I remembered Ghost saying Silas and his crew wouldn't leave town until they recovered their gold.

Silas said, "There's one more gold bar that I'll need and then you boys will never see me in this town again."

I looked into Silas's eyes. "You'll be here until Jesus comes back if you stay to try and find that last gold bar."

Silas laughed at this. "Yes, you're probably right."

He stood then and Badger and Cooper watched him warily as the big man walked down my front walk to his car parked in the street. I then bluntly asked, "Do you ever think your heart might change?"

He gave me a puzzled frown and said, "What's wrong with my heart?"

I said, "You belittle a man like Mose because of the color of his skin. You quote scripture to make yourself sound right. You claim Mose planted a Bad Seed when he got Gracie with child, and yet you don't even know that you got a sickness yourself. No offense, Mr. Vance, but you are really nothing more than a racist bastard."

Silas stood there chuckling, "Why, yes I am."

Silas Vance climbed into his car and we could hear him still laughing as he drove away down the street, hopefully leaving our town for good.

Two days later, when I figured Richard wasn't getting out of the State Home anytime soon, I talked Dec and Kat into confronting Mary Kay about where he might have hidden that last bar of gold. I figured she would be the least likely person to blow a gasket if we asked her nicely. On the walk over to the Long Soldier's house, Kat talked about the upcoming court hearing regarding the London murders.

Andy had posted bail and was free until the trial, but Loyd was still locked up. The talk of the town and the gossip to spread like wildfire was the reason three members of our community took revenge on Doctor London in the first place. With over 900 sterilizations there in the State Home, most residents were outraged that so many had been subjected to the procedure and the Beatrice Sun newspaper was filled with articles about sterilization to correct behavioral issues in troubled mental patients. The story got national attention because a lot of doctors had written open letters into Public Mind, expressing their opinions about the subject. Many were especially interested in attending the trial.

It was a hot topic at my house, because Dad and Mom were still livid that the State Home had taken it upon itself to sterilize my brother. They had tried to sue them once, but when the lawyer demanded more to take it to trial what was done to my brother was forgotten as time passed.

It was sunny and warm that day as the three of us approached the Long Soldier house. Kat was telling about the large enclosure that Mose had built in the garden behind Gracie's house. It was made with chicken wire and took up the entire sunken garden connected by the walkway attached to Gracie's back door. Mose had built it so that Bandit and Miracle could roam all over the backyard. The moment we started up the front walk to Mary Kay's house, Gracie opened the front door, gesturing at us to join her inside. "Shh!" she whispered. "If all goes well, Chris and Mary Kay are going to reunite. Your brother, Kat, is such a good boy, and Mary Kay's baby is going to need a father."

It stung me a little, because I figured Gracie knew who the real father happened to be, and although she was speaking so highly of Chris Catlin, what she wasn't saying about my brother made me feel sort of bad inside. But she was right, Chris would make a good father, while the real father was locked up for stealing dozens of weathervanes off the barns of local farmers. And he wasn't going to change anytime soon.

Gracie led the three of us to her kitchen window overlooking her backyard garden. It was a large area, surrounded by a thick stone wall that ran in a circular shape forty feet to the alleyway. Some twenty feet from the window Chris and Mary Kay sat on a bench inside a gazebo laced with vines and bushes. They sat far apart on the bench with Bandit and Miracle planted between them.

"Sweet Sleeping Jesus!" Gracie whispered as Miracle placed her front paws against Chris's chest. A green glow emanated from her tiny fingers. The emerald traces of light formed a web work pattern across Chris's chest. Bandit held up his paws, aglow with a deep shade of blue. The luminous glow slipped out through his fingertips and both threads of blue and green lines blended together and changed to a violet shade that burst quite suddenly, causing Chris to silently weep.

Mary Kay reached over the heads of the two monkeys, gently running her fingers through the tears streaming down Chris's cheeks. "Let what was broken," she said, her words drifting through the open window in front of us, "now be healed. Allow your broken heart to be mended. Let our love for each other strengthen us both as we weather this storm."

Bandit crawled up to Chris's left shoulder. Miracle dropped to the floor of the gazebo. The little white-faced monkey peered up at the house, placing one finger against her lips, gesturing to the four of us to not whisper a word about what we had just witnessed.

Inside the kitchen, Dec asked, "Did she do that for us?"

Gracie nodded. "Yes, there is something special about those two little creatures. Something happened to them while being confined out on Rivermoon. They both have some mysterious power to heal hurt and pain. Mary Kay is making plans to take them to the Children's ward at the hospital to see if those two might heal sick children. Such mo jo allows them to use their powers for the greater good."

In the coming days, as Spring rolled in, Kat told Dec and I that Chris and Mary Kay were planning to be married near the Fourth of July. As a gesture of good will toward my brother, Chris had asked him to be his best man at the wedding. According to Kat, Chris had gone out to the State Home to visit my brother. Although I would have liked to have been a mouse in the corner, listening to that conversation, I would never know what was said on the matter. Somehow, Chris Catlin showed his true nature and made peace with Richard.

When Kat told us the story, Dec said, "That would be too weird for me. Standing in front of a church full of people, pretending everything was okay between the three of them. Mary Kay cheated on Chris. Richard betrayed his best friend. And poor Chris, dumb fool that he is, forgave both of them. Wonder what he'll tell the kid one day?"

Quicker than Jack the Bear, Kat shoved Dec up against the oak tree beneath our tree fort. She doubled up her fist, raising it even with his face. "My brother is no fool, Declan! He's got more heart than you'll ever have! Thanks to whatever those two monkeys did to him, Chris was able to move past this. He forgives because he refuses to harbor anger and bitterness. He and Mary Kay are going to have a long, good life together. Just be happy for them! Besides, I am going to be an aunt and Hawk is going to be an uncle."

Chapter Forty-Five

In the month before school let out for summer vacation in May, by then, no one in town talked anymore about the shooting. No one mentioned Mary Kay's abduction nor the stealing of that gold from Robber's Cave. That subject just faded away and became a thing of the past. The new talk in town was the frequent spotting of Tyler Burke.

Big Ty sightings spread like wildfire.

Harv Brindle heard a mad cackle one night out in his garden. When he peeked out his window to investigate, Ty stared back at him on the other side of the glass pane. Harv fainted in fright. Marge Temple was practicing by herself at church on the organ. Big Ty had appeared behind her and leered at her. Marge fainted, too. Chester Giest had been carting sacks of garbage out to his burn-barrel after sunset. Ty sprang up beside his barrel and reached through the flames to poke Chester in the chest. Poor Chester had a heart attack and barely survived.

Late one night down at the Catholic cemetery, two kids were trying to see the souls of the dead, a common initiation dare that sent many kids in town out to the cemetery gates. Most never made it past the first headstone before turning tail to run, claiming a ghost had touched them. Well, these two boys bravely walked to the middle of the cemetery when a horned owl with glowing red eyes had swooped down at them from the branches of overhead. One boy dove to the ground, cracking his head wide open on a tombstone jutting up from the ground. The other froze in terror as the owl made another pass at him, its talons raking the top of his head as the owl changed into a flying monkey.

Later that night, in the ER, Mac took the report that the two boys hysterically gave him. They claimed Ty and an entire pack of stubby goblins had surrounded them, poking and pinching them. Big Ty howled like a madman and chased the boys back to town. Those two kids were so upset, that Doc Wilson had to sedate them to calm them down.

Things were becoming serious. No one wanted to be out after dark. Townsfolk started locking their doors, checking their windows, and bringing their dogs in at night to stand watch beside their beds. Folks working second shift in most places left their jobs in pairs to stay safe. People getting up early in the mornings, weren't too keen to open their shades until after the sun came up for fear Ty might be peering in at them. Mac and Noah were constantly getting called out of the sheriff's office to go and investigate Big Ty sightings. To add an extra man to the police force, Sheriff Mac hired Ghost to take Ty's place as his second deputy. Thinking that Ty might go to ground and return to hide out at Andy Tate's house, Ghost kept a close eye on his place for several weeks. Mac started to patrol all three cemeteries in town, especially after dark when most people spotted Ty roaming around. When Mac was out on night duty, Dec stayed at our house instead of being home alone.

   Dad kept a loaded shotgun beside his bed at night, and Mom slept with a frying pan on her night stand. She said her she wasn't taking chances that Big Ty might come to take revenge on Dad for the dressing down he gave him when he'd taken our dogs over to Rome's place.

   Dad and Mom had urged Gran B to move in with us so that at night she wouldn't be alone, but Gran stubbornly refused to let Ty scare her out of her own house. Besides, Gran said she was ready to pick a fight with Ty if he came calling. She thought Ty was plagued by a wanagi, which meant demon in Lakota. Gran said a wanagi from the spirit realm had hitched a ride with Ty from out there on Rivermoon. Gran had a vision of wild horses running loose through town. She said she'd tamed the herd by touching each one with an eagle feather. That next day after her dream, Ghost invited me to Gran's den. He had a leather pouch with him and in it were what he called "weapons of warfare." He drew two eagle feathers out of the pouch. He handed one to Gran B and took the second one for himself, draping it around his neck with a leather thong. He then attached the three bronze arrowheads I had been carrying to three leather strands. Ghost placed those strands around my neck so that the arrowheads could be worn beneath my shirt. Custer, Wild Bill, and Buffalo Bill engraved on those medallions were talismans that would protect me against evil.

It was upon hearing the haunting stories that Henry finally snapped. Dec and I watched Henry go from being unstable since he shot Jon Kennedy to going nutty in zero flat. It was just too many scary stories about ghosts, demons, and spirits of the dead that pushed Henry over the edge. He took sanctuary in St. Joseph's Catholic church one night, carrying a sixteen-point buck's head mounted on a board that he'd ripped off the wall of the Huntsman's Lodge, where the Shriners held their meetings. Dec and I spotted King Henry carrying that deer head down the street. Henry was also armed with a long sword and he used it on the church door to pry it open. Dec said we should run two blocks to the courthouse and report the break in to Sheriff Mac, but even before we started in that direction, sirens came blaring down the street. Upon seeing the red flashing lights quickly approaching the church, Dec and I decided to sneak in behind Henry and just watch as the calvary arrived.

We darted up the stairs and huddled down at the front of the balcony overlooking the chapel below us. We didn't have to wait long for the show to unfold at the altar at the front of the chapel.

King Henry had removed the large wooden cross from the back wall of the chapel. He had wired the sixteen-point buck's head to the top of the cross and had it leaning against the pulpit at the front of the altar, so that the buck was facing the rows of pews. Working by the light of dozens of candles at the front of the church, he scattered little wooden crucifixes before the large cross. Henry then shoved the basin of holy water over so that water splashed all over the floorboards of the altar. Taking his sword hilt in a two-handed grip, he kneeled before the cross adorned with the buck's head and froze there, facing the rows of pews.

Ty appeared there below us in the sanctuary. I stared at him in disbelief, for the medallions I wore dangling from leather thongs around my necks made it possible to see the spirit realm unseen by mortals in this realm. Ty was encased in a bright red aura. An evil miasma leaked from his inner being, emanating from his soul in wisps of luminous vapors. He raised his hands, clenching them into fists. As he struck at the air before him, a horde of green-scaled goblins exploded across the altar as if expelled out of a rip between the realms. Small, pudgy creatures with shiny bald heads. Bug-eyed with bulging lemon-yellow eyes, and long fangs protruded from their gaping mouths. At a command from Ty, the squat creatures swarmed up onto the altar, surrounding King Henry.

Suddenly, King Henry surged to his feet, wildly swinging his sword and shouting, "In the name of Jesus, Son of God, King of Kings, Lord of Lords, I command you demons to fall! In the name of Cernunnos, Wild Stag of the Forever Forest, of Herne the Hunter, whose symbol is the White Stag the leader of the Wild Hunt!"

And there on the altar below us where the wooden cross had stood, there was now a stag-headed swordsman taking his place behind Henry. He was a large, muscular figure who wore no shirt, and yet no demon swords touched his bare skin, for he moved amongst the goblin horde with all the speed of a striking viper. Slashing. Poking. Stabbing. Using overhand cuts and underhand strokes, he wove a path of death through the goblin ranks. Where his sword struck, goblins wailed and evaporated, leaving behind puffs of black smoke. Above his brow, his white antlers shone with a brilliance that blinded the remaining goblins. A horn appeared in his hand. He raised it to his lips and gave three loud blasts, summoning a pack of wolfhounds from a rent in the Otherworld behind the altar. The huge, transparent dogs sprang forward into the ranks of goblins, making short work of the last of them. Goblins and hounds vanished, blinking out one by one, until only King Henry and Ty faced each other. Herne the Hunter vanished as well, just as Mac and Noah came running into the chapel. Henry stood there, his sword raised above Ty's head. "Henry?" Mac said, his pistol drawn and held before him. "Drop the sword! Drop it now or I'll shoot!"

Ty slumped down on the altar, splashing through puddles of holy water scattered on the floorboards. I could see blackish smoke wafting from Ty's large frame, each one resembling tiny ghosts that whiffed out with an airy puff in the purple flashes created by the holy water. As if scorched by his contact with the water, Ty screamed. Henry tossed down his sword, raised his hands, and backed away from Ty wallowing between them in misery and anguish.

Mac and Noah brought out their handcuffs and arrested both King Henry and Big Ty. I was just getting ready to speak to Mac and Noah, but Dec nudged me with his knee and placed his finger against my lips. It was as if he read my mind, and knew that I was going to sound like a raving nutcase if I told Mac and Noah about what we'd seen. So I sat there in silence as Ty and Henry were escorted out of the chapel. The spookiest part of the whole episode was five minutes later, when Dec and I slipped outside the church.

Noah had already driven King Henry away to take him to jail, but Mac was pulling away from St. Joe's with Big Ty seated in the backseat of his cruiser. Standing there in the shadows of the church, Dec and I froze in sudden fear as we saw Ty looking through the back window of the car directly at us.

And he was smiling.

Chapter Forty-Six

Ronan Catlin was born to Chris and Mary Kay shortly after their wedding in July. My brother was released from the State Home in time to serve as Chris's best man, but due to an investigation into a church explosion on the west side of town, Richard did not stay in town long. Westside Baptist Church, on West Court, was leveled by an explosion that demolished the church at 7:30 July 4th. Choir practice was scheduled for 7:30, but the explosion ripped through the church at 7:25, but no members of the choir had shown up. Reverend Kempel said there would have been 12 members of the choir inside. Miss Paul, church pianist, would have gone to the church early, but she had fallen asleep and was just walking out the front door when the explosion hit. Mrs. Estes and her two daughters were on their way to the church, when they had car trouble. The Reverend and his wife had both been detained at home. Normally, he said, they would arrive at around 7:10. Windows in homes near the church were shattered. Mrs. McKinney who lives a block away from the church said there was a loud explosion.

Firefighters determined there were three reasons for the explosion. 1.) Coal gas 2.) Natural gas 3.) A combination of both. The power line from the tower on the west edge of town was cut and the radio went off the air at exactly 7:25. The grocery store directly across the street from the church, had large damage due to broken windows, but no one was in the store at the time. When fire men arrived it was feared that some members of the church might still be trapped within the rubble, but after 30 minutes, Reverend Kempel accounted for all 12 members. Insurance paid for most of the damage, but glass dealers in the area reported a booming business. Insurance adjusters had been busy making adjustments to homes and buildings in the vicinity.

The explosion blew three walls of the church apart. Men from the gas company found a small leak in a line 100 yards east of the church. The church had a gas line in the basement for heating a Sunday school building. However they found the gas line turned off at the meter and this had authorities puzzled. It had been just two weeks ago that a water heater was installed but the gas had been turned on at the meter at this time. Sheriff Mac wanted to know who turned that meter off and why?

Mom told Sheriff Mac it was preposterous to think my brother had been involved in the suspected arson as Richard had been still locked up at the State Home, and although Mom was Catholic she said it was a shame to go suspecting the church explosion had anything to do with the Baptist Minister, let alone that Sheriff Mac wanted to question my brother about the cause of the explosion. The destruction of the Westside Baptist church was never solved. No one knows to this day whether there was foul play involved or not. My brother swore he had nothing to do with it.

The investigation drove a wedge between Dec and I for that next few days. I had never defended my brother on any account before, but when Dec swore if Richard was involved in the crime, his soul would go to hell when he died, I scoffed at the notion, telling Dec it was only a building built by men and not god. I didn't believe that God would send any one to hell for blowing up a mere building.

I then brought up the London file he'd stolen from the evidence room and for several days Dec fretted over how he was going to get that back in place before the trial started. He was too busy sweating over that to even think about where my brother's soul would end up at one day. In the end, Dec turned the file into his dad, confessing that he'd swiped it, and ended up grounded for two whole weeks. Before he was even off of groundation, Andy and Loyd were sentenced to ten years apiece for being accessories in the London murders.

Ironically, on the day they started their sentences at the State Pen, King Henry was released from the State Home on supervised home visits. He was heavily medicated and shadowed by his wife and an orderly during his weekend visits.

Big Ty was locked up in solitary confinement at the State Home. His strange encounter with the ghost of Bobbie Martin still haunted him and some doctor out there told Mac that Ty might never recover from his weirdness. Dec and I heard he was still babbling like a loon, and we once swore we'd heard him howling at the full moon late one night when we were sleeping out in our tree fort. Just to know Tyler Burke was locked up out there and that he might escape one day, gave Dec and I the creeps.

    Dec became so worried about Ty breaking out of his cell out there at the State Home, he eventually told Sheriff Mac about Kat's haunted dreams. Concerned about the welfare of his only son, Mac was over sensitive about the two of us witnessing the shootout between Rome and Lawrence. He even suggested we see Gran B to get things settled in our heads. Mac shared with Gran the farfetched story about what we'd seen and experienced on Rivermoon. The thing is, Gran already knew the entire story, including the winged monkey and the mind control of Wraith over those mad baboons. She did not laugh at us when Dec and I shared these same stories with her. To help us overcome our fear about Ty ever escaping from the ward he was on, Gran urged Mac to take Dec and I out to the State Home so we could see for ourselves how many locked doors Ty would have to go through to leave that place. There were seven in all, and Mac assured us Ty wasn't getting out anytime soon. Still, we were on edge that entire summer.

It was two months after my brother left town, when school was just starting, that Mary Kay came to see Dec and I about a matter of great importance. She even asked us to start a fire in the fire pit so that her meeting with us could be all official like. As she joined us, taking a seat on a half-log across the fire from us, the last thing on our minds was what she shared with us there on that bright spring day beneath our tree fort.

    Mary Kay said, "I left Ronan at home with Chris. I wanted to meet with you two alone so that there would be no interruptions."

    She reached inside her purse and drew out two small bank booklets. She handed them over the fire to Dec first, and then me. "What's this?"

Dec asked, opening his booklet and getting a strange look on his face. I opened mine, too, and nearly fell off my log seat when I read the amount that was listed in a savings account in my name. "Ten-thousand dollars?" I gasped in surprise. "What is this, Mary Kay?"

She said, "Despite his dark side, Richard's got an angel on his shoulder. He just needs to listen to him more often, rather than the demon who whispers in his other ear. Before he left for Chicago, he cashed in that bar of gold that was never recovered. He put the money into five separate accounts. One for me, to help raise his son. One for Chris, to purchase our house. One for Dec. One for you, Hawk. And the last one for himself."

To even think that my brother had thought that highly of me that he'd left me money from that gold bar, choked me up inside. Tears welled up in my eyes. Pretending not to notice me crying, Mary Kay said, "He had a rough side, but he was a sweetheart deep down. When I wrote to him to tell him I had named our son, Ronan, and that he would be taking the last name of Catlin, he said he was okay with that, agreeing that Chris would make a good dad."

Dec took the money matter quite seriously. He made plans for his future, naming his bank account his *college fund*. Yes, even at 13-years-old, Dec vowed he would grow up to be our town sheriff one day. And he swore he'd hire me to be his deputy. I thanked him for the offer, but I had no real goal of becoming Dec's sidekick.

No, I had other plans, and the first thing I did was get in touch with Ghost to set up a meeting with Rod Kramer and the Nine Poor Knights. Rod and his biker club rode into town two days later and he was surprised that I invested most of my money in a new dog rescue ranch to be run by the Knights. The ranch was set up on the west side of town, and I got to visit there quite often, working with dogs that the club brought in to be rehabilitated and re-homed.

Rod suggested we name it something Native since I was Lakota, but in the end it became Storm Haven, a ranch for troubled dogs, which set a course for me for the rest of my life.

Chapter Forty-Seven

In 1964, Dec, Kat, and I turned 13. While I bonded with the dogs I was working with at Storm Haven, Dec and Kat grew closer together in their own way. It wasn't until I caught them kissing one night that I figured they were serious about each other. Kat was never destined for me anyhow. So I just accepted the fact that they had fallen in love.

The thing that bothered Dec about this version of Kat was the fact she started tapping into her Cingane roots, which came with her gifts. These gifts were scoffed at by a Catholic like Declan. In fact, he was often afraid that God was none too pleased with Kat anytime she used her gifts, for they caused her to veer over into the supernatural. A realm that Dec considered taboo. One night Dec and I came to visit Gran B, and damned if Kat didn't have a crystal ball on the table before her. Gran offered me a smile, letting me know she was okay with the crystal ball. Gran knew there was the Otherworld, and since she was both Irish and Laktota, she believed in magic and the spirit world. It was part of her makeup.

Kat said, "Plum Island was a germ warfare lab run by the Federal Government. Researchers there specialized in animal diseases that jumped to humans. There was once an investigation there into the murder of two Plum Island scientists, suspected of being terrorists for a biotech company. These scientists created the Montauk Monster, which washed ashore at a beach near Montauk, New York. The creature was dead, but it came from Plum Island. Although it looked like a hairless coyote, many said it was a raccoon. When a Pakistani scientist was arrested in Afghanistan, she had planned an attack on the Plum Island Animal Disease Center. An Al Quada terrorist, who knows what would have happened had she stolen germs from there?

"Ever heard of Lyme disease? When a deer tick bites a person passing along the disease, it seems like the flu, then goes dormant for weeks, even years when it comes back, ten times worse, attacking the heart, the brain, the spine. Some years trees produce few acorns, other years a bumper crop, which means an increase in mice. And deer ticks love mice. A single mouse can have dozens of ticks on it, and those mice pass Lyme disease to those ticks. A surge in acorns means a surge in mice and a surge in mice means Lyme disease spreading to more humans.

"The SARS coronavirus came from bats which in turn infected civet cats which jumped to humans in China. In Africa, poachers killed elephants and rhinos, and when they butchered them became covered in blood. An infection in an animal leap frogs to humans from such contact, then humans pass it along to another human.

"An infected person who fails to get a proper rabies shot endures a slow death. After a week, rabies swarms the brain. A man once shot a rabid coon, and its brains got on his hands, then into his mouth. The virus went dormant for a month, then rose in him like a winged demon. He was dead in seven days. Rivermoon was known as Germ Island, where animal diseases passed to humans. Somehow, Ty became infected with rabies, and ticks who sucked on Ty's blood became infected."

Kat ran her fingertips over the crystal ball and in the swirling red mist inside the glass globe we saw a sequence of events. One scene showed tiny ticks detaching themselves from Ty's legs, and dropping to the floor of his cell. Scene two showed mice being swarmed by the ticks, attaching themselves to them. These mice left Ty's cell and slipped into a hole in a wall. Scene three showed the mice scampering away into a wooded grove, where one mouse was pounced upon by an owl. Another mouse was attacked by a yellow cat. And several more mice flittered away into a herd of deer grazing nearby. Ticks from these mice ended up attaching themselves to the deer, the owl, and the cat.

Kat said, "Just this year, in 1964 the murder of a nationally known cancer researcher set the stage for a covert operation. It involved cancer outbreaks, contaminated polio vaccines, and biological weapon research using infected monkeys. Simian virus 40 is a monkey virus that was administered to humans by contaminated vaccines produced in SV40 cells. 98 million people have been exposed to the contaminated vaccines. SV40 was administered to humans between 1955-1963. Doctor Mary

Sherman, a senior surgeon in New Orleans, was found dead in July. She died of a stab wound to her heart. Rumors were she'd discovered a cancer causing agent in the polio vaccine and she was going to expose the Medical Association for administering this to the American public."

Inside the crystal ball swirling red smoke evolved the owl, the cat, and the deer. Twin balls of light drifted over their heads. One sphere was dark green, the other brilliant blue. Stepping out of the globes of light, Bandit and Miracle moved into the clearing. Bursts of lightning shot from their outstretched paws, connecting with the owl, the cat, and deer. Oily black puffs of smoke leaked out of them, resembling ghosts with red eyes. Tendrils of the lightning scored hits on them as they tried escaping from the clearing. The crackling light zapped all eight ghosts, leaving behind red-gold embers swirling in a swift wind. Freed of the contamination, the owl, the cat, and the deer left the clearing, healed and whole. Behind them, looking on, Mary Kay scooped up the two little monkeys and turned and left the wooded grove behind.

"This Dr. Mary Sherman," Kat said, "was not only stabbed through the heart, but one side of her body was incinerated. Rumor has it, that she was experimenting with a Linear Particle Accelerator, a machine that took up an entire building and was being guarded by soldiers with machine guns. It was suspected she had an accident with this machine and was burned badly by it, and her death was made to look like a murder.

"Someone went one step farther with this Particle Accelerator, increasing the kinetic energy of charged particles, by implanting such a device in Bandit and Miracle. You saw how they destroyed those infected specters with the lightning they generated? Someone monkeyed with those monkeys! They have super-charged powers that can either heal or destroy. Mary Kay is convinced they have stopped Ty's rabie virus from spreading by using their accelerator powers six times now. God only knows what will happen if Ty ever escapes from the State Home!"

Dec said, "The Zombie Apocalypse will then begin, right?"

"Maybe," Kat said. "I don't know. I only know that so far Bandit and Miracle have eradicated six strains of that virus by using their powers.

Mary Kay has received six different warnings whenever Ty's virus breaks free of his cell. Each time there is danger of the virus infecting others, Mary Kay has been summoned by the Summer Kin."

"The who?" I asked, most curiously.

"Summer Kin," Kat said. "Gran calls it the Otherworld or the Unseen Realm. The Elves of the Summer Country claim they have been chosen as guardians in a battle that has been waged for ages, and they have formed an alliance with Mary Kay's son, Ronan, who they claim is a Champion of the Celtic Road, as well as a Red Road Warrior, due to his Irish and Lakota heritage. Creed Blackstag, a Bard Chieftain from that realm has declared that Ronan is destined one day to accomplish many deeds and feats that will serve a greater purpose."

In the year 1974, Dec and Kat married, and Dec became Sheriff of Beatrice. One month after Dec was sworn in and put on his badge, Mac and Noah retired, to spend the rest of their days fishing on the Blue River. Although Dec begged me to become his deputy, I pursued a career in dog handling and as a Paranormal Investigator. My nephew, the son of my brother, followed me like a shadow. When Ronan was 12-years-old, he followed me one day down Standing Bear Trail on the south side of town. He looked a lot like me at his age, with shoulder-length raven hair, and a dark complexion due to his Lakota heritage. He was a skinny little kid with the bluest eyes I had ever seen. He was a happy kid, too, always smiling, always laughing. A good-natured kid despite being born out of defiance and pity.

Chris had shared with him by then who his real father was, and instead of resenting it, Ronan loved Chris fiercely. Richard only came back once on his fifth birthday, but he was off on his escapades soon after and never really got to know his son. So, I took it upon myself to always be there for him as he grew up.

Ronan became a legend in his own right, for with proper guidance and training from Ghost Running Thunder, he started his own practice as a Ghost Hunter, delving into the Unseen Realm on quests that he returned from, carrying tattered books, rare parchments, strange potions, and swords that actually shimmered with some mysterious inner light. Ronan named them jewel-blades, for each sword was shaded the color of the large jewel each had embedded in their hilts.

It was there that day on Standing Bear Trail that I finally met the Summer Kin. Ronan had a mischievous grin on his face as he gestured at the four gems he'd scattered on the ground and said, "Remain standing still, Uncle Hawk, or you'll be trampled by the Wild Hunt!"

A black stallion burst from the undergrowth to one side of the trail. The steed snorted as it raced past me, then wheeled about, its rider tugging on its reins. I felt furry forms brushing past my legs as hounds raced to keep up with the stallion and its rider. Huge, shaggy dogs bred in Ireland to hunt and kill wolves. Each one was enormous, with long legs and narrow heads. I looked up at the stag-headed figure mounted on the horse, his white antlers glistening with magical light. He was barechested with muscles rippling beneath the darkly-tanned skin of his chest and broad shoulders. A shimmering sword appeared in his hand. A burst of the bluish light erupted from the tip of the sword's blade.

I said, "Herne the Hunter?"

The stag-headed rider laughed, reaching up to remove the antlers crowning his head. Long, black hair spilled down around his face and his shoulders, unruly tangles that gleamed blue-black in the glow of the sword blade. "Herne was of another time and age. I am Creed Black Stag, and I've come to gift the boy with a book from the Lodge. I am one of the Summer Kin, who battles in the Unseen Realm."

Creed handed a large, leather-bound book down to Ronan, whose eyes widened in surprise as he read the title, saying, "Monster Compendium, the facts on werewolves, vampires, and the undead!"

He hooked his antlers to his belt, then produced a rolled parchment from his saddle pack. He handed this down to Ronan, saying, "A map leading to the locations of a vast array of weaponry to aid in the Hunt. Relics are scattered in your realm, and so must be retrieved by you.

Read about your many enemies, know their strengths, learn of their weaknesses, develop your skills and talents to defeat them. Your days ahead will be filled with missions and quests.

"First, to Koyasan Monastery in Japan, founded by Kōbō-Daishi, Grand Master of the Buddhist Teaching. There, you shall learn Daito-ryu, Japanese martial arts first taught by Takeda Sōkaku.

"Second, to the School of the Winds in Scandinavia where you shall learn Sword Skills and Master Bladework.

"Third, you will visit a company of Buddhist monks in Tibet to learn the Ways of Silence and Meditation.

"Fourth, you will visit the Jesuits in the Vatican at Rome, to learn the Way, the Truth, and the Life, from the Brotherhood of the Rose.

"Fifth, you will travel to Israel to be trained in Hebrew verses from the Torah by priests of the Essenes.

"Sixth, you will travel to Iran to learn the verses of the Quran, for you will be constantly harassed by the jinn of Middle Eastern origin.

"Seventh, you will spend a night in the haunted Asylum in Switzerland to confront demons, ghosts, and entities of the undead. During your Hunt, you will confront creatures infected with viruses and plagues. Your battles will be many, and each victory you stop more evil from being spread. In many of these confrontations, your allies will be priests, shamans, mullahs, imams, wizards, Templar Knights, healers, druids. As a Servant of the Light, May the All Father watch over you.

"A monster is a creature, whose powers of destruction threaten the human race. Monsters pre-date written history, and the study of monsters is known as monstrophy. Well-known monsters include Count Dracula, Frankenstein's monster, werewolves, mummies, and zombies. Although there are dozens more, the list starts with: Behemoth. Centaur. Cerberus. Changeling. Chimera. Cyclopes. Demon. Dragon. Freak. Ghoul. Goblin. Gorgons. Jinn. Kelpie. Loch Ness Monster. Hydra. Leviathan. Minotaur. Ogre. Troll. Warg. Wendigo. Werewolf. Yeti."

Creed Blackstag and his hounds were then gone from this world and raced away into the Unseen Realm.

Chapter Forty-Eight

Ronan often Gated out of town, stepping through dimensional portals that teleported him to places all over the world. Ghost went with him on these trips to hunt down entities of Darkness wherever they cropped up at. It was Ghost, too, who taught him martial arts and fighting skills, for to defeat many of these demons and monsters, he needed mad warrior skills in order to prevail.

Ronan was protective of me, his mom, and step-dad, Chris. He forbid any of us to join him on any of their excursions, claiming it was way too dangerous. Kat was often chided by Ronan for using her crystal ball to keep track of them when ever he and Ghost went questing. He told her that one of these days some powerful demon was going to notice her eavesdropping by looking on in her magical globe, and there was a real fear that one of these entities might follow an ethereal trail that would lead a dark, malevolent apparition back to Kat watching in the safety of her den at home.

Mary Kay was always there at the end of such dimensional trips, with Bandit and Miracle at hand to deal with any contagion that may have infected Ronan or Ghost in the completion of a quest. The little monkeys had so far healed the two of several real nasty viruses that left unchecked, could have spread to any of us. The two squirrel monkeys utilized their Linear Particle Accelerator skills to annihilate any spores, bugs, or toxic chemicals that hitchhiked back from any war zone Ronan and Ghost had traveled to.

Ghost claimed ghouls and vampires were infected with vicious spores that were air-born and could easily infiltrate one's immune system. The Undead, such as zombies or werewolves spread another savage disease through scratches or bites, and in almost every case, resulted in a virulent strain of rabies, which left their victims stark raving mad lunatics.

Ronan and Ghost joined the ranks of the Order of the Hunters, an elite force of Paranormal Investigators who tracked down and destroyed monsters wherever they threatened the human race.

In Tel Avi, Ronan and Ghost eliminated a demon-inspired terrorist cell plotting a chemical attack in Israel.

In Tehran, they assassinated two fanatic brothers who planned several bombings in nearby Iraq. Both brothers were not only crazed Extremists, but also being manipulated by a band of jinn who hailed from the deserts of Saudi Arabia.

In northern Africa, Ronan and Ghost took out an Extremist faction connected with Boko Haram, yet also influenced by a war-mongering demon whose devoted followers had already killed hundreds in savage attacks along the African coast.

In Bosnia, they eliminated a terrorist group determined to bomb a dozen schools there as a political strategy to use children as targets of their attacks.

In Egypt, they halted the transportation of Sarin gas over the border there and coming from Syria. This attack, too, was influenced by a demon who had waged warfare on mankind for one thousand years.

In each of these places, Ronan and Ghost prevented attacks in the physical realm by taking the fight to the spiritual realm, because in truth, the evils in this world have a basis in the spirit world. To truly win against Darkness, there are countless demons to be dealt with properly.

While I longed to be a skilled warrior in the supernatural realm, I had another gift entirely. I would have loved to tell my grand kids one day of my prowess and skill in defeating evil entities much like Ronan, but from my experiences on Rivermoon, I came to realize my gift was just as necessary in defeating evil. To set free those who were bound here in this realm so that they could move on to the Otherworld was a much-needed component in the battle in the spirit realm. Bobbie Martin, the little cadet from Lawrence, Kansas, set that stage for me, for in sending him on his way, I accomplished a great feat. One in which, Bobbie and the other trapped ghosts on Rivermoon, all passed to the realm beyond. Their spirits had been bound there, and they desperately needed freeing, their shackles removed, so that they could rise to the next level.

Ironically, it was two other boys by the name of Martin that set a course for me in the coming year. These two boys from Nebraska needed freeing in a bad way. And by helping them to pass on, I received my calling then for the rest of my life. Despite the fact that I had soundly defeated Wraith back on Rivermoon, wielding the two tomahawks of Crazy Horse and Gall, I was not to be known amongst the Order of Hunters as a demon-slayer. No, the title I was given by Ghost Running Thunder was the Deliverer, my skill freeing those who were bound.

Years had passed since I freed Bobbie Martin, but the two other Martin boys had called to me for several weeks, before I climbed in my car and drove to Alda, Nebraska. There I discovered their memorial to commemorate their deed which was remarkable under the circumstances.

In August 1864, Nate age 15 and Bob age 12, were helping their father with a load of hay when the three were attacked by a band of Sioux and Cheyenne. While the father held off most of the warriors with his rifle, the boys jumped on a horse and fled, with Nate holding onto Bob. The Indians followed and shot Nate twice with arrows, once in his elbow and once in his side. The second arrow passed through Nate and lodged in Bob's back. The boys, pinned together, fell off of the horse and were left for dead. Nate and Bob eventually made their way to a doctor and were unpinned. Bob survived and died at age 47, while Nate died as an old man at 79.

The two brothers being pinned together by the single arrow left their souls anchored to the place they fell from their horse. Yes, the boys painstakingly made their way to a doctor in the nearby town, and yes, he freed them from the arrow that pinned them together, but they survived and carried on for years after the savage attack. When it came their time to die, several Native demons prevented them from leaving this realm, and ended up chasing them with fiery arrows in the spirit realm. As I stood there that day before their memorial, the boys relived their terrible adventure, mounting up on a horse, being skewered by an arrow, pinned together, and falling from the horse. It was that arrow that anchored them to the earth here, and would not allow them to pass on.

I used the Buffalo Bill medallion to destroy the arrow, for Nate held onto it and carried it with him to the end of his days to remember their miraculous ride away from the Indian attack. As soon as the medallion disintegrated that arrow shot by a Cheyenne bow, the spirits of both Bob and Nate were set free. They thanked me for my deliverance, and passed onto the other realm.

I continued my role as a Deliverer for many more years.

Many of you reading this, will want to know what became of ex-deputy Tyler Burke. Did he ever escape from his cell at the State Home? Did the virus he was infected with ever spread to others?

Many will want to know what happened to Oscar? Rosie the elephant? Hiney Scrabble? Lawrence Shank? Badger and Cooper?

I would have to say, that's a whole other story now, isn't it?

Author's Notes

My great-grandfather, Amos Hawkins, was a steam boat captain on the Missouri, Mississippi and Ohio rivers. During the Ohio floods, he met my great-grandmother, Rebecca Bower, a Lakota woman who practiced Native medicine. When a young boy was burned badly down in Beatrice, the doctor wanted to amputate both of his legs, but Rebecca Bower, used her healing skills on him. That boy grew up to be the Chief Fire Marshall of Beatrice, thanks to my great-grandmother.

The son of Amos and Rebecca, was my Grandfather, Amos Hawkins. He had a great sense of humor. As a kid, every time we'd go down to Beatrice to visit, I would end up seated on the porch, listening to his stories. He'd always offer me a chew of his Redman, but as I reached for his open pouch, he would cackle and withdraw it, slipping me a stick of Spearmint or Juicy Fruit instead.

Once when he and my Grandma got into a heated argument, Amos drove his buggy downtown and bought a big block of ice. He drove it home and pulled up beside my Grandma who sat fuming in her rocker on the front porch. Amos dumped that big block of ice at her feet and said, "Here, old lady, sit on that and cool your ass off!"

Another time, since he was of Lakota heritage, some snooty white lady walked up to him in downtown Beatrice, held up her hand, and said the traditional Indian greeting, "How!"

Amos grinned at her, offered her a sly smile, and said, "Me already know how! Me want to know when?"

Every time I think of him, I smile.

I loved my grandfather and wept the night he escaped from a Nursing Home down in Wymore during a bad winter snowstorm. He froze to death a mile from the town and was found the next day beside a set of railroad tracks running back to Beatrice.

When I started this story, a memory surfaced. Once while seated in the back seat of my dad's 57 Chevy, I sat beside Amos while Uncle Richard and my dad carried on a conversation in the front seat. As we pulled up to a corner, there were three little black kids standing there. My Grandpa, who had been chewing Redman, spat a brown stream at them and laughed, "Here, catch that, you little jungle bunnies!"

I was so shocked that tears came to my eyes, and that image of those poor little kids dodging his tobacco juice stayed with me for years afterward. I vowed that day never to be so cruel toward anyone. As I write this, I think of my cousins, who are African American, and I can't help but think of their feelings being hurt by such a shocking deed by Grandpa. And Grandpa being Lakota, should have known better than to pick on three little black kids who had never done anything to offend him.

Oscar the monkey did live in a cage on the side of a tree there around 1940. Rosie the elephant lived there, as well, and took frequent baths in the Blue River. Hiney Scrabble and Lawrence Shank were real people, as well. I thought Hiney was short for Heinz when I first introduced him to the story, but later found out his name came from the fact his hind end was all most people saw of him as he dug around in trash bins in Beatrice alleys.

God only knows the real reason Lawrence killed his wife and young daughter. I just remember Uncle Richard telling me about the time Lawrence gave him money to go buy him a pouch of Redman and how surprised he was when Richard brought him back his change and the tobacco. The irony was not lost on Richard that there was the town killer thanking him for being such a honest young boy.

As far as delving into the paranormal with this story, no one can blame Stephen King for that. I have never read one of his books. I did, however, read *Boy's Life* by Robert McCammon, and it was in reading this that I was prompted to try my hand at emulating his flair for nostalgia and quaint characters who populate small-town America.

If you liked the story, drop me a line at:

authorfrye@gmail.com

Characters

Hawk Declan Chris

Mary Kay Mac Noah